Copyright © 2020 by Simon Gary.

First printed and published in the United Kingdom 2020.
Edited and typeset by MJV Literary Author Services.
Cover designed by Maja Kopunovic.

ISBN: 978-1-9160525-4-3 (Ebook)

ISBN: 978-1-9160525-5-0 (Paperback)

All rights reserved. This book or any portion thereof may not be reproduced or used in any manner whatsoever, without the express written permission of the publisher, except for the use of brief quotations in a book review.

Any references to historical events, real people, or real places are used fictitiously. Other names, characters, places and events are products of the author's imagination, and any resemblances to actual events or places or persons, living or dead, is entirely coincidental.

THRYKE

The Man That Nobody Knew

SIMON GARY

INTRODUCTION

Success came late into the life of Cornelius Thryke.

Today, when the name of the late star is mentioned, most will recall the sit-com *Gone to the Dogs*, via which he truly entered the public eye. A fading few may even cherish the beautifully dappled black-and-white films in which he starred, although they may not recall the titles, nor the roles that he played.

His success on television during the 1970s has been well documented in the book *Gone to the Dogs*, and it is not my intention to revisit that material here, except where it naturally forms the end of our story. It is, however, my purpose to uncover and present the life and times of Cornelius Thryke, prior to his foray into the televisual arena. This investigation will, quite naturally, cover his extensive filmography, but also deliver insights into the man that he was away from the screen.

This journey has been made possible, to a greater degree, through a great gift from Cornelius himself: Thryke was a ferocious diarist, filling many journals throughout his lifetime. These are accompanied by clippings and other stories of interest, which have been pasted into the now delicate and fox-stained pages.

After his death in 1977, the diaries and other personal effects were archived at the local museum. It was here that, as a young curator, I first came across them, in several dusty boxes on a high, forgotten shelf. When I pulled them down, it was like receiving a sparkling, Egyptian treasure. For many months, I read them hungrily, drawing the wealth from their pages, unseen since the pensmith's hand had passed over them, all those years before. Thryke's was a truly wonderful and unsung life, which deserves to be shared with all, and this is what I attempt to do here. I achieve this with a mixture of his diary entries and my own painstaking research.

I never set a course to find Cornelius Thryke, but it seems he has found me. This book is my acknowledgement of and gratitude for that fact.

I hope, dear reader, you will take some joy from this book.

Quentin Prowler; author, archivist, compiler and potential television historian, 2019.

Part One:

Beginnings

SIMON GARY

EDITOR'S NARRATIVE
Quentin Prowler

Cornelius Arthur Thryke was born on 14th March 1915, in the small country village of Little Sodbury-on-the-Wode. The last of the winter snows had since receded, and there were early signs of the daffodils coming into bud, when Cornelius plummeted onto the bedspread of his dutiful mother, Vera. Little did she know that a star had been born.

Cornelius was born to Bartholomew Augustus Thryke (b.1868) and Vera Elsie (*nee* Summers, b.1891). There were those in the village and its environs who thought the Thrykes to be a strange match. Bartholomew, or "Bartie", as he was known within the family, was well into his forties when he had begun to woo the then-nineteen-year-old Vera. Their first meetings were stuffy and formal affairs, as Vera had originally caught the eye of bachelor Bartie at a small church picnic, in 1910. The dalliance began with furtive glances – mainly from Bartie – which, by the spring of 1911, had developed into a bold "Why, hello Miss Summers," one Sunday morning, after the communion service.

It should, by way of padding, be relayed that Bartie was the parish priest of All Saviours' Church, Little Sodbury-on-the-Wode. It was a position that he had taken in 1900 and, as such, he was something of a heartthrob amongst the female parishioners; one must imagine that, over the years, many had tipped their Sunday hat in his direction. But, it was a fresh-faced Vera who won his heart – or, at least, a small portion of it – from God.

Of the photographs which remain, it is clear that the Thrykes were a striking couple. Bartie stood, black-haired, at almost six feet tall, and was lithe and wiry. He was often to be seen clad in his cassock and a wide-brimmed hat. Cornelius recalls him thusly:

"Father has always reminded me of a crow: black, distant and watchful. His mind is full of God; he has no time to consider the lowlier things. He passes through the house like a shadow, barely touching any of us. Perhaps this is how all fathers are."

His mother he recalls more fondly. Here is an extract from 1925:

"Mother has a beautiful face and, when she offers her rosy cheek, I kiss it gladly. She glides around me, in an aroma of lavender and freshly-baked bread. My tummy feels warm, and I feel as brave as a polar explorer! Her smiles are squishy and glow with peppermint. She tucks me in tight at bedtime and places my book softly on the dresser. She is so gentle. She is my mother."

The details of Bartie and Vera's courtship were originally rather sketchy. However, I was lucky enough to make a recent discovery, amongst the papers of Cornelius.

I remember it well. One Tuesday, the summer before last, I was working late at the museum, cataloguing the last of the Elizabethan shoes. I had been the custodian of the Thryke archive for a number of years, but the sheer number and volume of his diaries had kept me busy for the whole of that time. Also, to be honest, the Thryke collection had played second fiddle for some while, prioritized behind several successful public exhibitions, which I and the Little Sodbury Museum had put on. Chief amongst these has been the acclaimed "Gentlemen's Pipes Through the Ages", which drew an astonishing 127 visitors during August of 2016 alone. My pamphlet accompanying the exhibition is still available, by mail order and online, for those who are interested, including any television executives looking for wholesome and educational broadcasting material. But, I digress.

With the last of the Elizabethan shoes placed back into the display case, I retreated to the dusky quiet of the archive rooms. The shelves, for which I am responsible, stand at the back of the private rooms, and I am fortunate to have secreted a small armchair amongst them, which I am fond of visiting during breaks. It is from that very chair that I write now. I like to think that it will one day find itself a place in a grand museum one day, under its own merits, as worn and threadbare as it is. But, again I digress; let us return to the Tuesday night in question.

As I have elaborated, the chair is of some import, as it is into this very location that I wearily crashed on that wonderful summer evening. I looked at my watch: it was already half past five, and I did not feel ready to don my helm and cycle home; I would rest a little first. It was then that I decided to have a look through one of the boxes, in which, to that date, I had not yet spent much time. I dragged it from a lower shelf, positioned it next to the chair, and began to idly paw through the papers, boxes and mixed trinkets, from that stratum of our host's life. It was then that I found it, hidden at the bottom: an unassuming cigar box, its once regal colours now tarnished and dulled.

My keen archivist's sense told me that I had stumbled across a find of some significance and, with breath held fast, I squeezed and lifted the lid, much like Cornelius would have done, all of those years earlier.

And, there they were...

Presented to me, dear reader, was a small cache of letters, bound with a fray-faded ribbon. What a wonderful treasure to behold!

In the excitement, I fought my urge to dive in, fumbling like a bike-shed lothario. Quickly, I located and donned my white gloves and gently pulled the ribbon. The bow relented and the pages fluttered, stretched and revealed. I recreate them here, much as I found them. They are the courtship letters of Bartie and Vera Thryke.

Tuesday 25th April, 1911.

Dear Miss Summers,

I do hope my "good morning" at this last Sunday service did not render you startled! One did not wish to appear impertinent or forward.

Sincerely,
Reverend Thryke.

*

Monday 1st May, 1911.

Dear Reverend Thryke,

Your concern flatters me, sir. I was neither startled nor found it an impertinence.

Sincerely,
Miss Summers.

*

Wednesday 3rd May, 1911.

Dear Miss Summers,

Your response gladdens me – I had been troubled. Such an ejaculation is not within my nature but, if I may be so bold, you looked handsome in your Sunday bonnet. Perhaps I shall see you in the congregation this coming Sabbath? My sermon promises to be rousing.

Sincerely,

Reverend Thryke.

*

Friday 26th May, 1911.

Dear Reverend Thryke,

Worry not, I have already forgiven your bold ejaculation of a pre-luncheon greeting – though I found, like your rousing sermon, it left me all of a flutter!

Perhaps, in moments when we are alone, you may wish to address me by a more intimate form?

Sincerely,
Miss V. Summers.

*

Wednesday 31st May, 1911.

Dear Miss Summers,

Your last letter had such an effect on me! I have seldom encountered such abandon, despite being a man of the world!

It is the church's Summer Fayre next Saturday. Perhaps (am I being animalistic and wanton?), perhaps I might stand near you with a glass of punch and whisper your name – when the other parishioners have wandered out of earshot, naturally!

My dear Miss Summers, I must tarry no further and close here – I am afeared that you have been sent to tempt me and steer me from my righteous path! But, at the same passing, I am full of wonder and curiosity at the avenue your femininity presents to me! Oh, such joyous confusion! Could I call you Vera at the Summer Fayre?

I must post this letter with haste, before my ardent bravery does leave me. I do so hope it does not shock you!

Sincerely,
Reverend Bartholomew Thryke.

*

Monday 5th June, 1911.

Dearest Bartholomew Thryke,

Shocked, dear one? Why, not at all! Though, like you when your nib scratched across the page, I could also feel the blood coursing through my veins as I read the passion in your words! My naughtiest Bartie! I would consider it caddish, in the least, were you not to fill my summer cup this Saturday next!

Sincerely yours,
Vera Summers.

*

Tuesday 13th June, 1911.

My Dearest Vera,

There are now two pages in my diary that I have revisited again and again: they are those leaves of this Saturday and Sunday last. You carried such a serene and innocent beauty at the Summer Fayre, trussed in your ribbon and finery. I was much sorry that we could only exchange a few utterances. Still, it was right and proper that you remained in the company of your esteemed mother, such that she could deflect the attentions of myriad gentleman suitors. So, imagine my delight when we, tossed on the tides of fate, did find ourselves alone in the churchyard for those few brief moments! The sun glinting from your best bonnet was so becoming! Forgive me, my sweet, that my nerve did fail me, and I could but croak "My dear Miss Summers!" before the town clerk did accost us both!

If only I could be so bold, in the light of day, as I am as a candlelit pensmith! Could that any understand this dichotomy of feeling and expression!

Perhaps you and your mother would be so kind as to call at the vicarage for tea, on one of your visiting days?

Sincerest wishes,
Bartholomew.

It is clear from these letters that the infant Cornelius was born into a nurturing and passionate marriage, built on a foundation of genuine love.

The Thrykes were wed on Saturday 30th September 1911, in Bartie's own church, All Saviours', Little Sodbury-on-the-Wode. The ceremony was performed by Bartie's old seminary chum, Biggleswade Smart, the celebrated parish priest of nearby Corinthian Thatch. He appears in many of Cornelius's diary entries, including this, from 1956:

Dear Diary,

Well, my old friend, I read something rather sad in the newspaper today. I may well be coming to that age when I shall begin to peruse the obituaries with a more significant air of dreadful expectation than I approach the columns of births and marriages – it is many years since I was announced in the first, and long since have I given up on the idea of being included in the second. The obituary column, however, seems to loom large, and I search it for my name on an almost daily basis. If it does not appear, then I assume that I must go out for milk.

But, today jarred me a little. Written bold, with an obituary commensurate with his life, was the name Reverend Biggleswade Smart.

Biggles was no ordinary parish priest, and the fact that he was firm friends with my father always struck me as strange and incongruous. Uncle Biggles, as he insisted that we call him, lived a lionhearted life, bursting with joy and colour. He kept a deep-red motor-racing car, which he careered around all of the best tracks, collecting arms of garlands and silver. On a Saturday, he was always to be found with the bonnet covers folded back, tinkering away with some wrench or tool.

Father felt him frivolous - you could tell by the way he rolled his eyes at the giggles of our fireside, cocoa-stained stories. But, I also think that Father lived vicariously through the deeds and successes of his chum, Biggles, the champion motor-racing vicar.

Reverend Smart was also a fine opening bat, and always scored well when he strode onto our square. Mother claimed that father had once petitioned the bishop to have Uncle Biggles banned, on account of his expertise with the willow. It was said that Biggles had a first-class batting average of nigh on sixty, and that the England selectors had begged for his services on more than one occasion. I do not know if this is true, but I do know that I once saw him smite a mighty six, which spun the weathervane atop of the church spire.

Such was the larger than life character that was Biggleswade Smart. Lives are seldom lived that way, in these modern times. Perhaps I should write a screenplay in remembrance of him – I would play him myself. It was said, in my youth, that there was a remarkable resemblance between us.

To our modern standards, Cornelius's early childhood must have seemed idyllic. In the years which preceded his schooling, Cornelius was free to gambol through the fields and meadows, under the supervision of his elder siblings, his beloved Henry and Martha.

Henry was the firstborn, arriving in March of 1912. Athletic and blond, much like the young Cornelius, he led the merry Thryke troop, as they roamed the verdant territories of Little Sodbury and the surrounding villages. Henry was a natural outdoorsman, who shuddered at the shackles presented by school. His numerous escapes from scripture or Latin prep were legendary, and parents and teachers alike soon gave up on any pretence of capturing or luring him back. Cornelius used to boast that Henry could "mimic any birdcall, name any tree and catch fish faster than an otter on shore leave!" When hungry, or not sated by foraging, the youthful Henry would eventually return home and regale the young Cornelius with tales of his adventures. "To me, he was a hero," Cornelius remarked, in 1945.

Meanwhile, Martha was born on 28th October 1913. She was thin and dark-haired, and was immediately favoured by her father, Bartie. Less robust than her brothers, she did, however, try to follow them across the streams and fields. This would often lead to her arriving home first, coughing, spluttering and with her smock pocket laden with frogspawn or other such delightful substance. The cruel japes she received would inevitably lead to immediate retribution from Bartie. Such reprisals were often directed solely at the junior Cornelius, particularly as Henry grew and filled out, into a strapping, often absent, teenager.

A thirteen-year-old Cornelius writes this moving tale, for a school essay competition on "The Importance of Disappointment":

ESSAY ON THE IMPORTANCE OF DISAPPOINTMENT
by Cornelius Thryke

The red woodland was crisp and slippery, as we set forth into the morning trees. The sun was not long up, and our breath was swirly, and nipped from us with quick, tell-tale signals, as our company strode forth, beneath the canopy. Captain Henry – dear Captain Henry – was our leader.

He was almost three years to the day older than I, and had earnt his pips in earnest conflict. We would do anything for Captain Henry: cross the fastest stream, climb the tallest oak or sneak into the darkest, most terrifying barn. Captain Henry led – whistling his tune, as he always did, warming strength into the limbs of his men – and I followed behind, second in command, with my stick glooping into the leaf fall.

I am Sergeant Cornelius. The skipper calls me "Corny", as only he can. Major Mother forbids it, but here, amongst the birch, the blackthorn and the beech, it steels my heart as the march grows long, and the shadow of the enemy grows thick.

"Hi-ho, Corny!" he calls, cheerfully. "Keep up! We shall make fishing poles this day. Come now, Martha; stay the pace! Are you sure that pack is not too heavy?"

Henry speaks fondly to Private Martha, who scurries behind at the rear; our captain is so patient. She is not as strong as Henry and I, but she manfully volunteered to staff the logistics billet. We are tall, strong and blond; she is short, wispy and dark. Perhaps this is why she is the favourite of the chaplain general, the C.O. of our corps. I fear that Private Martha will soon outrank me, as she has seniority of almost a year and a half. But, as long as I have my captain, I shall be alright. I had the honour of receiving a promotion and commendation in the field, this spring last, for bravery in the face of the strange man yonder. The captain gave me a fantastic citation. Alas, I could not share it with the general and major.

We walk on into the dank. The skipper has his own pack, I have my stick and Martha carries the sandwiches. She is brave, to a point, but I wonder for her place here, in the Sodbury Fusiliers. The air grows thicker, as the trees loom around and over us. Even my heart is beginning to tremble, though I push on, following the leaf-litter dints left by our intrepid captain. Deeper still we march. The trees grow closer, thicker and taller, each reaching high for a spot of sun. The enemy could be anywhere, dug in beyond any barky girth. Days like these are keenly appreciated, for we know not when they will end. The sniper's is the bullet you will never hear.

Eventually, we drop down into the dell and the tree crowd thins. The leaf carpet gives way to grass and the suggestion of a smooth boulder. A back wall of rock looms over us like a shadowy spectre and, silverine, a flashing yet slight cascade descends into the ink-blue pool we have come here to see.

"Set up here, Corny," cries the skipper. "I'll see about cutting some likely canes."

"Roger that, Captain!"

Strong, tall Henry laughs and glances back, over his shoulder. "And keep an eye on Martha; see that she doesn't get up to any mischief!"

"You can count on me, sir!" I give a thumbs-up and feel immediately childish and wanting, for my military bearing. I turn quickly, in time to see Martha skipping amongst the rocks, shiny and slick. I look beyond her and see her pack, lying half-open on the ground.

"Martha," I scold, "you'll get creatures all over the sandwiches! And, the scent may attract unwanted nostrils!"

I walk over to where the pack lay flapping. Deftly, I draw the straps back into the buckles.

Then, I notice a sod of earth, disturbed and lying to one side. Has the enemy bivvied here? Are they watching us even now, taking bearings from Martha's errant pack? I scoop up the earth and, in one movement, I spin and hurl it in the direction of Martha's satisfied gurgles; "And, don't let it happen aga—"

But, before my words have tumbled free, they are faltering. The clump speeds directly toward Martha, right as she turns to look at me; the clod explodes, with a sickening thud, against her forrid.

She shrieks, topples and falls, with a splash, from my view. *Oh, beastly grenade!* Fear floods me as I scramble, in an instant, to the place from which she fell; I glance down, both looking and without looking.

Martha emerges, spluttering from the murk. Her screams pierce, as the water sprays and pours from her mouth. Her face is awash with scarlet, which blobs thick and dark, from the gaping wound on her forehead!

"Martha!" I cry. "Oh, Martha!" I reach down and grasp a flailing hand. As I drag her onto the bank, she stumbles and grazes a knee.

"Oh, Martha – please, I am so sorry. Please forgive me. Please, please do not tell Father!"

She is gasping for air. Her eyes are glassy and rolling like marbles on a drain-head. She is white, and too shocked to even cry.

"Martha, please!"

It is now that the skipper re-enters the clearing. He drops the sticks and is with us in a single bound.

"What has happened here? She's bleeding!"

I sense panic in his voice.

"It... it was an accident!" I stammer. "She got in the way!"

"An accident?" The skipper looks me square in the eye; I look downward. "Father will flail me alive!"

"But..." Tears now sting my eyes.

"I am in command here; Father will hold me accountable! He will beat me, Cornelius. Do you hear? He will beat me so!"

"But, Henry!"

Martha, now in full awareness, screams another piercing scream, as she sees the blood staining her hands and her tabard. I begin to cry. I glance at Henry; he too has begun to sob! He, too!

I swallow, and know I must say my piece: "Skipper, I will take her home. I will shoulder the blame in your place."

Henry's tears halt.

"My brave Corny! Yes! Yes, I think you should. It is time for you to show bravery in the line of fire. This tragedy is your burden to carry."

I lower my head and nod in the affirmative.

"Do you know the way?"

"Yes."

"And, you will take good care of her?"

"Yes."

"And, you will leave me some sandwiches?"

"Yes."

He nods. "Then go, brave Corny. Carry the injured back to base, report in and godspeed. I shall stay here and complete the mission."

I know what I must do. I stand and brush the tears from my face. As she still wails, I nurse Martha to her feet, and we begin to traipse off into the wood.

So many hours must have passed. So many. The blood has stopped running, but Martha is left with a nasty-looking wound. Dried blood cakes her face, her dress and one knee, as she limps along.

"Do try and keep up!" I call.

"We are lost, Cornelius! We shall die here. We shall be eaten by wolves!" She starts to wail once more. It is true; the light is fading and we appear to be no nearer home.

"Nonsense!" My voice is shaking. "I know exactly where we are. We shall be home in time for tea."

I feel the hot sting of tears on my cheek. Why did Henry have to let us go? Why could he not come with us and guide us back home? Did his bravery really fade?

Night has fallen. We trudge on, through owl hoots and rustlings. Suddenly, I halt. Martha, weak with fatigue, catches me and falls forward, into the murk.

"Shush! Listen!"

Sure enough, we can hear voices. They are calling: "Martha! Martha!"

My sister runs past me, instantly refreshed.

"Martha, Martha!" the voices call.

"It's Mother and Papa!" cries Martha. "They are searching for me!"

She stumbles over a hidden root, but her relief drives her headlong, into the dark. I hasten to follow, even though I know the way.

"Oh, Martha, there you are! We have been…"

The voice stops.

The voice stops, then screams: "My dear goodness! What have *they* done to you!"

It is Father's voice. It is shrill with anger; leaden with revenge.

"Where are they? Did they leave you? How did they allow you to become so terribly injured? *My* poor girl!"

I emerge from the trees; they see me. Father and Martha shrink back, like black crows, in Mother's lamplight.

"You, boy!" snarls Father. "You did this!"

He springs forward, his cane held high! His anger is complete.

It is Mother who eventually carries me back. They have shrunk back, black and wiry, into the village lights.

The essay, Cornelius notes elsewhere, was disqualified from the competition for having "nothing to do with the theme". Furthermore, Thryke was also given the slipper and additional lines, for "wanton fantasy" and "failing to respect the sanctity of family" – the Reverend Batholomew Thryke himself approved the punishment, personally.

On 28th July 1914, the world fell into war.

Cornelius was born in the following March, his early years shaped by conflict. By 1914 Bartholomew was in middle age, being forty-six years old and, in a reserved occupation, he was charged with delivering spiritual guidance on the home front.

As Vera Thryke carried the foetal Cornelius, it was his beloved Uncle Biggleswade Smart who answered the nation's call: at the earliest opportunity, he enlisted with the Army Chaplains' Department.

Biggles was commissioned as a chaplain, fourth class, and with the local Gentlemen Farmers Regiment, he arrived in France in 1915. He, and many of the local men of Little Sodbury and the surrounding villages, found themselves attached to the 14th (Light) Division, as part of Kitchener's K1 Army. Biggleswade was eventually assigned to the Duke of Cornwall's Light Infantry, as part of the 6th Battalion, where he was to give spiritual guidance to the men.

Our account of Biggles's time on the Western Front, aside from the Army records, owes a great deal to the occasional letters which Biggleswade sent to both his own parishioners in general, and Vera Thryke in particular. Those which survive are housed either here, in the museum war records or, touchingly, amongst Cornelius's personal papers.

When I first came across the letters to Vera, it was a very moving moment. I had read and handled the epistles to the parishioners of Corinthian Thatch, and there is a definite warmth amongst those, but the personal letters were a joy to behold, if not representing a harrowing snapshot into the plight of those ordinary men – the soldiers on both sides – who went to war, confused and afraid, and never returned.

The Somme, 1916.

My dear Vera,

It is with a heavy heart that I write this letter. How is it that man can do these things?

I trust things are lovely back in the villages? Are the flowers in the fullest of bloom? It is summer here, although one would be forgiven for forgetting it; the sky remains grey, full of smoke and ash. Even the sunbeams find it inappropriate to shine upon our upturned faces, such as it has all of our summers.

I hope that you will forgive my less than elegant prose. I can no longer discern if we are each shelling, or whether it be a chronic ringing in my ears. Perhaps they have become clogged with mud – it is undoubtedly in plentiful supply; even my bible has not been spared from the occasional coating. Wherein this madness shall we find pockets of God?

Having grabbed a few moments of reflection, I felt the need to write to my dear ones, back home. So, you shall know that the good Lord has granted me further life, for now! Many, many others have not been so fortunate. I do not know what news does filter back to you, but there is no glory here. Yes, there is bravery in the face of fear, but no glory.

Yet these blasted fields throw up serendipitous slices of God's dark humour. Amongst the many thousands of men here, faces of home still cross and fade. Yesterday, there was Albert. I do not know if you knew him, but he was a farmhand on the Steadings acres, until he joined up and travelled here. He had never once left the safety of the villages and, when he did, he was shown that the security of home was real. We prayed together yesterday – there was peace in it. He clutched my tunic with a strong, bloody grip, as my words soothed him into rest. I held his gaze, but I am not sure if he saw me; his eyes were Heavenward, as he reclined in the trench, wounded and so terribly afraid. He knew that he was going, and I could not bring myself to tell him otherwise; what point in such a lie? As his fingers released the coarse material of my jacket, I blessed him into readiness and gently closed his eyes. It was not two years ago that he made that delicious cider for the Corinthian Thatch fete. Do you remember? We shared a cup or two in the barn. I revisit that moment in the fleeting shards of my dreams.

But, I should ask of you and yours!
Why, the young one would have had his first birthday, this March last? Is the child a girl or a boy? I must know, dear one. I picture him a boy – young, strong and full of life, like his brother, Henry. My! I calculate that he has turned four, some months back! Where do the years go? Faster then; now slow – stuck in the mud.

I do not know if you should be able to write; sometimes the odd letter can find its way through. Remember me to Bartholomew and Martha.

Yours, in fondness,
B.

The following letter, to Reverend Smart's parishioners, caused much consternation and fervour at the time, particularly when it found its way into the *Sodbury & Corinthian Gazette*:

Dearest Flock,

In this time of war, I think of our joyous Sundays together. In this hour of conflict, it can be challenging to remember which grey morn falls upon the Sabbath. Time has condensed into a sequence of noise, mud and searing fire. We, in our frailty, have created our own Dis, here on this our very perfect Earth. But, goodness shall prevail. It is law.

But, this Sunday, I would like for you to pray for us all. All. *I shall illustrate with a story of what has just befallen me:*

It was but two days ago that I found myself out in the mire. My task was to bring back any wounded men, to comfort them in their journey, and to bless those whose passage was already westward bound. As the shells and stray bullets whistled around my ears, I happened across him.
He was lying on his back, on the edge of a shallow crater. His boots were obscured by the stagnant puddle of filth which had pooled in the bottom of this terrible dell. Instinctively, I went to him, tripping over body parts as I went. He needed me. He needed the comfort of our Lord. As I arrived at his side, his eyes widened. His uniform was muddy, torn and stained black. A hand across the stain was red – red with holding back that which was within him. Knowing that he was not long for this

world, I drew a small crucifix which I carried upon me. At its sight, his breathing slowed and I began to pray. I looked into his face. It was young and beardless, and his skin was as white as snow, flecked only by the berry trickle from his mouth.

"What is your name, young man?" I asked.

"Bitte?"

"Wie heißen Sie?" I responded.

He smiled, "Fritz."

"Bless you, Fritz." I cradled his head in my arm and drew myself next to him, my own boots now obscured by the healing waters.

I held him for what seemed like hours, but in reality was only a few minutes. I guess I had closed my eyes, for mere seconds, but when I opened them, he was there. Standing over us was a German officer. As he knelt beside our scene, I noticed that there were tears in his eyes. From his pocket, he also produced a small crucifix, much similar to my own. He too cradled Fritz, and our prayers were doubled and aligned.

"Lob sei Gott," I said.

"Praise be to God," the German chaplain replied.

Fritz passed into the arms of our Saviour, shortly after. We both bowed our heads, as his young, innocent life expired. The horror of war seemed to fall into silence, as we both lay there, commending our comrade to Heaven.

Fritz had not been my enemy, any more than any of you are.

He was a young boy, as your sons are, longing for the loving apron of his mütter.

Nor was my brother in Christ my foe. Yet, we both came to the sad realization that we must return to our trenches to continue this madness. Together under God; asunder under Man – this was our truth. This was our truth, and I hate it. Be sure, there is no glory in what we do, we sons and pawns of men!

As we were to head our separate ways, he held out a manly hand, the cross still dangling from it. I offered my own, the chain of my silver cross fresh with the blood of the fallen.

"Farewell, my friend," he offered.

"Lebewohl, mein freund." I reached out and drew him toward me, and I sobbed. I sobbed for the fall of Man. And, he sobbed. I don't know if he made it back to his trench.

So, I beseech you: pray for us both. Pray for the confused soul of sinless Fritz. Pray for an end to this madness. There are no enemies here, just countless, dismembered victims.

Your humble shepherd,
Biggleswade.

The Sunday after this letter was received, from his pristine pulpit, Batholomew Thryke condemned it in the strongest terms that the Church allowed. Cornelius, as a babe in the arms of his mother, knew nothing of the vitriol at the time, unless he felt it through the bond he held with the weeping Vera. Whatever lesson in humanity Biggleswade thought he was sharing was undone from the pulpit of his once great friend.

Upon his return, in 1918, Biggleswade was a changed man. The community to which he felt himself naturally drawn had much changed, also. In the following year, he packed up and left Corinthian Thatch for the last time. Cornelius saw him only infrequently after that.

Part Two:
Becoming

EDITOR'S NARRATIVE
Quentin Prowler

In the September of 1922, at the age of seven years old, Cornelius Arthur Thryke was sent away to school. It was to come as something of a shock, to a child more used to roaming freely through the soft countryside, playing pirates and soldiers as he went.

A similar plan had been laid out for Henry, a few years earlier, but such had been the elder brother's consistent escape attempts that he was, by then, home-schooled by mother Vera. Bartholomew would accept no such outcome for Cornelius.

"One of your sons will receive an education!" he is recalled as screaming at Vera. "Cornelius shall go away to school!"

The establishment chosen was Greyowls Preparatory School for Boys, which was a three-hour steam-train journey from the comfort of Little Sodbury-on-the-Wode.

Cornelius's school days feature heavily within his writings, so much so that I can pass the baton directly onto our host for the time being; the following pages are extracts from Cornelius's own memoirs and diaries…

THE MEMOIRS OF CORNELIUS THRYKE.

I

In 1921, I was sent to Greyowls Preparatory School for Boys. I was kitted out in my grey flannel shorts, blazer and cap, with a bright-red tie clutching at my throat. As Mother walked me to the station, carrying my small case for me, it was still sunny and warm, and I longed to throw off the shackles of my new, itchy uniform and dash off into the fields and copses behind the station house. But, I could not. Mother was holding my hand tightly and looking straight ahead, as she strode.

We arrived somewhat early for the train, though I could only tell the time from the sky, back then. Mother took me into the tearoom, where she ordered a pot of breakfast tea and two small macaroons. We sat at the corner table, so that we might observe the platform from the comfort of our seats. I am not sure, to this day, whether I knew what was happening or not, but I remember the silent tears that rolled down her powdered face.

When a pipe-smoking man leant out from behind an enormous newspaper to gaze upon her, I felt a flush of anger: this was my precious time, in the company of my mother; I would not allow it to be sullied.

"You do remember where you should alight the train?" she enquired, presently.

"Yes, Mother," I replied.

I looked at the tag, tied to the handle on my case. I was to become this label, whatever and wherever it was. Would I ever come back here, to the warmth of mother's gingham folds and floral pastry scents? Even Father had shaken my hand this morning, and pressed a penny into it. Was I coming back? I felt the hotness of tears upon my cheek.

"You must so try to be brave, my soldier," said Mother, trying to soothe us both. "It will soon be the holidays, and you will come back for a while."

For a while?

A couple of days before, in the fading light of a late-summer's eve, I'd had a similar conversation with my brother, Henry. How worldly-wise he had seemed to me at that time! We were sitting in our den, deep in the woods, chewing the fat and righting the wrongs of our world. As I reflect, years later, I now realize that as that new autumn sun was lowering, my childhood, blissful as it had been, was also fading into shadow.

"Will I like school, Henry?" I had asked.

Henry raised himself onto his elbows and looked long at me; I wondered if I had misspoken. Presently, he removed the straw from his mouth and gave a reply:

"Perhaps you shall."

I was heartbroken! Even at that young age his words shook me! Were we not of the same cloth? He had run away so many times – would not I?

"I shall not!" I spat, indignantly. "Shan't so! I shall be back here the very next day! Even if I must run all night!"

Henry reclined once more and cupped his head in his hands. "Then, I will wait for you here."

There was venom and intent in my words but, as I bade Henry farewell on that morning, some of that strength left me. And now, as Mother and I sat in that station tearoom, quietly sobbing into our macaroons, the rest of it faded into nothingness. I was to be an unwilling schoolboy – as if there were ever any other kind?

Presently, Old Jack, the stationmaster, poked his head around the peeling red door. "Ma'am?" he said, gruffly.

Mother bowed her head. I climbed down from my chair and grabbed for the handle of my case. Her hand came down on top of mine and our eyes met.

I'm not sure how long we remained there, but Old Jack coughed loudly, to gain our attention. Behind him, steam was billowing onto the platform. "It's time, ma'am."

As I began to drag my case along the floor, she collapsed back into her chair and let out a shrill wail.

Jack placed a hand on my shoulder. "Let me help you with that, young master," he purred, in a kindly drawl. "Be a brave lad for your mother."

I did not dare to look back. The world had scooped me up, and I was bundled onto the train.

Greyowls Prep was housed in a large, bleak, gothic building, with several equally dank outbuildings, serving a variety of tortuous purposes. It loomed over you from all approaches, with towers and battlements extending into the sky, like elongated and sharpened fingers. That it was home to anyone was a source of mystery to me. It had been built in the early 1800s, by eccentric cotton magnate Aubrey du Montague-Pipe. All I can say is that he must have been fond of long corridors; the architect, at Pipe's behest, had left plenty of routes for bitter draughts to howl along the halls – even, it seemed, in the height of an English summer. What little natural light there was beamed through thick, leaded windows, most of which appeared to carry displays of various disembowellings and martyrdom; I believe that Montague-Pipe had been a deeply religious man. It was ironic in the extreme that this terrible gothic folly had plunged its creator into depression, bankruptcy and, eventually, death. Some of the boys claimed his tortured soul still walked the passageways on certain eerie nights.

An old, open-topped bus ran from the station to the school. On "arrival days" it would shuttle until the last of the boarders' trains had called in. On that first afternoon that I arrived, I was one of the earliest.

A guard shooed me off of his platform and bade me stand in an adjacent field. "The bus will arrive shortly," he stated, in a rather matter-of-fact manner, as if catching this peculiar form of ancient transport was something that I did every day.

I dragged my case along, occasionally lifting it off of the ground, and entered the field by the entrance the guard had indicated. And, I waited.

I had placed my valise down, slightly under the tree-line, at the front edge of the field. Perched atop, I was able to survey the other boys as they arrived, with the luxury of them not immediately spotting me. I have to say that I was utterly petrified. Before long, clusters of boys had assembled in tall, gangly groups. I sensed a few were looking in my direction, so I kept my gaze upon the tips of my tight and shiny shoes.

"What-ho, old chap!"

Startled, I looked up in the direction of the voice. A bespectacled young fellow, perhaps even smaller than myself, was standing beneath a mass of blond hair. His hand was extended confidently in my direction.

"I'm Watkins – Algernon Watkins – though my chums call me 'Algie'!"

I took hold of his hand. It was sticky. "Thryke. Cornelius Thryke."

"Cornelius? Shall I call you Corny?"

I felt my face flush with anger. Corny was my brother's name for me; I did not want it purloined so early, and cheaply, into my schooling. "Corny will be fine."

"Huzzah! I say, Corny, are you a new boy, too?"

I was tired and fragile, but I knew I must try. "Yes, Algie; yes, I am."

"Whizzo!"

I found his enthusiasm draining. I just wanted to contemplate my fate in silence. But, my new pal pressed on. He placed his case next to mine and climbed aboard.

"Don't worry, Corny; we can be new together! I have a feeling we're going to be firm friends!"

And, that was how I met Chief Superintendent Algernon Watkins.

Within the walls of Greyowls lay a culture of brutality, designed to toughen us up and turn us into useful men. My initiation into this life was smoothed, somewhat, by my association with Algie; he had a brother at the school, who had presumably coached him in all of the rules and strange customs. My knowledge meant that I was able to circumvent many of the unusual punishments – though, not all – which were meted out by the older boys, in retribution for the merest infraction of code. I remember my first encounter with these bizarre rules.

"Ah, youngling!"

I continued my progress along the bleak corridor.

"You! Youngling!!"

I turned and gazed, confused, in the direction of the cry.

An older boy, in a tailcoat, was glaring at me. He snapped his fingers and pointed to the ground: "Your shadow was cast across my shoe."

"I beg your pardon?"

"Do not play the innocent with me, youngling. Your shadow fell upon my shoe! You know the rules."

I did not. Though, I felt my interceptor was dutybound to tell me.

"Since the shadow of a youngling has sullied the shoe of a senior boy, I invoke a hatting!"

Now, I had no idea what this meant, so I just nodded.

"Well, don't just stand there gawping, boy – cut along, before I punish you further."

I turned away and paced, as quickly as my young legs would allow. I knew enough not to break into a canter, lest I should be found foul of running in the corridor, which no doubt had a different infraction tariff attached than it did last week. Eventually, I reached my form room. I collapsed into my desk, hot and breathy.

"Are you alright, old man?"

Algie had adopted the strange habit of calling me "old man", even though I was seven. He was already around forty-five, if trapped in the diminutive body of a seven-year-old, bespectacled blond boy.

I was just about to launch into a tirade on the unfairness of it all, when our form master, Mr. Alexander Hillbrow (M.A., Cantab) entered the room. He clipped me around the ear as he strode to the board.

"On time means five minutes early, Thryke. Do try and be punctual."

I have carried that logic with me for a lifetime. At that moment it made no sense but, to this day, I have never missed a train. I have, however, spent many hours waiting for one.

"Good morning, first-years!" barked Hillbrow, from the front of the room. "I trust none of you were involved in last night's pillow fight debacle, as this morning you will need your energies focused on the delights of English grammar! Kindly, and with the minimum of noise, attend to the retrieval of your text and exercise books."

Thirty desk lids rose in unison. From the safety of the barricade, I shot a whisper across to Algie.

"Watty. Watty. What the devil is a blasted 'hatting'?"

Algie scrunched up his nose, just as another volley was issued. Clearly, it was not my morning.

"Thryke!" came the shrill, icy blast. "Do not consider that idle chatter behind a desk lid renders it inaudible to the intelligent human ear!"

I lowered my desk to an angle I now know to be approximately thirty degrees, and peered over the top. "I'm sorry, sir?"

"My point exactly!"

A stick of chalk was propelled toward me with frightening velocity. Instinctively, I re-raised the lid, and I assume it shattered on impact, as the boys in front were treated, spluttering, to a cloudy, white downpour of debris. Hillbrow looked both impressed and disappointed at the same time: it was quite the feat of expressionism – if one might use the term in that respect.

Thirty desktops applauded in a domino run. It was then that I noticed Algernon straining, his hand reaching for the light fixture.

"What is it, Watkins?" asked the master, wearily.

"Please, sir; it wasn't Corny's fault, sir. He has a question, sir."

"Ah! Well, why didn't you say? Of course, class; Thryke has a question so burning – so vital; so critically acute – that the study of His Majesty's English grammar should be put on hold for each and every one of us." His eyes shot to me, full of malice. "So, Thryke, enlighten us. Share with us your brilliant question; your wonderful piece of wisdom! Chop chop!"

I glanced at Algie. He nodded, so I slowly raised my hand: "Sir, what is a 'hatting'?"

I can only liken the next few seconds to plunging into a deep swimming pool: the air whistled from the room, and the boys around me began to gasp like drowning mariners. Everything closed in and became heavy. It was some time before I rose to the surface.

Hillbrow stood, stock still, at the head of the class. He looked pale and pulled taut.

"There is no such thing as a 'hatting'."

"But sir, one of the—"

"There is no such thing as a hatting!"

"The older boys, sir—"

"There is, Thryke, no such thing as a hatting!"

I remember, to this very day, feeling my face colour with confusion – confusion and rage. No such thing as a hatting? But, hadn't I...?

What even was this place? All at once, I wanted the familiarity of home.

"No, Father," I blustered.

My comrades burst into guffaws. With a sweep of his gown, Mr. Hillbrow tutted, as he spun back to the board. My humiliation was complete.

It was during recreation that the mystery deepened.

I was watching the other boys buying tuck; Algie was in the queue, but I had no funds. As boy after boy trotted away from the line, pockets bulging with wizard treats, I imagined how they would taste.

There was no money being sent for me from home – Father forbade it. I was in the school as a "dog-collar boy": a chap whose board was paid for by the Church. "D.C.!" they would hiss, from nooks and niches. "D.C.!" I swear even Algie, my only friend, looked down upon me sometimes. You see, because Father drew his small salary from the same Church coffers which paid for my meagre schooling, he felt that he was already shouldering a significant financial burden for my education. Further expenditure on the "peacockery of nougat" seemed to Father to be somewhat frivolous, and not in keeping with his self-imposed law of frugality. So, I watched.

With fellows rushing this way and that, as a lowly "younger" I was used to being buffeted around the mahogany corridors. Only, on this occasion, I endured a particularly fierce collision. My stripling of a body bent double and I collapsed to the floor, clutching my midriff.

As I gulped for air, my staccato breaths began to flutter a piece of paper, which had become entangled in my garments. I picked it free. Whilst folded neatly, it was clear that it had been torn hurriedly from a jotter and roughly folded in twain. On the outer layer, in a spidery hand, were written the words: "Give to old Cowans."

As luck would have it, that afternoon was the sadistic rite of the fortnightly cross-country. During our lessons, our masters would tut, as they observed endless white lines of boys snaking around the perimeter of the grounds, while the gales blew and the rain inevitably slanted in. As the youngest year in the school, we were permitted to escape with a rigorous four miles, while McNair, the games master, shouted various slogans of abuse in our general direction.

Fortunately, it was also a widely known fact that McNair liked a drop of Scotland's finest. The crafty fellow had planned his curriculum such that all cross-country runs took place on the same day – a Wednesday.

"Old McNair is at it again, is he?" This was often the plaintiff muttering which accompanied a classroom sighting of these distant, mud-spattered serpents. At the time, we did not understand that crafty McNair spent his athletic supervisory day slowly drawing from a hip-flask, which he surreptitiously refilled between lessons. As I look back on it now, he must have been three sheets to the wind by afternoon tea.

So, on this afternoon, under the less than careful eye of Mr. McNair, Albie and I scrambled back into the school and quickly pulled on our uniforms. With the sheet of paper safely ensconced in my inside pocket, we darted through the ghostly corridors, only once having to avoid a gliding fleet of masters. Soon, we had arrived at the glass-panelled door of the library.

Mr. Cowans was known to dislike the boys of Greyowls Prep with avid diligence. He despised them borrowing his books with even more intensity and, through a perceived necessity, he had spent many years creating a labyrinth of ever more complex rules and regulations to prevent it.

"What are you boys doing in here?" he barked, without raising an eye from the desk.

Albie, now slightly behind, elbowed me in the ribs. "Go on," he urged.

I reached into my blazer pocket and pulled forth the piece of paper. "Please, sir, we have been sent for this."

I placed the paper, at chin height, onto Cowans's desk, then retreated a pace. Cowans drew his glasses down onto the end of his nose and hooked at the fold, with the point of a pencil.

"Please, sir."

In a single, occidental swoop, he pencil-flipped the paper, caught it in mid-air and drew it up to his eyes. In a simultaneous oriental swirl, his glasses were pushed back into place, and the tip of the nose was scratched. "Well," he sighed, "let's see what we have here, shall we?"

He opened the sheet back, as to unfurl the information hidden therein. I would share that same information with you here, if I could but, to this day, I am not sure what message lay within the folds. What I do clearly remember was his reaction, which I shall now share.

"Where did you get this?"

"Please, sir; I must have it."

"Where, young man, did you get this?"

"An older boy, sir. I must have it, sir."

My sheet disappeared into the top pocket of the grumpy librarian. He flopped down from his stool and drew himself up to his full height. From this position, he held my gaze. I knew that I should stand firm. Cowans then opened an unseen drawer and pulled forth a set of keys.

"Not here," he said. "Wait for me in Ancient Rome."

I looked back at Albie and shrugged my shoulders. Behind me, Cowans was already striding away. "What do we do now?"

Albie grabbed be me the sleeve. "Come on. Old Cowans meant to cut along to the Ancient Rome section, silly. It's over there, in that shadowy corner."

I was not sure what cut me more, Albie remarking that I was slow on the uptake, or realizing this myself. We set off at once, and arrived in Ancient Rome via Mesopotamia, Greece and Junior Sheep Husbandry.

I was curiously engaged in studying an artist's rendering of a particularly brutal-looking North Ronaldsay, when both myself and Albie became aware of books shuffling on the shelf. Cowans, in Egypt, slipped a thin tome between a copy of Niebuhr's *Roman History* (translated by Hare & Thirwall) and Pattermonger's *Colosseum Disembowelments for Boys*. No words were spoken, as I reached up and grasped it between my thumb and forefinger, pulling it down toward me. Then, through the shelving, I saw Cowans slink off, back to his counter, as I fell to my rump, book in lap.

"It's just an old exercise book!" exclaimed Albie, with more than a hint of disappointment. "What use is that?"

"But, it's not," I replied, thumbing through the pages: "it's something akin to a guidebook, Albie! It's full of wheezes, dodges and schemes!"

"You don't say!"

"I jolly well do, old boy!"

Albie beamed and plonked down on the floor, beside me. "Cor! Well, let's have a look!"

I was flipping through the pages, unsure where to stop and browse. The rush of such esoterica was breathtaking.

"Stop!" cried Albie. "There! Look!"

My rifling had come to a halt, on a page written in a loose, spidery hand.

"I'm not sure if I can make it out," I said. "Perhaps it is in Aramaic?"

"It's no more Aramaic than the tip of your nose," replied Albie, with a snort. "Here, pass it to me. Right there – don't you see? 'Hattings'!"

Albie grabbed at the book – I made no attempt to stop him; I think the subterfuge had knocked the wind from my sails. "Read on," I said, shuffling around so I could lean back against the oversized bookshelf. "Read on."

"*'Hattings'*," began Albie, grandly: "*'A hatting is a level three punishment. During a hatting, the receiver must rise early and take a position in the entrance hall. It is advantageous to arrive early, in the event of a glut. Once in the foyer, the receiver must jockey for position around the school mascot.'* Do they mean Alan, old boy?"

I assumed so; Alan was the name of the stuffed boar which lived beneath the grand hall clock.

"'Boys must remain in contact with Alan at all times, during the hatting'."

The image of boys jostling around a serenely indifferent and hirsute porcine seemed pointlessly ludicrous to me, even then. "Go on," I said, with an ancient sigh.

"'Then, while contact remains, all hattees must recite the home counties' ten most important top-hat manufacturers, as agreed by the school's 1900 Hatting Committee. These must be recited in alphabetical order.'"

"Good grief, Albie! How is one meant to know that? I mean, really!"

"Fret not, old boy! It goes on to say that there are three acceptable variants: the classical, the volume and the exports list. Alphabetized lists are available in the appendices. Well, that certainly is a wizard stroke of luck, wouldn't you say, old boy?"

"Is there much more?" It was all that I could muster.

"A little, yes. It goes on the say that when you have completed the recital, to the satisfaction of your nominator, they will call out 'hatting' from the staircase. You are then to double away to their personal study and prepare their breakfast toast."

It was the punishment of nothing for nothing. "All that, just to secure some toast?"

Albie shrugged.

"Then, why don't I just do that? It amounts to the same thing."

Albie came from a long line of boys who had been pettily tortured at Greyowls. I knew that he respected these grim traditions, built up over generations of misplaced revenge, but I could not. The trees and streams of home had never poked and twisted in malice. Sitting there, on that cold library floor, I fancied I saw a large crow, expanding and looming over me.

"Shall I scribble down the classical list for you?"

The crow drooled the ash of singed scripture upon me, as it tried to engulf the gap between us.

"Corny?"

I knew what I needed to do.

"No."

"But, Corny!"

I rose, looked Albie in the eyes, and gently removed the book from his grasp. "Come on," I said. "Come on, old boy."

Brave Albie's lip trembled, and he gave a sniff as he pushed himself up from the floor. "But, Corny! Wait!"

I was already striding back to the desk of Old Cowans. He could have his set of rules back; I would not follow them.

I slept through my hatting, the following morning.

The prefect I had encountered did not.

He found me a couple of days later, enjoying my hobby of watching the other boys buy tuck.

"You dare to disobey me?!" he squawked, sweeping down onto my childish frame. His blow struck me, swift and hard, and I was propelled back onto the floor.

Silence fell, as a hundred sugary eyes descended upon me. I could only glare back in rage – the rage that I had always carried. I made no sound, no whimper, even though tears were stinging for release.

My tormentor, Cadwallader, looked on, open-mouthed, expecting me to blub. There was a murmur of discontent amongst some of the boys.

"Silence," screeched Cadwallader, his torso becoming long and thin. "You will complete the hatting tomorrow, do you hear?"

There was another murmur of discontent, only this time louder and more rumbling. Red-faced Cadwallader swished his tails around him and seemed to spin, like a top, down the corridor. "Tomorrow!" he shrilled, in his wake.

When he had passed into the once there, I could not stave off the flow, and had to cry openly. At that moment, I longed for the softness of Mother. I felt vulnerable, weak and ashamed.

But, in that instant, I felt boys pulling me to my feet, brushing me down and straightening my blazer.

"Straight bat, Corny," said one, who I did not know. He reached his hand around mine and pressed a sherbet lemon into my palm.

Others surged forward, ruffling my hair or patting me on the shoulder. When I looked down, my cupped hands were full of the most wonderful array of tuck. For a few seconds, I forgot my torment and, a good foot taller, skipped off to my next class.

II

Over the coming weeks, various groups granted me sanctuary in their break-time activities. Cadwallader could not get to me in class, so it was only in these regulated moments of freedom that I was truly prey. My one lament was that I could no longer observe the colours and sights of the tuck queue – it had been a little window to me, like watching a Pathé reel of a sporting giant, but now it was gone.

One club which extended me welcome was the painting class. In the main, it was quite a ragtag bunch, but there was one boy, around thirteen years of age, who had a quite remarkable talent. It became my habit to place my stool slightly back from his left-hand shoulder, like a slip fielder with full view.

"What is your name?" he called back, on my second visit.

"Thryke, sir."

I felt I noticed the hint of a smile play on the corner of his lips. "Thryke, eh? Yes, you have made something of an impression, wouldn't you say?"

I looked down at my sandals.

"I am Constable. Before you say anything smart, be aware that, yes, I know it is an appropriate name, and no, I am not."

"Not what?" I ventured.

Constable sighed and recommenced mixing browns on his palette. "It is so hard to get the right tone, wouldn't you agree, Thryke?" He looked over his shoulder at me with watery blue eyes. "You're not much of an artist then, Thryke?"

His head spun back. "I find her hair to be of the entirely wrong hue; I am looking for chestnut. Do you think this is chestnut?"

Constable rotated slightly, giving me full view of his canvas. The woman staring back at me had a beauty, a strength and a poise. For the first time, I noticed a small photograph propped against the bottom, right-hand corner of the work.

"I think it is magnificent." Immediately, I blushed.

"Your compliment is noted. But, I don't know... it's... it's..."

"Who is she?"

Constable spun on his stool, now fully turned to face me. "What was your first name?"

"Cornelius. Chaps call me Corny."

He nodded, almost imperceptibly. "Well, Cornelius, she is my very own and dearest mother. I plan to present it to her this coming Yuletide."

"It will be a fine gift."

The boy turned back to his canvas. "Yes," he said, slowly.

In my next letter home, I declared my intention to paint.

Editor's note:
It is never mentioned in any of his diaries or notes, but Cornelius's letters home were never opened; in amongst his artefacts, we found the intact envelopes, like small capsules, bearing his gathering childhood thoughts – they were tied together with ribbon. On dark, winter evenings, I have tried to comprehend the events which would

have led to such a tragic turn of circumstance. If, dear reader, you can piece together some comforting scenario from these pages, I beg you to share it.

I also spent time in the theatre group – a small band, who were looking to put on their own productions. You may be forgiven for thinking that this disordered but well-meaning team sent me on my way to stardom but, in truth, they did not. I only went there, or to the chess society, when I felt it was too risky to appear in the art school.

I did not perform. Not at first. I was content to hand out the scripts at the beginning of the rehearsal and collect them all back in again at the end. It was the safety that I sought, not the spotlight. I was happy with the solitude I could draw, as I sat in a corner, farthest from the door. There, obscured from view, I would drift away and, once again, find solace in chasing through the meadows.

But, Cadwallader had spies in all corners. Slowly, they began to infiltrate the hobby rooms – one here; one there. I did not know who they were and, in my homespun reveries, I do not feel their eyes upon me. But slowly, inevitably, the net was being drawn in.

It happened a few weeks later, in the chess club. I was just about to succumb to a fiendish rendition of the King's Indian, when the door burst open, and in strode the irate Cadwallader, flanked by two of his cronies – one from art, one from theatre. Before, I had not noticed them, but now, reflected in the light from the evil prefect, they appeared as gargoyles: twisted, gnarled and of ill intent. They swept a channel for their leader – boys on either side were shoved or dived for cover – then they were upon me.

My opponent toppled his king, rose and took two steps back.

Cadwallader laughed. It was a cruel, hot roar.

"Well, Thryke, it appears that you have triumphed in your tawdry battle on the board." He swished around, addressing his words to all who would listen. "But, there are some battles that you cannot win. Some that you *must* not win!"

Cadwallader's cane cut the air and swept the pieces from the board. The single, last pawn circled, sighed and dropped from the edge.

"We are a society, Thryke," continued Cadwallader, "and societies have rules. Societies have tradition. Societies have order! When these pillars are disrespected, the punishment must be swift and public! You, Thryke, you… you little worm, have disrespected the traditions of our great institution! You are a stain, of which we are all ashamed. There is to be no forgiveness for the destitute church-boy!"

With practiced grace and speed, his silver-topped cane spun through his fingers and came crashing down across my shoulder-blades. As the pain sprung into my tiny body, the air was simultaneously driven from me. I was sent tumbling forward, across the squares, eyes wide, too shocked to cry out.

Thwack! The cane came down again and again.

I was now in a ball on the freshly shone floor. Blood was trickling from… where?

Thwack! Thwack! Thwack!

I do not know how the frenzy dissipated and stopped; I heard, only later, that Cadwallader's own goons had pulled him away, and a perfect circle of boys had gathered around me.

"Oh, my goodness!" – I thought I heard these words. I felt it was the voice of our kindly housemaster, Mr. Cooper. He seemed far, far away. I felt myself being scooped up; perhaps I was ascending! Was the life draining from me? My mind seemed to make the decision not to fight.

"Such unnecessary brutality!" the voice muttered.

Then, I passed from memory.

When I woke, it was as black as pitch. I tried to move my arms and legs, but I felt nothing but the searing soreness of beaten flesh and bones. I let out a curdling howl.

As I moved my head around, I noticed a warm glow, off in the distance – it seemed to be shaped by the glass of wiry windows. I howled again, aware now that tears were streaming down my hot face. I sensed a figure glide from the glow and float, noiselessly, across to me.

Was I? Could I be?

The bedclothes which restrained me were pulled back, and I was lifted, still sobbing, into the warm embrace of the apparition.

"It's alright, Cornelius. It's alright."

"Mother?"

"Shhh... No, you're in the school sick-dorm," she soothed. "You've been in the wars, have you not?"

The nurse grasped me to her starched bosom, and I sobbed into the fragrant material. A hand rubbed my back, gentle and soft.

"That's it, Cornelius: you let it all out. You've had quite a couple of days. But, you're safe now. We'll fix you up; we'll look after you."

The overwhelming kindness broke my heart further, and I wailed once more. All the pain of leaving the countryside, of leaving Henry, rushed upon me. The raw wound, from where I was torn from Mother, swirled into this moment of release. My body burned all over, yet my heart flooded it all with a higher, crushing grief.

"Shhhh. There, there." She kissed my hair. Perhaps she had a lost son somewhere.

I remember that moment with the greatest of clarity. While my body healed, my heart never did. In that instant, I promised that I would never cry again. To the best of my knowledge, it is a promise I have always kept, though to what I cost, I dare not tally.

"There's a good boy. Try and rest now; sleep and dream sweet dreams."

I stayed in the sick-dorm – the lone patient – for a couple more days. Masters came and went; boys peeked in from the double doors. Nobody asked me what had happened.

Eventually, the local doctor came in and signed me off fit, to return to school. As I perched on the bed, struggling with my laces, he placed a bag of dolly mixtures by my side.

"Your prescription, Master Thryke. For your use only, may I add; not to be shared with the other boys."

I thanked the doctor and pulled on my blazer; there was still blood staining the collar.

The nurse strode across and took my hand. "Let's get you to class, shall we?"

I nodded and, together, we walked out into the main school. Before long, we reached the door of my form room.

"This one?"

I gazed through the pane and saw my empty desk. I nodded.

The nurse smiled, then dropped to her knees and grasped me tightly. "God speed, Cornelius Thryke, you brave little boy. You come back and see me whenever you want, do you hear?"

I did not reply. I merely reached into my pocket, grasped the bag of sweets and, holding them up, I offered them to her.

"But, they're…" I think the earnestness in my face stopped her in mid-track; she held her soft hand beneath the bag and accepted them with grace. I like to remember that she wiped a tear from her eye, and could only mouth the words "thank you". Then, she stood, turned and disappeared into the depths. I exhaled audibly, pushed open the door of the form room and stepped inside.

My rehabilitation back into school life was slow and painful. Boys would see me approaching along the corridors and avert their gaze. Others, braver, would approach and nod. I felt like a small monkey viewed through the bars of a dismal cage, occasionally being tossed a glowing butt end, for the amusement of the voyeurs.

Even Algie, it seemed, had made new alliances in the short time that I had been laid up.

But, before long, hope was on the horizon.

The school became busy with the currency of Christmas. I still attended my clubs, as the shadows lengthened and the rooms grew colder. Boys began to receive parcels of hats, mittens and scarves – those in the house colours were permitted to be worn in class.

In the art club, Constable finished the portrait of his mother. It was magnificent to behold, and he unveiled it to much ado. Even a smattering of masters applauded, as the cover hit the floor.

Meanwhile, the chessmen had temporarily abandoned their jousting, to go about the critical business of making paper chains. There were great armfuls of them appearing everywhere, though they somehow managed to disappear when lessons recommenced.

The theatre group had been subsumed by the official school nativity production, which meant there were more experienced chaps on hand, who were a dab hand at handing out and gathering in the dog-eared scripts; my services were no longer required.

But, it mattered not. With my breath crystallizing before me, I would sit on my hands, to circulate the warmth, close my eyes and envision myself climbing trees with my dear brother, Henry.

It was during one of these meditations that Algernon and I were reunited; it was his hand that shook me back to life. Splendid Algie was standing next to me, clutching a parcel – one end had already been opened.

"I have something here for you, old man. Just to say, you know…"

I dragged my frozen hands from beneath my thighs, and looked up in puzzlement. "For me?"

Algie nodded. "Sorry I've opened it, old chap, but I had to check what it was."

He held out the brown paper gift, like the nativity doll: "Call it an early Christmas gift."

"But, I…"

"Go on. You've done more for us boys than you will ever know."

I took the package from him, unaware that the room had fallen silent and was watching. Algernon nodded in encouragement, as I slid my hand between the paper folds. When I pulled it back free, I was filled with joy.

"They're just like mine!" enthused Algie. "I asked mater to craft two sets. I'm sorry yours took a little longer, but the knitting circle came down with the cold."

I was holding in my hands a marvellous set of boy's apparel, which adhered beautifully to the house colours.

"Try them on."

First, I pulled on the mittens, then the scarf, then the joyous bobble hat. As the wool enveloped my ears, and the pleasure began to rise, the room broke out into a spontaneous cheer. Algie and I clasped hands raised in salute, accepting the plaudits from all around.

"Top show, Watkins!"

"Looking spiffing, Thryke!"

"Hooray for Watty and Corny!"

The cheers inevitably attracted the attention of a passing master. It was Cooper who happened upon the scene, the same master who had transported me to sick-bay, those few short weeks before. He strode into the room as the commotion died down, and his eyes fell upon Watkins and me.

"It appears you have received the gift of warmth, Thryke. Perhaps there is hope for us all, after all. Gentlemen, as you were."

This is my penultimate memory of the term.

It was the final day of that first Christmas term.

The plays had been played, the carols had been carolled, and small presents had been presented. I had wanted to gift something to Algie, but I had nothing to give. He seemed to understand.

Some of the early coaches had already trundled off to the railway station and mine, I hoped, was due to go within the hour. One must know that, through no fault of theirs, I had not heard from home in the time that I had been up at Greyowls; I did not even have a train ticket home. I thought that perhaps a master might provide one, but none had been forthcoming. One supposes I should have asked, but the mind of a seven-year-old boy is not a fertile field in which to harvest rounded suppositions.

"Thryke! Cut along to Mr. Cooper's study!" The shock of the

announcement shook me from thought and soon had me trotting along the corridor, in nervous anxiety. What was to become of me? Was I to stay in the school alone, over Christmas?

I arrived at Cooper's study, sooner than I had anticipated. Painfully, I was greeted with the sight of a heavy, closed door. I rapped my knuckles against it, hoping that I had registered a sound.

"Come!" It was like a bark, but from a smaller dog.

I twisted the brass knob with both hands and, at the edge of my strength, the door yielded. I pushed it back just enough to see Cooper, standing at his desk, grasping the hand of another man.

"It's always wonderful to see an old comrade, however hideous those days were. You were an inspiration to— Ah, young Thryke! Come in, Thryke, and look lively! Have yourself a warm by the fire. I have someone here to see you!"

Cooper pulled the door back, stepped between the figure and me, and out into the hallway. My attention was disrupted, as he pulled the thick, oak-panelled beast back into the doorway, leaving me in the room with... who?

"Uncle Biggles!"

I recall flinging myself toward him, grasping him around the waist. It was, I know now, the spontaneous release of those months of loneliness and pain. His great arms enveloped me.

"Oh, Uncle Biggles. How wonderful – how *wonderful* – to see you! Am I to come with you?"

He beckoned me toward Cooper's empty desk. "Have a sit in Gerald's chair. Warm by the fire for a moment."

I did as I was bid, and hoisted myself up.

"You've had quite the term, haven't you?"

I felt the emotion welling up inside me – the emotion I had promised to conquer. "I won't blub!" I stated, defiantly. "I jolly well won't!"

Uncle Biggles sat silently, for what seemed like an age, weighing me in his steely gaze. He twirled the ends of his moustache.

"Am I to come with you?" I repeated.

Although almost fifty, his hair was still thick and hazel – not black and lank, like Father's.

"I sat with you."

A look of puzzlement must have crossed my face, but the gentleness of his words was tugging at this young fellow's soul. He was a wonderful man.

"That first night that you were in the hospital wing."

"But...?"

"I admit, it was a wild coincidence that I was local, and I am sorry I could not be there when you woke."

"You... you watched over me?"

He smiled. "One greater than I is *always* watching over you, Cornelius." He tugged, playfully, at his dog-collar. "But, from that day on, our mutual friend Gerald – I mean Mr. Cooper – has kept an eye on you for me. That is what brings me here today."

I buried my head in my hands, desperately trying to hold back the floodgates.

"Don't hold it in, young Cornelius; let it all go. You will find comfort in it."

I drew my knees up to my chest so that I could hide my face behind them.

"But, yes, brave sir: you are to come with me. I shall accompany you on your journey home.

I immediately forgot to wallow in my woes and leapt up with joy!

"Come, Uncle Biggles, let us go and find my case!"

He let out a thunderous laugh. "Calm yourself! There is time yet. Sit a while; enjoy the peace."

We did not speak, as we shared a bench on the charabanc back to the station. I had bagged the window seat, but recognized nothing, of course, and each bump or rumble sent me bouncing around like an errant top. Occasionally, though, I would catch the eye of kindly Algernon who, from across the aisle and two seats up, beamed back at us both. I returned his gaze, I recall, with something approaching pride, as a single snowflake melted against the windowpane.

It was not long into the train journey that Uncle Biggles and I found our carriage empty, save our own two restless souls. He stood, stretched, and in a blink had crossed the chasm between the seats and now sat opposite, weighing me once more, like a battle-scarred Anubis.

"Are you staying with us for Christmas, Uncle? Please say that you are?"

He winced and looked wistfully from the window. The snow was drawing in now. "No, no, I am afraid I cannot. I will take a room at the Crown for a night or two, but then travel beckons once more."

"The Lord's work?"

He smiled and turned his head back. "The Lord's work."

My head dropped a little.

"But, Cornelius, if you will permit, I will walk from the station, back home with you. It will be nice to see Henry."

He closed his eyes and sniffed the air, extravagantly: "Do you know, Cornelius, I can smell it – can you? The wonderful baking of Vera! Mince tarts, hot from the oven. Is that cinnamon?"

I closed my eyes; "It is, Uncle, it is! And, unless I am mistaken…"

"What is it, Cornelius?"

"A steaming hot ham pie. See the thick, golden crust?"

"Ah yes, I see it. The glorious aroma springs forth with a hiss, as the knife portions it away. Oh, and Cornelius, there is a jug of thick, unctuous country gravy!"

"With plum duff for afters! My belly is so full!"

I held my sides in mock agony, and we both let out howls of laughter, which echoed into unseen tutting from first.

"I have so missed Vera, you and Henry!" sighed Biggles, lost in his reverie for a moment.

"And Martha?" I added, helpfully.

"And Martha."

"And Father?"

My words sat on the *rat-a-tat-tat*, for a few rhythmic cycles, before the door was drawn back.

"May I see your tickets, please? Much obliged, sirs. Ah, Little

Sodbury-on-the-Wode – alight, if you will, at the very next stop. A merry Christmas to you both – young sir; Reverend Biggles."

We walked in silence from the station.

Many years, it felt, had passed since I was last there; all seemed old. The light dusting of snow heightened the berry red. But, as I searched my body for the roaring delight of homecoming, it was not there – not even with my beloved uncle at my side. I clapped my breath between my hands, as Uncle carried my case, and I leapt around, playing the fool, though more for Biggles than myself. Then, as we rounded the swerve of the lane, emerging from behind the lonely church tower, there it was.

Home.

I stopped and stared at the small rectory – the place to where I had always returned. My shoes sank into the snow, and new flakes blew across them. I felt a steadying hand between my shoulder-blades.

"Are you ready?"

I nodded.

"I'll be right beside you. You are loved here. You are welcome. Come, let us enter."

I strode forward, pulling on the arm that had instilled me with – at least, temporary – bravery.

The door had been freshly painted, I estimated, back in the autumn – it only added to the sense of not belonging. I reached up and clattered the brass knocker ring, as I had done many times before. Uncle Biggles and I stood and waited in the chill, for the door to yield.

With a clunk, I heard the bolt go back. The door eased open.

There was no one there!

"Down here!"

"Ah, Martha! How good to see you! It is me, Cornelius; I am back from school for the holidays."

"Well, of course you are, silly! Don't linger there in the cold; hurry in, and bring Uncle Biggles with you!"

I chuckled at her tone: she seemed much surer within herself. Hurriedly, Biggles and I stomped the snow clinging from our soles and entered.

The house seemed dark, and my eyes took some time to adjust; what little light there was came from the low glow of the embers in the grate.

It was Mother that I saw initially. She looked pale and drawn. Sitting to her left was Henry – he, too, looked weak, and dark rings seemed to surround his eyes. In my confusion, I dashed to Mother first.

"Oh, Mother! How wonderful it is to see you! To be back from school!"

She wrapped an arm around me and I inhaled, deeply. Her hug was not as I remembered.

"Henry!" I addressed my older brother. "What Christmas adventures we shall have, out in the snow."

He smiled, without energy. "Welcome back, Cornelius." He glanced over to the chair in the corner.

There, the jagged outcrop of Father was waiting.

"Would you not address the master of the house, first?" he spat. "Perhaps they are yet to teach you Christian civility."

"I am sorry, Father." With slow paces, I moved toward him and stood where he might better see me. I held out a hand.

"Father?"

A bony-ice hand enveloped mine, lank and loose.

"Then you are returned, I see, and labouring under the impertinence of growing."

It was then that Uncle Biggles stepped from the shadows. Father, and his fading eyes, had failed to spot him.

"What is this?" exclaimed Father, looking about him like a gazelle.

"I'd have thought that was rather obvious, wouldn't you?" boomed Uncle Biggles, joyfully.

I surveyed the scene: Mother and Henry were both smiling.

"What brings you here, Reverend Smart?" questioned Father, black and cold.

"Somebody needed to collect the boy; to look out for him. I was in the area, so—"

"How fortuitous."

"Indeed, Bartholomew. He is but a boy; an innocent."

Father remained silent and seemed to recede into the dark.

"Come, Bartholomew," Uncle spoke: "we will leave this scene and talk in the vestry."

For a while, there was silence.

"I am content here."

"You will walk with me." There was a tone in the words – one which I had, until then, never heard used toward my father. I felt the air drawn from the room, on the collective intake of breath, all wondering what manner of reaction would spew forth from the Reverend Bartholomew Thryke.

But, none was forthcoming. In silence, he rose, walked to the coat rack and pulled his thick, black cape about him. Then, he placed his stiff-brimmed hat atop his dank, black hair and left. I watched as he and Biggles passed by the window, walking up the path to the church.

With that, mother was upon me.

"Oh, Cornelius, how I have missed you so!" She pulled me deep into her bosom and, with a free hand, beckoned to Henry. He crashed into the huddle and, in an instant, both he and mother were in floods of tears. I looked across to dear Martha who, for a second, stood with a scowl on her face. However, amid this outpouring of warmth, she too relented and dived into the melee. We hugged until the tears had dried.

"Now, Henry, light a couple of those lamps. Give us some light, so that we might better see our Cornelius. And, Martha, put some more coals on the fire, so that we may observe him in some warmth. Then, we shall all to the kitchen, where the Christmas baking and decorating shall commence! Our family is restored!"

The snows were deeper when it came time to return to Greyowls. I trudged with the same dread, my case dredging a channel in the drifts, as I paused and looked back up the lane at my tracks. Would it always be like this? Moving from one place to another, burdened by the dull ache of unbelonging? As I dragged myself through the cold, I lost the sensation in my limbs and drew warmth from the luxury of memory.

Uncle Biggles had visited on a couple of further occasions, even dining with us once, and instigating some laughter-filled parlour games. In the company of his friend, even Father had warmed, if only a little; Father succumbed to frivolity, and acted in a couple of the games with some freedom and joy. It was, I am supposing, a good Christmas.

But, now it was over, and the drudgery of Greyowls loomed large. I took no solace from the ride on the train.

"Ah, Thryke! Welcome back."

"Thank you, sir."

Mr. Cooper reached into his pocket and withdrew an envelope: "For you, I believe."

Cooper must have read the quizzical look on my face. "I trust, Thryke, that all will remain a mystery, unless you are to take and read it."

"Yes, sir." I grasped the envelope, which was Cooper's cue to glide off into the hallways.

"Master Cornelius Thryke."

My legs chafed against the coarse material of my blanket, as I eased my finger under the flap. A letter? A letter for me? Was it in a hand that I recognized?

Dear Cornelius,

I wish to thank you for the time that we spent over Christmas. It did a tired old soldier some good. Where once I prayed on those shell-pocked foreign fields, I am now a wandering soldier of God, trying to help from parish to parish. To have some remembrance of home gives me, at least, some semblance of foundation. I think, young Cornelius, that you alone, out of all of the wonderful Thrykes, will understand this.

To this end, I have sought to make your school days a little more palatable. I have arranged that a small allowance be made available to you at the tuck shop. Enjoy the luxury of a few sweet things when the inkling takes you. My wish is that you join the other boys in their mirth.

My good friend, Mr. Cooper, has also informed me of your desire to paint. Art is a fine endeavour for any man. I knew many a good artist during the war and, even in the depths of that despair, they found a rugged beauty. I have arranged for the extra subscriptions required for you to join the art club;

canvas, paints, easels and instruction shall all be made available to you. I know that you will become a magnificent artist, for the finery of God's countryside is within you. Reach deep, young Cornelius; draw forth God's love and let the brush be your pulpit.

I shall leave you now to return to your studies. The world awaits you, Cornelius Thryke – prepare yourself wisely. If I can render any further service, please do confide in Mr. Cooper. There are those of us who look over you.

With God's love,
Uncle Biggleswade.

I read the letter perhaps ten times, each time with the pangs of loneliness and joy. Then, I slid open the drawer of my bedside locker and placed the envelope reverently inside.

As I pushed the drawer slowly closed, Algernon Watkins trotted into the dorm. My first act, as a fully-fledged schoolboy, was to buy him some sherbet lemons. I was grown.

III
Summer Term, 1931.

Since it had opened, in 1926, it had become a tradition that the oldest boys put on a summer play for the girls of the nearby St. Winifred's, and that they, in turn, would reciprocate within the confines of their own, much grander theatre. As a leading light in the art club, I had been roped in by Maitland Cavendish-Pelham, our finest actor and cricket captain, to paint the sets.

"As lovely as they are, do you have to go into such minute detail, Thryke? No one will be able to see the veins in the leaves from out there!" Pelham pointed out into the auditorium and sighed.

"My dear C.P., if a job is worth doing, it is worth doing well. *I* shall know; I am only off here at the side. You shall have to rehearse around me."

"As you wish, Cornelius. Oh, and by the way, I take it you shall be free for the house match on Thursday evening? I have you down to bat at six."

I smiled. Cricket had become such a joy to me. I had no real aptitude for it, but I could nick a few runs, or the odd catch in the deep. "Aye-aye, skipper; I shall see you on the square."

I was negotiating some bark. We had performed *A Midsummer Night's Dream* several years before, so I was able to touch up some of the friezes. Others, like this one, had become too distressed to use and had been whitewashed. This necessity provided me with a fresh canvas.

"If you can drag yourself away from your woodland!"

"You would not understand, Pelham. I am a soul of the countryside; I was born to roam."

"As was Caesar, but he didn't clog up my stage! Oh, very well! Places, everyone!" he cried. "We work around our renaissance man here! As you were: Act One, Scene Two."

It was the afternoon of opening night. It was warm and sunny, and I found myself sitting on the veranda of the cricket pavilion, waiting for my turn at the crease. Our two in the middle were moving along at a fair clip and, although I was padded up to go in next, I felt confident that a high enough score would be amassed before my services were called upon.

I allowed my attention to drift. I scanned the trees that surrounded the oval, felt the light breeze and listened to the call of the birds. I pictured myself striding through the ferns, stick in hand, exploring my mental woodland. In my mind, I went down to the stream, fast-flowing and life-filled, and sat on the grassy bank, staring intensely into the inky depths. A group of shimmering, silver roach swept by on the current, in effortless progress, onward to where the waterway widened and the waters calmed. This was my place.

A hubbub from the middle shattered my vision. There was a circle of boys at the far end of the pitch, and a couple of masters were dashing across the outfield. I stood and, still carrying my bat, began to walk to the middle. When I arrived, I saw him, flat out on the ground, blood trickling from a head wound.

"I say, chaps, what happened?"

"Weren't you watching? Latimer caught an unfortunate one to the head."

The circle split and a blanket was spirited onto the victim.

"An ambulance has been called," said the games master, gravely. "Here, Pelham: place this jersey under his head; make him comfortable. The rest of you, go back and get changed; this match is over."

I turned and began to trudge back to the pavilion. The inquest had already begun amongst the fielding side. I was just about to chime in, when a shout called me back.

"Thryke!" It was C.P.

"What is it?"

"That dastardly short pitch ball – it's put us in something of a spot."

"But, you heard Llewellyn: the match has been abandoned."

"Not the cricket, you clot! The play!"

I ignored C.P.'s pointless insult, though I was still somewhat confused; "I don't understand."

"Latimer! Latimer is our Snug."

"So?"

"What do you mean, so? We open tonight! Latimer is hardly in any fit state to go on, wouldn't you say?"

I still could not understand the urgency attached to C.P.'s words. "Then, use an understudy."

C.P. looked down at the stricken Latimer, who was just starting to move his leaden limbs. "There isn't one," he mumbled.

"Repeat again your last."

"There isn't one, Thryke – not for that part. Our company did not recruit enough players."

I shook my head gently, and my quizzical look returned. At sixteen, I had perfected it.

"Look, Thryke, you were there; you were working through all the rehearsals. Perhaps you picked up the part. I saw you, saying all the lines to yourself, while you were painting."

"Now, just you wait there—"

"Thryke, if you go now you can get a good couple of hours of cramming in. You know it all, already."

"But, let's just say that I did know," (I did know) "I'm not an actor; I am an artist."

"And, a jolly fine artist you are, too, Thryke; we have the most meticulous sets this side of The Globe. But, don't you think you deserve to take some credit front and centre?"

I remained silent. Something within me wanted to shout: "Yes! Yes, I shall do it!" But, equally, I knew that I had been happy in the background, as I had been all those years earlier, handing out the scripts in my first term. Now in my last semester, had fate finally caught up with me? Surely there was another solution.

"Surely there is some other solution?" I said.

"I fear not. The school needs you."

If there is one thing that Cornelius Thryke has never been, it is a shirker. I have always stood for king, country and what is right. As I looked at Maitland Cavendish-Pelham, it was clear what I must do, even though in the midst of this knowledge, I felt nauseous, trapped and pursued. I was a quiet man of the country. In a few short weeks I would return home and find myself a situation in the open air, tending to nature and being the silent hero. These were not the actions of a reflective country gent.

"Okay," I said, with a sigh, "I will do it. But, just for tonight. Just until Latimer is fit to resume."

"But, of course! You are a scholar of the highest order, Thryke. The school thanks you for doing your duty."

And that, dear reader, was how I made my first forays into acting: it came from a nasty bump on the head.

After all the trials and tribulations that I have encountered over the years, I sometimes wonder if it were not my head that got thumped on that fateful June afternoon. It is funny how random twists and turns shape our destiny.

On that opening night, my first of many, the cast milled around nervously, filling the space with silence. Boys who were previously gregarious and loquacious now isolated themselves, in the enclosures of their thoughts. I watched it for a while, as an outsider, before getting distracted by my own fears for the painted sets, or remembering my cues.

I had, as Pelham had suggested, pored over the play with the eye of a scholar, with what remained of the afternoon. Latimer – whom at that moment I detested – had been carted off to the hospital and, as yet, no word had reached us players on his condition.

Not an hour before, I was convinced that I knew the play backwards. Now, I was totally discombobulated; I doubted my own name.

"Are you ready, Thryke? I understand you have selflessly stepped up?" It was Mr. Hancock, the drama master.

"Yes, sir."

"Well, I'm sure you shall do splendidly. There is quite a good crowd growing. The girls and their mistresses are finding their seats, and a few local dignitaries are enjoying an informal reception in the headmaster's study. It's been quite the topic of conversation down in the village, for many weeks."

I groaned.

"Chin up, Thryke! What's the worst that could happen, aside from forgetting your lines, or your cues, or tripping over, or the set falling down? Well, you get the idea, Thryke. But, none of that ever hurt anyone; just part of life's rich tapestry."

Hancock wandered off, no doubt to spread his unique brand of uplifting doom to some of the other fellows. It was strange how he and many of the other masters had dug out their gowns and mortarboards for the evening. Local dignitaries, indeed.

"Old Hancock is right: there is a jolly good gate." This time, my ponderings had been shattered by the presence of Smythe. He was acting as the production's lighting man so, naturally, he had been out into the auditorium. "Capacity crowd, I should reckon. And, some fine fillies in attendance, too, what."

"Oh, do trot along, Smythe. I am feeling bad enough as it is."

But I wasn't, it struck me hard, as Smythe disappeared with a grin; I wasn't feeling despair at all. Yes, there were nerves, but just enough. Just enough to make me feel like a lion! In that single instant, I hankered after one of the more significant parts. I wanted to get out there and make the stage – the one that I had spent all of those hours decorating: mine.

Time began to fly!

"Places, everyone! Can Theseus, Hippolyta, Philostrate and Attendants please make their way to the wings? Curtain up in two minutes. Break a leg, gentlemen!"

I still remember, five acts and nine scenes later, returning to the stage with my fellows, to receive the intoxicating adulation of the crowd. My limbs coursed with the energy and the electricity. I craved to do it all again, now wishing poor Latimer less than well in his recovery.

We joined hands, stepped forward and bowed at the assembled throng – our little band of gentlemen.

Then, it was back to the room behind the stage, where I began to feel alone, once more.

"Why so sad?" It was a female voice. I jumped, startled by its velvetine softness.

"I'm sorry," I stammered. I was lost in my own thoughts.

"No need," she smiled. "I'm Luciana. A few of us girls wanted to come back and meet the players who have entertained us so royally this evening. Here." She passed me a glass of lemonade. It was warm but, to me, it tasted like the finest chilled Champagne.

"Thank you."

"I thought you were very good. Your roar was quite booming."

"Thank you."

"Is that all you say?"

"I'm sorry."

"And that; you've said that once already, too." She laughed and tossed back her head, so that her blonde ponytail swung and bounced in the half-light.

"I'm sorry. I am Cornelius Thryke. I played Snug and I painted the set," I added, hurriedly.

"Well, you are obviously something of a dark horse, are you not, Cornelius Thryke? Do you have any other abilities that you wish to share?"

The air left my body, and I blushed to the tips of my ears.

"I'm just an ordinary kind of chap." It was all I could think of.

She arched a plucked eyebrow and held me in an azure gaze. "I wonder if you are. You will be sure to come across and see the offering of our little school, next week, won't you?"

I nodded. It was all I could do.

"Good. Perhaps you will attend our small soiree, too? It'll be much like this," she looked around her, "but a good deal swisher."

"I shall." My throat betrayed me, and the words tumbled out in many pitches.

She smiled again. "Until then."

"Until then," I said. But, she was already gone.

I spent much of the following days contemplating my encounter with Luciana. "Daydreaming again, Thryke?" became a constant refrain in my treacly lessons.

"You will amount to very little, Thryke, if you cannot concentrate! You are hardly the gifted academic, are you?" came another, as a torpedo of chalk whizzed by my ear, shattering into blades when it struck the corner of Johnson's desk.

"Sir!" exclaimed Johnson, protesting from his cloud.

"Don't whine, boy! You can blame your dusty appearance on the vague propensities of the cavernously empty mind of Thryke!"

Needless to say, the days passed slowly, and in a chalky haze.

It was Algie, fresh from tennis, who eventually forced me to confront myself and the strange, new feelings in my soul. He found me sitting on the edge of the fountain, judiciously stripping the bark from a small twig. Quietly, he sat down beside me and leant his racquet against the stone. "A penny for them."

I usually found that phrase annoying but, that afternoon, it scarcely registered. "What?"

"Your thoughts, old boy. You really have not been yourself these last few days."

"Oh."

Algie, who even then had tremendous interrogation skills, let my remark hang on the still, summer air.

"It's just…"

"Yes?" Algie replied, hopefully.

"I don't know what it is."

"Well," Algernon's patience was running thin, "it's just that you've been jolly distant, that's all. Ever since you trod the boards in that bally *Dream*."

"Ever since I saw *her*."

My chum and confidante threw his hands to the air, in exasperation; "Not you as well!"

"What do you mean?"

"Half the chaps in that rotten play are mooning about after her. What was her name?"

"Luciana. Lovely Luciana."

"That's her: Luciana Fortescue-Ripley-Jones. Do you know she has an official number of ascension? True, it's in the hundreds, but even so! C.P. has been swanning around, proclaiming eternal love for her – so has Hughes and Byfield. Mortimer is even writing some incredibly ghastly sonnets to her – he had thirty-two at last count; many of them weren't even in iambic pentameter!"

Algernon's news riled me.

"You seem to know a lot about her! Are you to be a rival of mine also, you bounder?!" I sprang up, with clenched fists. I have never been an aggressive man and, to this day, I do not know from where my sudden ardour surged.

"Kindly calm yourself, old boy! Have we not been firm friends all these years? Did I not stick by you in those early times? I am no rival in love! Tsk! She is not my type. Not my type at all."

It was inconceivable! How could she not be? To my shame, I was enraged further; "Then you, sir, have no type!"

I stormed off. It was a number of days until Algernon and I spoke again.

St. Winifred's School for Girls was a magnificent facility. Like Greyowls, it swirled around one of those country houses bequeathed by a slightly dotty philanthropist. Only, here the donations had continued: outbuildings had become gymnasiums, laboratories and theatres; lawns were manicured, and topiary peacocks strutted on their borders. I had half expected to find giraffe and antelope sweeping through the grounds, such was the sense of extraordinary. I think I spent most of the evening with my chin permanently disengaged from its housing.

Their play was also something fantastical. Everything the girls of St Winfred's did was more spectacular and polished. As we all rose to applaud the staggering virtuosity, I swear that Luciana Fortescue-Ripley-Jones – from her rightful place: front and centre-stage – looked me directly in the eye. Did I see a trace of a smile on her soft, plump lips?

In the general sated hum of exiting patrons, I spotted several chaps clambering over one another to get to the head of the queue. This queue, I should tell you, was not for the cloakroom, nor the confectionary stand; it was for those few of us who were to go to the small after-party, which the girls had kindly arranged. As a participant in our own, seemingly tawdry production, I was one of the privileged number whose attendance was requested. But, as I saw the other chaps almost climbing over one another to partake, my resolve withered and died: why would she select me, over the glorious Maitland Cavendish-Pelham? He was already at the head of things; a muscular, blond six-footer, bound for Cambridge, to gather blues in anything he wished. Or, why not Johnson, the son of an industrial magnate? New money, yes, but money nonetheless. Here was I, the lowly son of an embittered crow, impoverished, dull and unrefined.

It was dear Algernon who tapped me on the shoulder.

"Go on, Cornelius. Be stately. Walk with poise and purpose. You are as good as any of those fellows. If it is fated, it will find a way."

I turned, as Algie pushed his wire-rimmed spectacles back up his nose and sniffed.

"Go, my Cornelius."

I laid a hand on his arm. "A wretched fellow, such as I, does scarcely deserve a friend such as you."

"Go."

And, so I went.

I was the last to step through the door, into that strange, confusing paradise. The room was full of lilting laughter and sirens floating around, distributing drinks. I accepted a glass – I hoped – with good grace, though I don't believe I saw the source of its supply.

In the middle of the room, there was a buzzing ball around the queen bee, Luciana. Once again, I saw the futility in my pursuit. C.P. was striding around, manoeuvring like a tiger near a kill. Other boys tried to get near, but a sidestep from C.P. blocked the line of vision and approach. Luciana was tossing her tresses, laughing at witticisms and baited hooks of attention. At one point, Mortimer went to his pocket and withdrew a slim sheath of papers. Surely not! Surely he would not try a sonnet? Not here?

I slid back against a wall, not taking my eyes from the writhing mass of nascent testosterone. I raised the glass to my lips but, as I did, her gaze diverted and met mine. I felt that I had been struck dumb, with all the power of a lightning bolt. Though, in that instant, I also became devilishly suave. I released a semi-smile and raised my glass, slightly, in a toast.

It wasn't too long before the gathering was thinning, and the various suitors were spinning away. Against my wall, I supposed that I also should be heading back to Greyowls, to weep into my lumpy, shapeless pillow, while pleading for sleep in the summer heat of the dorm room.

Then, as I was preparing myself to leave, it happened: Luciana Fortescue-Ripley-Jones detached from the remnants of her group and walked, perfectly, toward me.

"And, to think that you have made me come to you! It is rather delicious of you, Cornelius."

She was intoxicating. I clung to the functioning of my mind as a drowning sailor clings to flotsam, praying it would not let me drown in circling sharks of drivel.

"Good evening, Luciana. Congratulations on your performance." *Very good.*

"I saw you from the stage."

"I know." I was growing emboldened by the accuracy of my opening. We moved into the mid-game.

"I am very pleased you chose to grace our little gathering with your presence – despite your insistence on ignoring me."

"I would not have missed it without heaviness of heart. Though, this moment has been my highlight."

"Thryke!"

It was Hancock, the drama master, calling from the doorway. "Cut along now, the last of you; it is high time we were bidding our hosts goodnight."

"It appears you are wanted, Cornelius Thryke."

"It is good to be wanted, Luciana Fortescue-Ripley-Jones."

I made to stride away, but she stepped in, holding me briefly. Her fragrant breath began to caress my ear.

"There is a stone moondial, in the arboretum near the lake. Do you think you can find it?"

I nodded.

"Meet me there at midnight tomorrow." She seemed uncertain. Her lips delicately brushed my cheek.

"Thryke," called the master, "I will not tell you again!"

I nodded assent and floated back off to Greyowls. As I passed him, Hancock shook his head sadly, and grabbed my arm.

"I should be very careful there, Thryke. Very careful, indeed."

But, I was not listening. I was drunk.

There were, of course, many recognized routes out of the school, for boys determined to nefariously leave the premises, so finding myself outside of the school grounds was not a difficulty.

The night was cool, and I was both comforted and made nervous by my blazer: it marked me out as a child – yet, this mission singled me out as a man. It was now half past eleven and the dangers, as I saw them, were being spotted by anyone who might be coming back from the village pub. While the methods out of the school were known, us boys had no real intelligence when it came to the nocturnal movement of the masters, or the caretaker; they might have been out there, concealed in every shadow – I just didn't know.

I had kept the appointment hidden from all – even dear Algernon. Whispers of a boy going out tended to amplify, like vibrations rolling across a drumskin. The masters, like spiders, would sense the disturbance and scurry to surround the culprits, before the crime could be committed. No; secrecy was vital.

The mixture of fear and anticipation was exhilarating, and I could feel my heart pounding in my chest. I thought of her, and it struck harder, sending my blood pulsing through my ears. I had to remain calm; in my current state, I was no good to anybody.

Emerging from a clump of bushes, into the lane, I recalled roaming the countryside with my beloved brother, Henry. But, he wasn't Henry anymore – not the Henry of my memories – he was a man of nineteen. Yet, if I could have spoken with anyone – begged for counsel and advice – it would have been my brother. I scurried across, into the safety of more trees, and prowled in the general direction of St. Winifred's.

It was not long before I arrived at the gates. It was with resignation that I held the cold padlock and chain in my hand. Why had I not considered that the gates would be locked? If the pupils were all like Luciana, it was probably more to keep girls like her in, rather than amorous boys, like me, out. I surveyed the scene. The gates were climbable, yes, but a gaslit archway extended above them; my physique, lithe and catlike as it was, would be easily spotted atop the gates. Besides, the iron and chain would surely send out an earth-shattering rattle of disapproval, as I battled with both the bars and gravity. No, this was not the place to go over, nor was it the place where I wished to receive a backside of rock salt, fired from the adjacent caretaker's lodge – not tonight, thank you. There would be a weakness somewhere. There *must* be a weakness; there always was. I began to track the perimeter, working in the direction of where my limited research had placed the arboretum.

All at once, my foolishness struck me. "Thryke, you're an imbecile!" I whispered to myself. "Even if you do manage to get over, you don't know where the moondial, the lake or the arboretum actually are! Neither do you know if she'll turn up! Then, you've got to get all the way back and into bed, undetected. You fool! You bally, bally fool!"

A sudden rustle in the undergrowth jarred me back to the external. I stood stock-still. I knew enough about country craft to realize that I had no clue what it was. Perhaps it was an enraged badger? Or, poachers? Maybe it was desperate poachers, armed to the teeth with serrated, ripping knives and blunderbusses! I listened for footfall. What if it was the headmaster and a handpicked team of men, sent to track and eliminate me? I wouldn't even know they were there: grizzled veterans, with the scent of blood in their nostrils. They might even be circling me now, their painted faces grinning at my adolescent jaunt.

The rustle intensified, stopped, then was replaced by an eerie scraping, like boots being drawn across the ground, making a mark; taking a position. The game, it appeared, was up.

In that moment of stark realization, the undergrowth gave up its secret: a shape shot toward me at a blinding speed, and my heart and body jolted.

There, in the bright moonlit clearing, our eyes met.

She was a vixen of indescribable beauty. And, when I say vixen, I am not using the vulgarities of youth to picture-paint a roaming daughter of Aphrodite. No, I am talking about a true vulpine vison, in the patina of old, burnt marmalade.

We stood, as in a trance, for what was probably no more than a few seconds, each trying to resolve and ascertain who was more startled; whose animal heart was beating the fastest. The schoolboy within me stepped back, and my oneness with the countryside rose, filling my soul with gentle wonder; she was wonderful. Her jet nose twitched as she attempted to sniff my intent, while the moon picked her out in flame.

She was plump at the flanks; she clearly had a stash of food somewhere – regular and easy. Perhaps it was by the bins? In the girls' school?

Sensing that thought, on the web of nature which held us together, she dashed and disappeared. I was once again left to gather my feelings and control the beating of my heart. Could I follow her?

In my explorations that evening, I found the most profound sense of joy that I had known in many years. Yes, painting and cricket, and latterly acting, had lent me some semblance of calm and distraction, but this is who I truly was: a free soul, born to roam the woodland, downs and hills. As I finally located and sat in the silver shimmer of the moondial, all was clear to me; on this point alone, I was glad that I had made this trek. It was ten past the hour of twelve.

"You came." She emerged, glistening from between a clutch of dancing Japanese Cedar.

"Of course."

"I've been watching you, sitting there in your blazer. I felt you had the weight of the world on your mind."

I gently tugged at the breasts of my jacket; "I'm afraid my dinner suit was at the dry cleaners."

"Well," she declared, clad in an elegantly cut dress and light, white cardigan, "may I join you?"

With gallantry beyond my years, I stood and motioned to the seat beside me. "It would be my honour, mademoiselle."

She smiled and stepped a chord through the circle. We sat in unison, and she gave a little shiver.

"Are you quite warm enough, Luciana?"

"Hmm, it was just the shock of the stone. It is rather chilly, though. I shall be rebalanced, momentarily."

I stood again and made to remove my blazer.

"It's fine, Cornelius. Come, sit with me a while. Let us enjoy this beautiful night."

The breeze carried her perfume to my nostrils. I breathed deeply and, for a moment, a smile played upon my lips.

"Do you know why I came here tonight?" Luciana asked, suddenly.

I shook my head.

"Because you are different. You're something of an enigma, Cornelius Thryke."

"I'm just me."

"And, there it is. It takes such courage to be that. I wish I were as brave as you; I'm someone different every day."

"The real you is in there somewhere – you already know her, and I'd wager she is wonderful." It was, up to that point in my life, the greatest thing I had ever said. Moonlit curiosity upon moonlit curiosity; it was like living in a Shakespeare play. All one had to do was remember one's lines, as they were already written upon the soul. The years have been so kind to this memory; I cherish it.

"What a beautiful thing to say!" She reached down and took my hand. I blushed to the tips of my ears.

"It was last evening, after the play, when you were watching me from afar. Those other boys... it felt like they were clambering all over me, with tales of athleticism, boasts of achievement, or sonnets of rank indecency. Yet, there I was, amidst the bluster, encouraging, goading and directing them. Is that who I am?"

I squeezed her hand. "Perhaps *this* is you."

"Maybe it is; it feels closer."

We sat in silence for a few more minutes, both staring at the moon.

"I wonder what's up there?" she asked.

"I'm sure we will never know. Some things are just best left."

"What will you do when you leave school?" she asked suddenly, not breaking her lunar gaze.

"Go home."

She laughed. "Silly Cornelius! I am to go to Paris, to complete my education as a lady. My father, the baronet, decrees it."

"Your father is a baronet?"

"Yes. Tiresome, isn't it?"

"No. On the contrary, I believe it to be wondrous."

"Really? And, how is your father engaged?"

"He is a member of the clergy. Rector of a small village, upon which he perches, like a giant, black crow."

"You paint such an appealing picture! Will you follow your crow into the clergy?"

It was delightful! I had never before sullied the name of my father with another. There was such a sense of racing intimacy.

"No, my religion is in nature. I shall roam, explore, fish and paint – that will be my worship."

She sighed: "It sounds idyllic. Or, perhaps you should come to Paris, too – live like a monk in the artisan quarter, painting endless portraits of me." She delighted in her words, and laughed once more, as she had amidst my rivals.

She leant in and kissed me on the cheek, before releasing my hand and drawing herself up to her full, elegant height.

"Do not change, Cornelius. Do you hear?"

I lowered my eyes in assent. "What now?"

"I don't know," she said, softly.

She began to glide back off into the cedars. "Perhaps you could write?" she called back, over her shoulder.

And that, dearest journal, was my last memory of school.

IV

It was perhaps a month later that I saw my dear brother, Henry. He had a situation as a farmhand, on the other side of Corinthian Thatch. He had written me a letter, requesting that I meet him outside of The Bell, early one July morning. The message, as jolly as it was, left me in poor humour: Henry's spidery hand betrayed a life without schooling. I felt ashamed, as I realized the gift that I had been given, while he was left to wander.

Meanwhile, at the homestead, my own future was being brought into question.

"He is a boy no longer, Vera. Is he to sit here forever, squandering the education that we sacrificed all to provide?"

"But, Bartie, he has not been back long. He will find employ."

"Not sitting there, he won't!"

I rose and strode between them. They both looked up at me, meeting my flicking gaze.

"But, Father, I have employment: I am an artist.

Father spat: "Is that not predicated on the assumption that, firstly, you have art to sell and, secondly, that people wish to buy it? If you are such a dab hand with the brush, perhaps you should paint the parochial house, in order to earn your keep."

So, I was not in the best of moods, as I waited outside The Bell. But, as I stood, leant against the whitewashed walls, I made it my intention to enjoy the day, for tomorrow I would leave and find a job, with lodgings. Perhaps I could ask Henry; maybe extra hands were required on the farm where he worked. I would not need to earn much: just a small allowance and three square meals a day. Yes, Henry would assist. I would be out of the rectory by sundown.

Given that it was his first day off in months, Henry had chosen a glorious day for it. Even at that early hour, there was a promising warmth to the low sun; rays clipped through the trees and warmed my face. I closed my eyes and breathed. I imagined summertime in Paris: I was hand in hand with Luciana, first wandering along the banks of the Seine, or later drinking coffee on the pavement of Loiseau's Café, on the corner of Cligancourt Street. Then, as an admiring crowd gathered around me, I would paint her portrait in the shadow of Tour d'Eiffel. With glimmering brush strokes, her face danced in my memory scape; when would I gaze upon it again?

I opened my red-lidded eyes, just as they passed around a distant bend in the lane. Was it? No... Yes! Yes, it was! Henry strode purposefully, broad, muscular and tanned. He was in the rudest of health; farm life obviously agreed with him. He wore a crisp, blue shirt, its sleeves rolled up and unbuttoned to the waist; the brown V of his chest spoke of a summer toiling under the sun. Henry had grown into a magnificent specimen but, at the same moment, I felt ashamed that he could not spell such a descriptive phrase. I drew my arms around me, trying to hide my own wiry physique.

I had been looking forward to this day alone with my brother so, for a second or two, I felt resentment toward the second gentleman, walking alongside him. His face was obscured by the brim of a battered Panama hat, but I smiled at the devil-may-care spirit of his headgear. He was tall and muscular, like Henry, and clad in a white shirt and tan trousers. He was broader, giving the appearance of greater maturity and age. Perhaps it was someone Henry had befriended at the farm. I supposed that when Henry described this day of folly to his friend, our interloper had mistaken my brother's words for an invitation, and Henry, as was typical of him, had not had the heart to put him right. I would welcome him too, if that were what Henry wished.

As they got closer, both Henry and our third waved vigorously. I felt this strange to begin with, then realized the joyful folly of my ways.

"My goodness gracious; now, there's a sight for sore eyes! Brother Henry *and* Uncle Biggles!" A surge of sentimentality zipped through me, and I sprang into the lane to meet them, lunging at them both, as they came into range.

"Careful, young sir!" exclaimed Biggles, with a laugh. "You'll squish the provisions! Speaking of which, you can carry this bag; I'm getting too old to be lugging weight like a pack mule!"

"A good expedition is one which is well-equipped!" cried Henry, grabbing me in a headlock and ruffling my hair. "But, the young scholar here must do his share. After all, is that not what younger brothers are for?"

He released me, deaf to my half-hearted protestations, and hooked the straps of the pack over my shoulders. My own supplies – sandwiches made by Mother and a small canteen of tea – hung at my side, in a satchel. I felt decidedly lop-sided.

"Perfect," said Henry; "our company is good to go."

"If you think Cornelius won't just walk around in large circles?" replied Biggles. We all fell into laughter, then Biggles and I fell in behind Henry, our leader for the day.

"Then, you are our guide," said Biggles. "Do you know where we're going?"

"I have just the spot. It's a bit of a trek, but it's worth it. Nothing us Thryke boys cannot stride with relish!" He slapped me playfully on the shoulder – I gulped back the pain.

"Nor the Reverend Smarts of this world," I replied. "Lead on, skipper."

We trekked through fields and woodland, for a good couple of hours, stopping periodically to drop the loads from our back. All morning I had been followed closely by the chinking of bottles.

"What have you got in here?"

"You'll see," said Henry. "There's a treat for each of us. It shall be well earned."

As much as I enjoyed the trek, I was not sorry to see the spot that Henry had chosen. There had not been much conversation on the journey; Henry had set off at a furious pace, which had stretched us out. Meanwhile, with Biggles, his military training had warned him not to walk too close to the other men in his column. Henry had promised us a spot which would make all the toil worthwhile, and he had certainly delivered. As the trees thinned, we entered a small, grassy dell, not twenty yards across. It formed an arc on the edge of the riverbank, and was lit beautifully by the mid-morning sun. Gratefully, we dumped our packs and began to remove our boots. I rolled up my trousers and dangled my feet into the cool, flowing waters.

"Not used to it anymore?" said Henry, placing a hand on my shoulder. "Here, make yourself useful and lodge these in the water, against the bank." He handed me six beer bottles, one after another.

With a shrug, I consented. I scooted along to a spot in the reeds, where the water was shallower and calmer. As dragonflies buzzed around me, I stowed the bottles, as instructed, and climbed back up into the grass, where my feet began to dry and warm.

It was a beautiful morning of fishing. The conversation was light, but what fish there must have been were thundering by on the current; nobody had had a nibble.

"Well, if the fish aren't biting, then I suggest we do," I said. "Mother has made me a large pack of sandwiches, for those who wish to share."

From the corner of my eye, I saw Henry lightly jab Uncle Biggles in the ribs, and cock his head in my direction. "That school did something for him, eh, Uncle? He's come back quite the leader."

"Indeed he has, Henry; indeed he has! Tell us, Cornelius, what will you do now that school is over?"

I positioned my back in the bow of a tree, as I opened the voluminous doorsteps Mother had prepared: half a loaf, interrupted by cheese and homemade chutney.

"Oh, I don't know. I thought I should be an artist, but I have recently discovered a passion for acting."

Henry burst into a peal of rat-a-tat laughter, but Biggleswade raised a hand to silence him.

"Fine trades, both. I have no doubt you could do either," said Biggles. "But, while you develop those, you may need something else."

"I know; you're right. Henry, is there any work going on your farm?"

Henry looked downcast; "If there were, I would take you back there tonight – believe me, Corny, I would. I don't know how you have stuck it in that house for so long, already."

"Now, Henry," warned Biggles, gently.

"Well, you know how Father is: full of Christian spirit."

The Reverend Smart ignored the protestations of Henry who, by now, was rooting through his pack for victuals of his own. My attention was taken by a kestrel, hovering in the distance.

"I wouldn't put you off of the Army," spoke Biggles, presently. "It's a career, and they'll give you a solid trade."

"I thought you abhorred violence," I replied.

"Do not get the Army confused with war, Cornelius. Yes, there is evil and violence in the world, and I saw my fair share, I can tell you. But, an army is a deterrent; it is there to defend, not attack. I have seen soldiers kill, but I have also seen them build. I have seen them deliver God's forgiveness, as well as his wrath."

"I couldn't be in no Army," called Henry, between bear-like mouthfuls. "Hmm, we're forgetting!" He crawled down to the riverside and withdrew three bottles of beer from the brisk water.

"Champion!" he declared. "Them's just right. Knock the top off of that for young Corny, would you, Uncle?"

A few seconds later, I was handed my first bottle of ale.

"For me? Really?"

"We're all grown-ups here, Cornelius. I should say you're old enough. Henry insisted we bring extra for you."

With a beaming face, we three chinked our bottles together and I took my first, deep draught. It tasted of… well… of the countryside and freedom; it was beautifully cold and refreshing. I wiped the back of my hand across my face and let out a satisfied sigh.

"Well, that certainly is the stuff! Thank you, Henry. Thank you, Uncle."

"Enough of the 'Uncle'!" shrieked Biggleswade, in mock anguish. "Call me Biggles – everybody else does. So, might you consider it? The Army, I mean."

"I might. But, I wish to pursue my dream; I wish to go to Paris."

Biggles and Henry exchanged glances. Henry shrugged, deferring guidance on that one to the more experienced man.

"Paris?"

"Oui, c'est vrai!"

"Cor," exclaimed Henry, "he already has the patter! Like Napoleon himself!"

"Do you know anyone there, Uncle?" I asked, more through hope than expectation.

Biggles patted his brow with a handkerchief and drew on his beer bottle. "I was there, but only fleetingly, I'm afraid, during the Great War. Those Parisiennes I met were merely brief acquaintances."

I must have looked down at his response. Henry scuttled across and put a hand on my shoulder.

"Does this news disappoint you?" asked Biggles.

"Yes, young Corny. You're only just back. Why all the sudden interest in the Frenchies?"

All at once, I felt foolish. "I shan't say: you would only mock me!"

Henry looked confused, but Biggles chuckled and brushed some detritus from his moustache. "I think maybe he needed that drink, Henry."

"What do you mean?" Henry's confusion had not yet relented.

"There is but one thing in this world that can make a man jump oceans and seek the uncertainty of alien climes."

Henry chewed on Biggles's words a while before, finally, the light came on: "Ah!" He draped his arm fully around my shoulder now, and drew me toward him. "Women! Now, if we're to talk about those, we will need another drink!"

"So, you've fallen in love?" asked Biggles, with solemnity and grace.

"Yes." I felt ridiculous and vulnerable. I took a swig of ale and hid my face behind the bottle, in a feigned examination of the label.

"Why the shame?" asked Biggles. "Love is of God, and God is love. Caring for another is not weakness, Cornelius; it is strength. It is the strength of putting others before yourself. You should be proud."

"He's right, brother. Come on, tell us about her."

"Her name is Luciana Fortescue-Ripley-Jones. When I am with her, I feel... I think... I become someone else: a better version of me. And, she is so, so beautiful; she was a vision in the moonlight."

The laughter never came.

Biggles asked how I came to make her acquaintance. I described the whole story: the cricket match, the play, our midnight assignation... Both listened quietly, munching on the last of their sandwiches. In the act of telling my story, my provisions lay practically untouched.

"The daughter of a baronet, off to a finishing school in Paris?" reflected Biggles. "All becomes clear."

"What should I do, Uncle Biggles? I am so confused."

His pale-blue eyes met mine – there was sadness in them. We held one another's gaze for what seemed like hours. The sad eyes sent a message, but I did not want to hear.

Henry emerged from the bushes, knelt and let the water run through his hands. Standing, he wiped them on his shirt front and prepared to distribute his wisdom. I took another mouthful of beer and recommenced the battle with my doorstep.

"I knows exactly what you're going through: I'm courting the farmer's daughter – only, she refuses to acknowledge so. Verity Parker – a real country beauty, not dissimilar to your girl, I should reckon. But, blast and botheration, is she not confounding and annoying in equal measure?! Half the lads on the casual are running around after her, but deep down – deep down – I know she loves me! I tell her I knows two priests, that will gladly step us up the aisle, quick as she likes, but she scoffs and accuses me of having the mind of a beast! Me!? Henry Thryke!? It's something in our name, young brother; not your fault at all.

"So, I say to you... I say you go to Paris! You go get your girl and you tell her straight. There's nothing worse than living in the knowledge of not knowing, if you understand my patter. But, there; I've said my piece, as is my duty as your brother. Life has a habit of working out, that's all – just know that. You've grown into a fine man – that's all I'll say."

While I listened to Henry's speech, I was watching the man we both lovingly called Uncle. He seemed pained. My own feelings felt small and insignificant, next to the life that he had led. But, I knew that the life I would lead would, in some way, be a tribute to his – he and the comrades who had served with him.

"Biggles," it was the first time I had ever addressed him such, "have you ever been in love?"

Henry arched an eyebrow. We sat in silence for a while.

"God is my love."

Henry looked on and drained the last from his bottle. I took another draught from mine, content to let the silence sit, eyes still boring into our esteemed war hero. He began to rummage in his pack and withdrew a metal flask. I'd seen enough masters surreptitiously drawing on them to know what it was, and immediately felt ashamed of my probing.

"Once," he said suddenly, recapping the flask and passing it to my brother. "It was many years ago."

Common sense told me to leave it there – to respect the privacy he was struggling to protect – only, my mouth had not read the stage direction, and followed a course of its own. "What happened?"

Henry looked confused, as he took a nip and screwed the lid back onto the flask. He offered it back to Biggles, who had again fallen silent under my questioning.

"Give it to Cornelius: he'll need a nip."

The flask was passed my way. I took a tremulous sip, as Uncle Biggles continued talking:

"As I say, it was a long, long time ago. But, it was complicated. I loved her from the moment I saw her, but I always knew I could not have her for my own. She, astonishing and worldly, and I a lonely old fool. It was her touch, her smile and her scent that I carried, each day, onto that forsaken battlefield – all in the knowledge that I was in sin. Not a day still goes by when I do not ask forgiveness for what transpired. Pah: 'what transpired' – I still cannot say it! For *what I did*. For the commandment that I broke, I am truly sorry. My punishment has been just and, like Odysseus, I am doomed to roam. Cornelius, you think me a hero, yet I am a coward: I went to war to hide from my shame – a shame which bore fruit through love."

I gave him back the flask and his desperation passed, replaced now by melancholy.

"And yes, my sin of love begat further love. I ask forgiveness for the act, but I do not regret the outcome. Just that I could be..." he paused, "...more."

"Come, Uncle Biggles," I rose and extended my hand; "let's get back to some fishing."

I often recall that day and puzzle over Biggles's words. But, one thing I do know: he carried on running. Henry joked that he was a Roaming Catholic, which never made sense, as we all knew he was C-of-E. But, with a few months of that expedition, he made passage for Africa, to take up the word as a missionary. He was already in his sixtieth year; his sense of shame must have been prodigious.

In the winter of 1932, Father passed away.

I was resident above a shop, over in Lumpton Mulberry, when Mother sent word that Father was ill. I had found employment as a decorator, working for a good man: Mr. W.A. Pond. It was his shop, you see. It sold all kinds of hardware and doubled as a studio. Clients could visit and choose wallpapers or paint hues, then, as the resident painter, I would offer my services.

It was unusual to receive a letter from my mother, though I was an enthusiastic writer of such epistles. I would sit in my room at night, scratching away by lamplight. I wrote many letters to Luciana, explaining how my funds were growing, and that I would soon be able to afford the passage to be beside her, in Paris. I would take a studio flat somewhere, among my fellow, multi-national artists. I would paint the Paris streets by day, the coffee shops, the bars and the restaurants. I would paint the rippling coloured awnings, as the populace smoked, drank and laughed beneath them. In the evenings, I would attend lessons, drink Pernod or dine modestly, with my fellow artisans. Our band would grow famous, and I would be regarded as one of the leading lights of the new movement; history would have to find us a collective name. But, the weekends would be ours; we could do whatever she wished. Perhaps we would take a train from the Gare Du Nord and spend a few days trundling the beaches of Fecamp or Vattetot-Sur-Mer. We would eat ices and dance through the foaming surf, under cloudless, blue skies, pocked only with the crescent of a screaming gull. The ozone would clear out our lungs, and I would paint her portrait amidst the iris moss, wrack and kelp. Then, inevitably, the city would call for us, once more.

Occasionally, she would send a reply but, as her letters became shorter and more infrequent, my resolve to see her grew more urgent. I knew that she was busy, and though my absence was surely making her heart grow fonder, she also had to contend with the distractions of Parisienne life. I saved as hard as I could, and took what additional odd jobs I could find.

Naturally, my mother's letter meant my entrepreneurial bent was placed on pause. She described how Father had fallen ill and requested that I come home, at once. I bid my leave of Mr. and Mrs. Pond and, a couple of days later, boarded the next train back to Little Sodbury-on-the-Wode.

It was a cold, October day, when I strode up the lane, suitcase in hand and coat lapels bent into the wind. I remembered those distant years, when I had dragged this same case across the ground, being short of leg, but long enough of arm. The underside still bore the scars of these mathematical disagreements, but now I was a grown man, entering the prime of life. My father, it seemed, was in the winter of his days.

It was Henry who opened the door. "Cornelius."

"Henry." We stood in awkward silence. "Am I... am I too late?"

He stepped aside and motioned up the stairs. "He's still with us. Probably waiting for you."

I ascended in footfall creaks and timber moans. Rising from the stairwell, I saw that the bedroom door was ajar. Low murmurings were issued from within. Slowly, I pushed against the door planks and eased my head into the room.

"Cornelius, my baby boy, you have come!"

Mother rose, ceased in worrying her handkerchief and threw her arms around me. "I knew you would; you are a good boy."

Over Mother's shoulder, Martha sneered and shook her head, sadly. My sister had none of our mother's beauty; she was her father's daughter. Even in her young face, she carried the bitterness that Father had so enjoyed. She was not quite nineteen.

"I came as soon as I could. Hello, Martha."

"Cornelius." She was already wearing black, and her long, black hair fell lankly over her shoulders.

Mother released me from her embrace and, in tiptoes, kissed me on the cheek. Then, placing a hand in the small of my back, she guided me lovingly to the chair that she had vacated. I sat opposite Martha and lightly placed a hand on my father's arm.

"What do I say?"

"Just tell him you're here," said Mother.

Martha dabbed at her eyes, with relish, before readying a flannel in the bowl.

"Father? Father? Can you hear me? It is I, Cornelius." I looked into his face. It was ashen, but the cruelty was gone; he had an expression of peace. Martha began to pat at Father's forehead.

"Your sister has been such a good girl," explained Mother. "I don't know what I would have done without her. But, I am so glad to have my boys here."

"What do the doctors say, Mother?" I asked.

"They say he has apoplexy. There has been more than one attack," she said.

"You have just missed Doctor Brown, Cornelius – I'm surprised he didn't pass you in the lane," said Martha. "He administered father with a heavy sedative, so now he sleeps. You have missed the nights of groaning and pain, I am afraid."

"Martha!" snapped Mother, in admonition.

"It is alright, Mother," I responded, soothingly: "she is right. One day, Sister, I hope you will forgive me."

And, that is what *I* tried to do. Not forgive Martha – she was just a child – but, Father: he was the one who cast me out. Now the old crow had flown his last, my only hope was that that particular baton had not been passed.

His eyes, which had been ebony and fizzing, were lidded now. They had once beheld the sin of the world and had been reviled. I did not know what my sin had been – nor Henry's, for that matter – but those eyes were focused on a different journey today. The long, jet cassock, in which he swept around the parish, was hanging on the front of the wardrobe, pressed and clean, ready to be his burial gown. In its stead, he wore a bright, white nightshirt, starched and shining. Even his hair which, in life, layered like blue-black feathers which bobbed beneath his jaw, had fallen back, slate, to reveal his large-lobed ears. *Corvus corone* no longer; he was the husk of a harmless man.

As dusk fell, we drew the window and lit candles on either side of the voyager. Henry and I filled the scuttle and put rather more coal on the fire than we knew Father would like – Martha pretended not to notice, and began dabbing Father's forehead with more considerable gusto and vigilance.

"Mother, shall I make some tea?"

She smiled assent from her chair: "Yes, and why don't you and Henry bring a chair up each, from the kitchen? You cannot stand all night."

I nodded and motioned for Henry to join me downstairs. The kitchen was cold and the range was barely warm.

"I'll get this fired up. You take up a couple of chairs."

"Yes, sir!" Henry snapped to attention. "I think Biggles was right about you: officer material."

The kettle was just starting to warm when he returned.

"It'll be a while, yet," I said.

"I don't mind. I just had to get out of that room for a bit."

"I know what you mean."

Henry sat at the table and toyed with the edge of the cloth. "How are you feeling?" he asked.

I swallowed. "Can I be honest?"

Henry nodded.

"Nothing."

My brother exhaled heavily and sighed. "Thank goodness: then, there's nothing wrong with me; I thought I was the only one who felt that way."

"Well, he was never the most doting father, was he? He left you to roam which, to be fair, you were exceptionally good at, and he packed me off to school."

"Well, there's neither of us turned out so bad. Not that it appears Martha agrees so."

It was my turn to be relieved: "So, she's been off with you, too?"

"Very bitey," confirmed Henry. "I've known enraged fillies to be less dangerous!"

"She's just upset, I suppose," I said, feeling the side of the kettle. "Getting warmer."

"Well, I just get the impression that she doesn't want us here, that's all," said Henry. "I don't mind it if I've crossed someone, but I don't see what it is I've done to earn her fury, I really don't."

I looked up, to the approximate spot where he lay.

"Ah," said Henry, percipient of the possibility. "He's been

whispering in her ear all these years; turning us black, in her mind."

"I fear so."

"Well!" He rapped his fist on the tabletop. "Would it be uncharitable to…" He stopped, checking himself.

"Hope he doesn't hang about?"

Henry rose and strode across to the range. "How much coal did you put in here? That kettle should have boiled a lifetime ago!"

He stopped and, in a nod-smile, told me that it would all be alright. At least Henry wanted me there.

Mother and Martha continued to sit at the bedhead, one on each side, wailing silently. Henry and I sat at the end, also on each side. Father, the man who had once loomed over me, in visceral strength and anger, was now small, white and weak.

The fire had now died down, and the glow was slowly fading from the embers. Across him, the blankets were pulled taut – perhaps Mother believed that if her husband's spirit were to escape, it would need to do so after negotiating the restrictions of very tight bedclothes. On either side, tapers flickered and anointed his skull in dull amber. His face had become quite grey now, and his eyes had sunk, deep, into ringed, gunmetal sockets.

We had been joined by the vicar from a nearby parish: the Reverend Seabert Hume, of Sharbury-Minster; he stood behind Martha and bestowed serenity upon proceedings. Father's breathing was becoming shallower.

"He is preparing for his joyous meeting with the Father," said Reverend Hume. "Let us all give thanks, in our own way."

We all fell silent, not daring to bow our heads. The mantle clock ticked louder. Then, with a gurgle and sigh, the death rattle was breathed into the room. With it went the dead man's soul.

It was done. Henry rushed to hold Mother, and Martha flung herself across Father's still chest. The priest began to pray:

"May the eternal God bless and keep us, guard our bodies, save our souls and bring us safe to the heavenly country – our eternal home – where Father, Son, and Holy Spirit reign; one God, forever and ever."

All I could do was watch, and stare at the remnants of a crow.

Part Three:
War

V

I never did make it to Paris.

Although the Church had looked upon them with sympathy, Mother and Martha had had to leave the rectory and move to a smaller cottage, on the edge of the village, and I had given what funds I had saved to assist them in their new home. Even in death, Father had had the last laugh.

He had been in the ground some seven years when my call-up papers came. It had just turned 1940. I was twenty-four years old.

"Arms up," barked the M.O. "Good. Any medical conditions?"

"No, sir."

"Very good. Move along."

And that was enough to mark me down as A1. Bosh! As simple as that!

I joined some other chaps in the line, to receive a rail warrant and my joining instructions. We were all to go to the same place: the Army camp at Brington. There, we would begin to be moulded into fighting men.

Once again, it was my old school case which came with me. I shoved it, unceremoniously, into the luggage rack, and sat down in the carriage, with four other chaps. I guessed we were all going the same way, but thought it might be an early chance to hint at my credentials. We all appeared to be in shock, but one of us had to take the lead – I had made up my mind to throw myself into it; there was no point to do otherwise.

"Hello, chaps. I'm Thryke: Cornelius Thryke. Are we all off to P.T.C. Brington?"

There were some murmurs and nods. It was time to up the ante.

"Would anybody care for a pear drop?"

I had taken care to buy a fresh bag from a sweet shop near the station, hoping they would come in handy, for a moment such as now. I offered the bag to each man in turn.

"Aye," said the first. He was a large, thickset gentleman. "I'm MacIntosh. You can call me Mac."

I moved the bag along the line. Sitting in the middle was a shy-looking man, with a full head of ruddy hair. "Thank you," he almost whispered, and his hand shook as he reached for the sweet. I would take him under my wing. As scared as I was, I would not let my new band down.

"And, what do we call you?" I asked. He wouldn't speak.

"Why, it's Ginger, of course!" cried Mac, with his Scots twang. "That'll be what they call him when we're in the Army! You see if they don't!"

There were no protestations from our timid friend; the name had already stuck. I could work on Ginger later; time to move the bag along. I paused it in front of the next man.

"And, I suppose you reckon yourself to be in charge?" he said, gruffly, in a timbre which seemed reminiscent of London. "Well, you're not in charge of me, see?" He smashed his hand into the bag and stuffed two pear drops into his mouth. Hamster-like, he skilfully stored them into unshaven cheeks, so that his mouth was free to carry on the volley. "I've never taken an order from anyone, and I don't intend to start now, either!"

Not to be perturbed, I maintained my cool and made my response: "I'm sorry, old boy. I hadn't meant to infer that I was in any way in charge."

If anything, this olive branch just seemed to rile him more. "*'Old boy'? 'Old boy'?*" He made as if he were addressing the rest of the carriage. "That's all we need: a toff on the train. You might be able to pick on young Ginger here, but not me: I grew up on the sites. We had men like you for breakfast."

"Well, I'll have a sweet with you, boy." It was the fifth man in our carriage. He was small and wiry, and evidently a Welshman.

"Geriant Jenkins – that's me. Glad to meet you all, though the circumstances could have been better, what. He's only trying to be friendly, see. No harm to it."

The Londoner sneered from his corner seat: "Well, let's get to know him then, shall we? Tell us, Pike, or whatever your name was, what did you do in civvy street?"

I knew I should say painter and decorator but, for some reason, that wasn't what came out. "I'm an artist."

The Londoner roared: "An artist! I know a few of them, mate, but they wouldn't like you! Tell you what, I'll call you Vincent van Toff!"

"I think I'd prefer Michael-flangelo!" Now, I've never been particularly quick with retorts – I was no music-hall comedian – but that was undoubtedly one of my finest moments. The carriage, led by the Londoner, fell about laughing. It was a full twenty seconds before he came up for air, wiping his eyes with two, bear-sized fists.

"Oh dear, oh dear!" he wheezed, regaining his composure. "Now, fair play, chief; that was good. I suppose you can't be all bad. Here."

He offered me his hand. I leant across and lost my hand in it. As his vice-like fingers closed around mine, he smiled through gapped teeth. "I'm Jack Bristow. Let's see where this takes us, eh?"

I smiled warmly, but the reality was that I was in staggering pain. Only a first, small blow had been won. This was my chance to become a hero and, further, win the heart of Luciana Fortescue-Ripley-Jones.

The train pulled out, and we fell into silence once more.

It was a jolt which woke me. I looked at my watch; I think I'd been out for a good thirty minutes.

"There he is; our leader's back with us." It was Bristow again, only this time there was warmth in his voice.

"You looked like you needed that, son," said Macintosh. "Slept like a cherub."

I yawned and stretched. "Morning, chaps," I joshed. "Any sign of breakfast?"

"Ha," snorted Bristow, "we've seen the last of a decent fry-up for a while. Cor, I remember the café near my last site – used to put on a real breakfast: bacon, eggs…"

"Sausage," I added.

Jenkins licked his lips and chipped in: "Mushrooms, tomatoes... We used to get our toms from the bottom of the garden, so we did."

"And, fried new potatoes," I offered.

"Aye, you'll be needing a few pots. And, perhaps some of those baked beans."

"Are you joking, Mac? Them things are rancid!" cried Bristow. "Believe you me, you don't want to be bricklaying in any confined space where the other fellow has had a dose of those!"

We all chuckled. "Of course, we'll need a hunk of bread, to mop up the juices," I said; "that's the best bit."

"Or, are we having a fried slice?" asked Jenkins.

We all thought for a second. The conversation was becoming quite the gastronomic dilemma, and I fancy a few tummies were beginning to rumble.

"You're both wrong," came a spirited response: "it has to be lashings of hot, buttered toast."

A cheer went up amongst the company, spontaneous and well-meaning.

"Ginger speaks!" said Mac, triumphantly, while grappling with the poor lad. "Good to have you with us, son!"

In the absence of a full-English, we had to make do with another pear drop each.

It was around two p.m. when the train began to slow.

"I reckon that's it," said Bristow. "I'll bid you all a cheerio now." He stood and began to rummage in the rack.

"Wait," I said, "why don't we try and stick together? It's got to be easier with a few friends?"

"Thryke's right," replied Macintosh: "there's no harm in trying to stay together. We had a fairly agreeable time on this trip." Even Ginger nodded at this remark.

"Nah, there's no point: they've probably already got us all on different lists. So long, chaps; I'll see you around." And, with that, Bristow pulled down his bag and disappeared into the corridor.

"Shame," said Mac. "No harm in *us* trying to stick as a band. What do you think, Ginger?"

"I'd rather stick with some chaps I already know; I'm not much of a mixer," responded Ginger.

"Jenkins?" I asked.

"Ah, sure; why not? You all seem like decent enough chaps – even Mac here."

"Then, it's agreed. It might all go for a burton, as soon as we get off the train, but we'll stick close. Okay?"

All threw their replies into the jumble of consent, and we made ready to alight, into the unknown.

On the busy platform, a smart corporal was barking out commands: "All men for P.T.C. Brington, board the trucks waiting outside the station!"

I smiled; "It's just like returning to school."

"Aye, except they weren't firing bullets at you."

"Maybe not, Mac, but I could dodge a high-velocity piece of chalk."

We all laughed again, tripping over one another's feet in our bid to stay together. Our laughter echoed over the din of the platform, and caught the corporal's ear.

"You, men! You're not on a beano to the lights! Conduct yourself like soldiers and get yourself in the trucks!"

We scuttled, eight-legged, up and across the footbridge, in the direction of the transport.

"Head for the farthest one," I commanded. "A lot of the chaps seem to be milling around the two in the middle; there should be space for us all in that one there." I was scared – yes, I don't mind saying that – but taking the lead was my way of coping.

We reached the truck without further scrapes with authority, and I helped each man up, as they threw their belongings over the tailgate.

"Come on," urged Mac, passing his hand down and hauling me under the murky tarpaulin roof. I swung my remaining leg over the gate and took a seat above the rear wheel.

I took a deep breath and leant forward. The other men were eyeing one another, with a mixture of nerves and curiosity.

"I'm Thryke and this is Mac, Ginger and Jenkins." I fished out my pear drops – they had served me well. "Here, pass these back and share them around."

"You may as well, chaps," said Mac, jesting: "they'll be putting this one in charge; best get used to doing what he says."

Shouts were still flying around outside, as the sweet bag rustled around in our truck. Someone screeched: "You, man! Stop smoking and find yourself a berth!"

I called out: "Room for one more in here, Corporal."

A puce, moustachioed face, beneath a buffed, bronze-badged beret, appeared at the back of the van. "That's 'Sergeant', to whichever wiseacre said that."

All eyes looked to me.

"And who might you be, sonny?"

I straightened my back and said, in a clear tone: "Thryke, sir."

"Don't call me 'sir': I work for a living, boy! You're all to call me 'Sergeant', do you hear? I'll be looking out for you, Thryke; I sincerely hope I get you in my lot." He looked away and called out: "Now, you get in here; the next field marshall says there's room in here!"

A duffel bag was flung over, into the space, and a familiar face appeared: "Hello, Thryke. Lads, fancy seeing you here. Help a fellow up."

I could see the sergeant starting to twitch. "That's twice I've heard that name in as many minutes!"

"Sorry, Sergeant, you'll not hear it again. Come on, Bristow, I'll help you."

The sergeant growled and rapped the side of the truck with his cane. "Get this lot back to the camp, and let's make them soldiers!"

The light was fading as we arrived at P.T.C. Brington. The trucks all pulled up in a line and men began clambering from the back. A corporal bounded up to our van, as Bristow was disembarking.

"Right, you men, I'm Corporal Harris." He did a quick headcount of the men in our truck. "Right. Good. It looks like you lot are with me. Take yourselves to hut twelve, find yourselves a bunk and stow your belongings there. When you've done that, fall in outside, in three columns, and await further instructions. Got it?" He didn't give us any time to respond, and was gone as quickly as he arrived.

Bristow turned to me. "Well, which way is hut twelve?" he said, with a grin.

"No doubt it's between huts eleven and thirteen. Come on, everyone, let's find our lodgings." I scanned the horizon, trying to find some bearing. "This way, I think. Is everyone down? Then, let's go."

Hut twelve, as it transpired, was on the end of the block, so our strategy to find hut eleven appeared foolish, when it turned out there was no ascending accommodation on its farthest flank. There was much grumbling, but at least we now knew where our digs were not.

"Back to where we started, then," I said, cheerfully, but there was now grousing and dissent amongst the group.

The corporal was waiting for us, when our rag-tag mob eventually located our hut.

"Unlucky, chaps. I admire your plucky logic, but it didn't pay off this time, did it? But, don't worry: we'll soon train that sloppiness out of you. Now, get your gear stowed and fall back in out here, double-quick."

Having eventually sorted ourselves into three relatively good lines, we were issued with a set of cutlery and ordered to march off to the mess hall.

"About time," said Bristow. "I could eat a horse."

"Oh, rather," I replied.

"Quiet in the ranks!"

We queued behind some other chaps, who were waiting in their working uniform. Most were spattered with mud; a few were shivering. I surveyed the scene. Some of the other chaps who were joining with us were already there, sitting below a murmur of discontent; it seemed that the food was not to the liking of one or two. Immediately, the older hands were at their sides, jockeying for the untouched scraps of meat, runner beans or mash.

"When you said you could eat a horse, Bristow, it looks like you might have to!"

"You're too namby-pamby, Thryke. Did they feed you swan every day, in that school of yours?"

"Only when the caviar was off."

Mac was queuing behind. "Looks like good, honest tucker to me. It'll stick to your ribs, that's for sure."

Meanwhile, poor Ginger looked decidedly green around the gills.

"Eat what you can, Ginger," I called, back down the line; "judging by these other chaps, we'll all be glad of any kind of meal in a few days."

"But, what is it they get you to do which makes you want to eat extra helpings of *that*?" asked Jenkins. His comment wafted across and into the ear of one of our uniformed predecessors – he looked us all up and down, and grinned.

Reveille was at 0600, but most of us were awake anyway. Only Ginger had trouble stirring, and he had spent all night mumbling in his sleep.

"Do you think the lad will make it?" asked Mac, motioning toward Ginger.

"We'll make sure he does," I replied, firmly. "We'll keep an eye out for him. Say, does anyone know how old he is?"

"That's all very well, Thryke," said Bristow, in a half-whisper. "But, this is the Army, see; we can't afford to be carrying passengers."

I threw my hands in the air. "Your point is duly noted, Bristow. As you say, this is the Army, but you couldn't be more wrong if you tried. One day, you might have to put your life in the hands of one of the Gingers of this world, and he might just pull you through. We leave no one behind."

"Agreed," said Jenkins.

"Aye," said Mac, "I'm in, too."

"Jack?" I set out one last appeal to his better nature. "Jack?"

"Okay, okay, but on your head be it, Corny. If we all get it for lagging, you're going up in front of his nibs first!"

"Deal."

It was a sunny, but chilly morning, as we clambered back into our trucks.

"Maybe they don't need us. Maybe they're taking us back to the station," enthused Ginger.

"Weren't you listening?" barked Bristow. "They're taking us off to the stores, to get us all kitted out. We have to go in the trucks because it's a couple of miles that way."

"Aye, we'll look like proper soldiers in our uniform," said Mac. "You may as well get used to it, lad."

Stores was a splendid affair, full of buzzing, humming and the occasional measuring. Mostly it was done by eye.

"Boots?"

"Size nine, please."

The corporal wandered across, as a few of us were trying on new footwear. "Must important bit of kit in a soldier's make up," he said. "Your boots will be your best friend. Keep them clean and supple and, don't forget, I want to be able to see my face in them every morning – like these." He raised his own feet, in example: it had to be said that his size tens had the most fear-inducing shine.

"How do those feel, Armstrong? Walk about a bit."

Ginger stood up and took a few paces, in front of the long counter.

"Armstrong?" I asked. "Is that you?"

"Yes, it is. James 'Ginger' Armstrong at your service."

The corporal nodded to me. "Right then, you lot, get the rest of your stuff together. The sergeant will have our guts for garters if we dally about here all day."

The rest of our gear consisted of a second pair of boots, two battle-dress uniforms, working denims, an overcoat and a respirator, amongst other items, such as a P.E. kit. It was rather like being at school – only, school didn't have an armoury. There was a strange sense of reflection amongst the men when we were issued with a rifle and bayonet. It was the first time that I had been forced to stare into the face of death – perhaps mine, or maybe an enemy's, at range from my rifle or, worse still, eye to eye with my bayonet. It was with a solemnity that we marched back outside.

Our next port of call gave us some reason for levity, but also brought us closer to what we had been asked to do: we were to enjoy a trip to the camp barbershop. Only, it was not like any other barbershop that I had been to: there was no badinage; no opinions swapped on Tommy Lawton's goals, or Paynter's Newlands double-hundred; nor any whispered aside regarding "something for the weekend". No, it was straight into the chair, to be sheared in the manner of a spring-born, emerging as a lamb to the laughter.

"Cor, look at you, Thryke! Don't you look different, isn't it?"

"I don't know what you're looking so smug about, Jenkins; it's your turn next."

In the afternoon, we were back in hut twelve, contemplating everything that we had seen so far. Maybe Ginger was right: perhaps it would turn out that they didn't need us, and we would all be sent home, after all. I could meet Henry in the Red Lion, or we could go on another fishing trip, if he could get time off. As an agricultural worker, Henry was exempt from the draft, and right now

I was so jealous of him. Maybe, instead of drinking and fishing, I could drive out to the Fortescue-Ripley-Jones estate and surprise Luciana.

I had written to her just before I had left home, but hadn't heard from her in some time. She wouldn't know where I was now. Perhaps she would ask the baronet to make enquiries, and he would locate me, pull a few strings and find me a cushy number somewhere – ahead of a summer wedding, at least. Baronet Cornelius Arthur Thryke.

I guess all of us had caught ourselves in the joy of that wishful thinking, in those first twenty-four hours, but the illusion was soon to be shattered further.

A couple of chaps from the admin office came in. They were carrying flat-pack boxes, brown paper, string and labels.

"Are you chaps planning on sending us home by post?" asked Bristow. "I'd rather have a rail warrant."

"The only warrant you're likely to get is an escorted one, all the way to the glasshouse," snarled one of the men. "Now, take this, see, and use it to wrap up your civilian gear to send home. They'll all need to be in the post room before six, for the van first thing. Got that?"

His blow had struck home. Obediently, we all took a supply of the necessary.

Our visitors about-turned and marched smartly to the door. "And, do wrap them nicely. We don't want to see anything that looks like a parcel of chopped liver. Got it?"

Shaven-headed, stunned and mute, we all sat on our bunks, staring at the piles of paper, card and cord. In the space of a day, we had been stripped down and equipped for a life of soldiering and war. While we had all believed – myself, sincerely – that we had processed and accepted the truth, few moments shattered that illusion with such total precision and speed. Scrawling one's own name onto the slip felt like registering a death. In a way, it was.

I think at least ten minutes passed in that grieving silence. Then, with a deep sigh, I took my trusty civilian coat and rolled it into a large lozenge. There was no need to check the pockets for pear drops.

The next day, and the next day, and the next, there was no other choice than to knuckle down and throw ourselves into army life. A few resisted, Bristow included, but they soon found themselves on the receiving end of short shrift.

It was approaching lunch on the third day—

That sounds like a cricket report: "Approaching lunch on the third day, and Thryke is just a few runs short of a Lords triple-hundred, against this talented Australian side. A magnificent effort, following on from the five-fer on day one—"

"Thryke! Are you with us?" yelled the sergeant.

"Yes, Sergeant."

"Then, come to attention, boy! Stand at ease! Attention! Stand at ease! Attention! That's better, men! There should a snap – an intent."

It was then that I spotted a lanky fellow, loping across the square toward our squad. He was in battle dress and wore a cap, not a beret, like us; he was obviously more important than we were. When the loping interloper came into his field of vision, the sergeant snapped to attention and gave a sharp salute.

"Your new men. Ready for inspection, sir!" he yelled.

"Very good, Sergeant." A floppy salute was returned. "Stand the men at ease."

"Stand at *h*ease!" At least, it should be written like that; Sergeant Puttock enjoyed sounding the non-existent *h*.

"I shall address the men."

"Very good, sir." The sergeant's voice then returned to its other default setting: very loud; "The officer will now address the men!"

The sergeant was not a short man, but this new specimen was a good head and shoulders taller than he. It was our first real encounter with an officer in the wild.

"Now, listen here, men," he began, "my name is Lieutenant Carruthers. I am the officer in charge of this platoon. I'm sure that you are here to do your absolute best, and nothing short of your best is good enough – one day, your life and the life of your colleagues may depend upon it. But, a troubled soldier is not an effective soldier. So, if you have any worries or distress, do not hesitate to bring them to me, and I shall make every effort to help, okay? And remember, we need you fresh on the parade ground each morning, so not too much wine with dinner. Thank you, men; keep up the jolly good work. Carry on, Sergeant."

We chewed over our various introductions at lunch.

"Cor, did you get that Lieutenant Carruthers?" complained Bristow. "Don't have too much wine with dinner, indeed? What a world he must live in."

"They say the food in the officers' mess is like dining in a fine restaurant," confirmed Ginger, sawing into a boiled potato.

"No, it can't be," I said; "it has to be the same as we have here, more or less. The chefs probably just call it something different."

"What do you mean?" asked Jenkins.

"He means that we had beef stew last night, and they would have got the same – only, with a bit of greenery and a dash of something in it, theirs would have been called *boeuf bourguignon*."

"Exactly, Mac," I said. "Are you a bit of an expert on food?"

"Aye, I've done work in the kitchens before. I told them when I came in; I think they've got me down for the catering corps after training."

We had all become close – Mac, Bristow, Jenkins, Armstrong and I – but we knew that our kinship was only for a little while. We had learnt to appreciate the small things, while we had them.

VI

The environs certainly knew that we had started training in earnest, because the wind became harder, the rains longer and the temperatures colder. I ached to my bones. Evenings were uniform, too; they became an endless round of drying, warming, cleaning and polishing. What made it all the more heartbreaking was that you were only really preparing to get your kit dirty again, the following day.

I became intimate with every inch of the parade ground, and with every twist, turn, climb and thumping descent of the assault course. I knew the inner workings of the Bren light machine-gun – every spring, pin, bolt and block – and I could strip it and reassemble it in the dark.

As the weeks passed, I was becoming a soldier. If an obstacle needed crossing, I crossed it; if a rifle needed stripping, I stripped it; if star-jumps needed jumping, I jumped them; if spuds need peeling, I peeled them.

One thing I did seem to excel in was shooting the machine-gun, down on the range. It was there that Sergeant Puttock watched me the closest.

"Load number three gun!" screamed the sergeant, from all of ten yards away.

"Loaded!" called Ginger, as he clipped the mag into the top.

"Fire five rounds!"

I lined up sights and squeezed the trigger! *Boom!* The whole gun seemed to lurch and kick like an angry horse! *Boom!* It smashed back into my shoulder. I pulled the trigger again and again, and once more for luck, before reaching up and unclipping the magazine.

"Number three gun clear, Sergeant."

There was some muttering between the sergeant and Corporal Harris, who was reviewing the target.

"He can't have done."

"It appears he has, Sarge."

The sergeant snatched the binoculars and sneered: "Get number four gun fired."

When all five positions had fired their rounds, the sergeant sprang onto the platform. We were all still lying by our weapons, awaiting the order to swap over.

"Stand up, Thryke."

I leapt to my feet.

"How many rounds were you ordered to fire?"

"Five, Sergeant."

His face started the redden. "Then, perhaps you can explain why there are only three holes in the target, Thryke? That sort of wayward shooting will not be tolerated!"

"With your permission, Sergeant, may I ask where the three perforations are roughly located?"

"Corporal, answer Thryke's question!"

The corporal joined us now: "They were all in the vicinity of the bullseye, Sergeant."

"All in the vicinity of the bullseye, Sergeant," Puttock repeated, mockingly. "So, he completely missed with two and got lucky with three? Either way, I want Thryke recommended for remedial L.M.G. training. I want him spending his evenings and weekends stripping and cleaning every blasted gun, rifle and pistol in the place."

His voice rose by a decibel or two; "So, let that be a lesson for all of you: shoddiness, in any military discipline, will not be tolerated! Do you hear?"

There were murmurs of "Yes, Sergeant," as the men shifted around, restlessly.

"There is one other explanation, Sergeant."

"What?" Puttock spun back to me. He looked fit to burst.

I remained stiffly at attention and stared ahead, into the distance, as Puttock began to circle me in constricting loops, leaving a trial of halitosis and ire. "Well, let's hear it then, Professor Thryke."

As he hissed the less than honorary title, fine droplets of spittle cascaded onto my cheek. I stood firm.

"It is possible that some of the bullets passed through the same holes, Sergeant."

Sergeant Puttock began hopping from foot to foot, displaying his gift for paraphrasing the previous moments in portamento. "Passed through the same holes? Passed through the same holes?! The lad here would have us believe that he is such a crack shot that he can blast the prophylactic from the member of a passing ant!?"

The rest of the squad burst into reams of uncontrolled laughter; I bit the inside of my cheek. I risked a glance at the corporal. He, too, was struggling with the image that the sarge had created.

"Stop your guffawing, now! This isn't *Davey Jangle's Variety Night!*" But, it was too late: the jokes were now falling, one into another; it would have been like trying to put a cork back into a Champagne bottle.

"Corporal!" barked Puttock. "I want these men polishing brass through their lunchtime. And then, on their march this afternoon, see that they are all carrying extra weight. Then, just for good measure, give them to the P.T.I.s; I want to see them passing out and puking. The lieutenant will hear about this."

Not one man complained, because not one man heard.

It was Corporal Harris who helped me into Lieutenant Carruthers's office, late in the afternoon.

"Stand to attention, soldier."

I dragged myself up to something approaching military poise.

"Get him sat down, for Heaven's sake, Harris. Then, go about your evening duties."

"Sir."

Harris pulled out a chair, into which I duly collapsed. Carruthers waited for the corporal to leave.

"Cigarette?"

"No, thank you, sir." I lolled in the chair as Carruthers lit up.

"I see that the sergeant has pushed you hard today."

I remained silent.

"I've ordered additional helpings for your squad in the mess hall this evening – as some countermeasure for you all missing lunch."

"Thank you, sir."

"I've also reviewed the target that you fired upon at the range. I'm satisfied that all five rounds passed through the centre of the sheet, in some way shape or form."

"Thank you, sir."

He stood and began to pace across the window.

"Yes, that is certainly some excellent marksmanship – the best the sergeant has ever seen."

"Sir?"

Carruthers turned, leant against the windowsill and drew deeply on his cigarette.

"You see, Thryke – and, I don't see that there is any harm in sharing this – you may think that Puttock and Harris have got it in for you; that they are singling you out?"

Again, I remained silent.

"Well, they *are* singling you out. On my orders."

Once more, I remained silent, but my mind was racing. The lieutenant was singling me out? What strange regulation had I now broken? It was hattings, all over again.

"We've had our eye on you for a while, Thryke: Puttock, Harris and I."

It was a bally conspiracy! And, it went all the way to the top! I would be lucky to get out of the camp alive! Was it even safe to report it to the major? Was he a willing accessory to my torture, too? If Carruthers was describing his vile plan to break me, openly, the top brass was surely in on it, too.

"You see, I've been receiving regular updates about the platoon, and you in particular; Sergeant Puttock informs me that there is a tight band of you." He crossed to his desk and sat down, running his finger down a notebook. "Ah, yes, these are the names: Armstrong, Bristow, Jenkins and MacIntosh."

"Permission to speak, sir?"

"Speak freely."

"I take full responsibility for any and all actions and offences committed by those men, sir. I am the ringleader."

The officer let out a light, feminine laugh. "Thryke, I didn't summon you here to admonish you. Wherever would you get an idea like that? I brought you here to congratulate you."

He stood again and crossed back to the window. Evidently, he liked it there. "Sergeant Puttock thinks you are an excellent soldier, as does Harris. From the off, you have shown leadership, grit and determination. Your fitness and strength have improved tenfold, and you show excellent military bearing. You also demonstrate above-average intelligence and superb aptitudes with weaponry and fieldcraft; you accept all orders unquestioningly and with good cheer."

"Thank you, sir."

"I'll be sending this report onward, to the C.O. at the I.T.C., Thryke. The Army needs men like you. My job is to provide those men; the Army's job is to place them where they are most useful, wherever that might be. Do you understand, Thryke?"

"Yes, sir."

"Now, go and eat; it's important that you build your strength back up. Dismissed."

I hauled myself to my feet and saluted as best I could. My mind was still racing – only, this time, it was wondering where my future lay.

The Infantry Training Centre was based at Crumpton, a pleasant seaside town in the northeast – it was the next stage of our training.

There were two delights in heading there: firstly, we were given a week of leave in between – it was with great joy that I collected my rail warrants from the pay office: one to Crumpton Camp, naturally, and one to my beloved Little Sodbury-on-the-Wode.

The second joy was that the whole group were to stay together; the chaps: Ginger, Mac, Taffy Jenkins and Bristow. And, that's how it would have been, had one of our number not met with an accident on the assault course.

I remember it to this day; despite all the things that I subsequently saw: poor Taff Jenkins, suspended by one leg, upside down on a cargo net. It was his screams of agony which stayed with me; sometimes, I still hear them now. It took a good half dozen of us to extricate him from the ropes, which we were strictly instructed not to cut. By the time we had him down, the medics had arrived. Taff was as white as a sheet and was drifting in and out of consciousness. They crashed him into the back of the truck and drove off.

I never saw him again. I often wonder what became of our friend from the Valleys.

EDITOR'S NARRATIVE
Quentin Prowler

As you can see, Cornelius Thryke's papers and diaries make superb primary sources of historical reference and, to that extent, I believe them to be records of national importance.

Thryke does not mention much of the period he spent on leave, in the early spring in 1940; he seems to have whiled it away in the bosom of his family, with his brother, sister and mother, Vera.

Of the few lines he wrote during this time, he expresses some concern over the wellbeing of Henry. Henry, it seemed, was suffering from the guilt of staying behind, which was common amongst those in reserved trades. As we have seen, Henry was a farmhand, involved in the important work of keeping the home front fed and supplied with daily sustenance. It is clear, however, that Henry struggled when his brother was called to serve.

One tremendously vital document does survive from that time, however. Waiting for Cornelius, when he arrived home, was a letter. I found it amongst his personal papers and, while I knew it was impactful, I did not realize the full significance until I began compiling this book.

The letter is curiously dated 29th February 1940, which of course was a leap day. On this day, Hitler issued a secret diktat to all Nazi officials, who were due to meet the American diplomat Sumner Welles: all were to deny German aggression and stick to the line that they (the Wehrmacht) had no choice but to fight, in the face of a British and French policy of German annihilation. The document you are about to read is scribed onto the finest, handmade scented paper; the slightest suggestion of the lavender oil still exists, if one closes their eyes and inhales, deeply. As you will see, the text makes mention of the enclosure of a photograph, and the top, right-hand corner of the foremost sheet bears the faint evidence mark of a paper clip: you can almost envisage the clip being applied and the photograph slipped, carefully, underneath. There is a photograph in the envelope, but it lacks the pristine nature of the letter; the picture enclosed is faded, creased and time-ravaged. The inscription on the reverse is barely visible, but it appears to match the hand of the letter writer. I assert that the letter was put away somewhere safe, but the photograph was not.

The primary sources of Thryke's own memoirs and papers mention a photo, on several occasions: one was carried on Cornelius's person, throughout his wartime endeavours – I am in no doubt that the picture in the envelope is the one and the same. In essence, the remainder of Cornelius's wartime reminiscences is also the tale of the travels of this small, black and white photograph. He carried it by his heart, to act as a beacon, when hope seemed lost. It all becomes clear when I reveal that the picture bears a small portrait of Luciana Fortescue-Ripley-Jones. It was a torch he carried into the darkest places.

The text of the letter now follows:

Thursday, 29th February 1940.

My dear Cornelius,

It seems our letters are fated to follow us around, to wherever the winds take us! I know I have not always been the most diligent of correspondents, but I do so enjoy receiving one of your letters; they bring me such happiness and laughter. It is difficult to keep track of you, now that you have been called up, so I thought it best to write to you at home. I hope you get some leave soon.

I trust the training is treating you well. I understand that you will probably be starting your infantry training now. However, you are not the only one in training! I have volunteered for the W.A.A.F.; I wanted to play my part, especially as my brave Corny will soon be entering the fray. I do so worry about you – write quickly, to let me know that you are alright. You will, won't you? Promise? If you continue to send your letters to my home, Father will arrange for someone to forward them on.

I had hoped to join the service in the Officer Corps, but the ability to do that directly ceased at the beginning of the month. Not even Dame Jane could pull any strings for me. But, I must not be too forlorn – all efforts are in defence of the realm, after all. However, I am confident that I shall be promoted with due expedience, so you may have to address me as "ma'am" in future missives! I jest, of course; I thoroughly insist that you continue to utilize the salutation "to my darling Luciana!"

Is it really coming up for nine years since we met at the moondial? I have seen you so seldom since! But, your friendship has been so constant, and you are rarely far from my thoughts. With hope, we shall meet again, before nine years becomes ten. Do you agree so? Protect your side of the bargain by keeping well and staying safe. Your bravery makes me fonder still. I have enclosed a picture of myself that you may keep. Look upon it, should you need some reminder of simpler times. Keep me with you always.

I must sign off now: I have many preparations to make, and my father must be placated. He knows this is what I must do, but it does not stop him fretting so.

Until next time, and with the deepest tenderness,
Luciana xx.

I am sure you will agree, it is a letter of unique tenderness, and one of the most important documents within the Thryke papers. One can imagine the lift it would have given the young Cornelius, heading out, as he was, on the next stage of his training.

The next step, as has been revealed, was the Infantry Training Camp, at Crumpton. Cornelius Thryke arrived at the camp in March 1940. In that month, he also turned twenty-five.

Again, Cornelius Thryke will take up the story, in his own words…

THE MEMOIRS OF CORNELIUS THRYKE.

VII

I continued my progress during infantry training. While we still continued with drills and P.T., we began to take part in training schemes, both during the day and at night. We were always out to capture someone or avoid being caught.

The I.T.C. meant getting used to a whole new chain of command, though most of the other chaps were all the same. We were lucky to get another decent bunch.

Corporal Weston was a pleasant enough chap, as was Sergeant Gifford, but it was Lieutenant Finlay who really struck me as a top-drawer fellow. He called me in on my first day.

"Come in. Thryke, isn't it?"

"Yes, sir."

He flipped open the buff folder on his desk. "I've been reading your record, Thryke. It's impressive. Very impressive indeed."

"Thank you, sir."

"But, listen – and, don't take this the wrong way – I've told Sergeant Gifford not to give you any section commands, at least not in the short term."

"Yes, sir."

"There are some of the other men in the platoon that we'd like to have a look at; we have a responsibility to bring through all of the chaps. They'll not always have a man like you to fall back on: your leadership abilities seem to come naturally; others have to be coaxed. You do understand, don't you?"

"Yes, sir. You can rely on me, sir."

"Good, good. Oh, and I see you have a regular allotment set up for Mrs. Vera Thryke. Your wife?"

"My mother, sir. I like to send her a little bit, sir; the Church pension isn't a tremendous amount."

"Church?"

"Yes, sir: my father was a vicar. It was on account of him that I was able to get into Greyowls, sir."

"Ah, yes, Greyowls... Greyowls. Sounds familiar." He began to drum the desktop with his fingertips. "Perhaps we played them at rugger once. Are you a rugger man, Thryke?"

"More cricket, sir. A middle-order bat, with some occasional off-spin."

"Really?" The mention of cricket seemed to cheer the lieutenant mightily. "Well, there's a small chance we might be able to get a game in, before either one of us gets posted. Any other players in the platoon?"

"I dare say we could get a decent eleven together, sir."

Lt. Finlay stood, walked around the desk and, with a hand in the small of my back, began to usher me slowly toward the door. "Good. That's jolly good, Thryke. Look, I'll leave that with you: ask around, get a few chaps and see the P.T.I.s for gear; see if you can get the odd net together. Good, good."

He reached for the door handle and gave it a twist. "Oh, and the military stuff: just keep up the good work, okay?"

When I got back to the barrack hut, Bristow and Ginger were waiting for me.

"Well?" said Ginger.

"He's put me in charge," I replied.

Bristow exploded into his well-rehearsed repartee: "I told you all, lads! Come along now and pay up! Make way for Colonel Thryke!"

I had to call out, atop of the merriment: "He didn't put me in charge of you lot!"

Bristow stopped in his tracks. "Then, what are you in charge of? The latrines?"

"No, the platoon cricket team."

The chaps all fell around, then. Above the din, I heard Caledonian tones cry out: "Trust Thryke to find a job that lets him keep his feet up 'til June! Didn't I say he was officer material?"

It was a good few weeks before I was placed in charge of a section, but I don't think it was a coincidence that it was on the first of our night-operations training.

"Listen up, men," said Sergeant Gifford: "our Major Inskip is holed up, with at least one full colonel and a few other senior officers, in a small farmland outbuilding, on the other side of that woodland. Now, the idea of this scheme is as follows: Lieutenant Willoughby's platoon has been charged with defending the command position. Our intelligence suggests they have three eight-man sections placed here, here and here. Thryke, you are to take your men and engage the enemy here. Got that?"

I nodded.

"Good. Meanwhile, I will take four men and Corporal Weston will take four, and we will engage the enemy at these points of cover – the plan is that this will allow Lieutenant Finlay to split his section, to track round from the east and west, to capture the command post and capture the high-ranking officers and their sensitive plans. Is everyone clear?"

We all nodded.

Sergeant Gifford started to wind up, with a motivational speech: "Now, as we all know, our Lieutenant Finlay has this ongoing competition with Willoughby, to see who has the best platoon. If we can see this off, he has promised us a decent drink on Friday night, as it pulls us level before the cricket final, on Sunday. Thryke, I hope for your sake that you've put a decent team together. The boss is counting on us."

I enjoyed those night schemes most of all. There was something thrilling about scampering around in the countryside, in the dead of night; the treks with Henry had prepared me for these moments. Chaps like Bristow and Mac – city dwellers both – didn't have the terrain in their blood, as I did. But, it was that sickly feeling of nervousness that I found most exhilarating; that feeling was always reminiscent of the night I escaped Greyowls and headed over to the girls' school. I tapped my breast pocket for good luck. I was ready for the off.

"Come on, lads, let's go."

My section marched, single file, into the night. At the head of the column, I hugged any cover I could find, even though we were still far from the enemy position. Eventually, we left the road and disappeared into the trees.

"Trust Mac to get the kudos, while we get sent in as a decoy," said Bristow, as we huddled deep in some bracken.

"What do you mean?" asked Ginger.

"Well, he's in Finlay's section. They're going to storm the building, capture the colonel and get all the glory."

I ignored Bristow – sometimes you just had to. Once he had voiced his frustration, you could usually rely on him to get his job done. I crawled over to Nolan, our radioman.

"Are the other sections in position?"

"Any minute now, Thryke."

"And, Atherton, can you make out their position?"

Atherton lowered his binoculars. "Looks like they're all behind a low wall, about eighty yards that way. They're dug in, Corny. They just need to rake our position with fire."

"Understood." Perhaps Bristow was right. I signalled all the men together.

"Okay," I whispered, "we've got to be quick, because the attack will start anytime. Here's the plan: Atherton, I want you and Ginger to head back around the tree-line, in the way we came; Nolan, Greaves, you two hold this position here; Bristow, Smith and Taylor are with me: we'll head up farther round, and see if we can't take them from their right flank. All clear?"

Everyone nodded. I looked at Bristow, who didn't disappoint: "We've just to be aware we don't go in on top of one of Willoughby's teams."

"Noted, Brissy, my old chum. We're just here to keep this westward section busy, that's all. Oh, and Nolan and Greaves, when the white flares go up, throw in a couple of smoke grenades – that'll keep them guessing further. Come on, my men."

We were just finding a better position, when the white flares started to climb into the darkness.

"That must be Sergeant Gifford's teams. The attack has started."

I scanned back to where I thought the rest of our section was. Sure enough, Greaves and Ginger sent up flares of their own.

"Right, time to send up ours; give those fellas something to think about," said Bristow.

"Hold a second."

At that moment, two red flares went off at the rear of the outbuilding.

"That's got to be the lieutenant's men," cried Bristow. "They've gone and set off booby traps. No one said anything about booby traps; that's just not fair! Come on, let's get back; the scheme's over."

"Not yet!" I barked; it was a sharp and authoritative order. "It's our turn to go to the party. Smith, Taylor, give Bristow and me ten seconds, then send a flare up. Come on, Jack."

We dashed off into the trees.

"What are we doing, Thryke?" asked Bristow.

"We're going to storm that building ourselves."

"But, how do we get across the open land?"

"Something will turn up."

And, it did.

"But, they're pig-pens," said Bristow, fully utilizing his gift for observation.

"Yes."

"And, the pigs are inside these little hut things?"

"Yes. But look: it takes us right up to the target. All their men are digging in, defending."

"But, you want us to crawl through forty yards of pig shit?"

"Don't over-dramatize, Bristow: it's more like thirty yards. And, it can't all be pig shit."

It turns out I was wrong, on both counts.

When Bristow and I eventually burst into the building, the shock was palpable.

"Sirs, could you come with us, please? Your position is surrounded."

"Inskip," barked the colonel. "Who are these fellows, and what is that awful smell?"

"They're two of mine, sir," replied the major, "though, in their current condition, it's hard to say which two. I'll order the scheme halted, sir. And, you two, do make sure you wash thoroughly when you get back to camp."

It took a few days to finally be free of the stench, though, on the plus side, Bristow and I were guaranteed our own table at mess times. We had to give up on the battle dress, which was eventually burnt, and replacements were sent down. Cleaning our boots was a challenge, though.

Throughout the next day, the men in my section were pulled out of various activities and summoned to the office of Major Inskip himself. Corporal Weston cornered me, during a smoke break.

"Not smoking?" he asked.

"No, I don't."

He took a deep drag. "You've got to have some pleasures in life?"

"Walking the countryside, enjoying a cold beer and fishing, Corporal."

"Ah, yes, you're a country boy; that explains it. Look," he blew out a funnel of smoke, "it's like this: the major is still investigating last night's scheme, you know? That colonel was sore at being captured; seems you interrupted his dinner."

"I'm sorry, Corporal."

"Well, apparently the colonel set up the defences himself, see. He had a couple of bob with Inskip that his men wouldn't get through."

"Oh."

"Yes, oh. Well, they're asking all the men in your section what went on, given that you weren't supposed to be anywhere near that outbuilding. Bristow is over there now."

"Bristow did what I told him, Corporal. They all did."

Weston flicked his cigarette butt to the floor and squished it out with a polished size ten. "Look, don't be so quick to fall on your sword, Thryke: martyrdom doesn't suit you. The benefit of the doubt lies in the uncertainty. Keep yourself in the grey area and you'll be alright. That's all I'm saying."

I nodded, and the corporal patted me on the shoulder.

"Look, you're a bloody good infantryman, Thryke. I'd be proud to have you in my section, you hear?"

I nodded again and waited for the inevitable call.

As suspected, Major Inskip saved Private C.A. Thryke for last. Sergeant Gifford looked at me strangely, as he ordered me to double away, over to the office block.

"Nice, smart salute when you get there, Thryke, and don't forget to stand to attention."

I took a deep breath as I paced the final few yards to Major Inskip's lair. I had never been in his office before, and didn't know what to expect. I stepped up and rapped on the door.

"Come!"

I opened the door and stepped across the threshold. The major, who was seated at his desk, deep inside the room, did not look up. "Close it behind you."

The door closed with a clunk.

I glanced to the far corner, where Lieutenant Finlay was standing.

"Private Thryke, sir," he announced.

The major finally looked up. I snapped into a salute and stood stiffly to attention. I placed my gaze over the major's head and through the large picture window.

The major began to speak: "Well, Thryke, we know all about the events of last night. We know that, as section leader, you issued orders in contravention to the orders already given by your platoon sergeant. Would that be a fair summary?"

"Yes, sir!" I called.

The major looked over to Lieutenant Finlay. "Stand easy, Thryke," said Finlay.

"Well, the postings will be released next week," continued Major Inskip, "but I'm going to recommend that you are given further training."

"Sir?" I thought there was going to be some fallout, but not this. "I want to get out there and do my bit, sir."

"Indeed you do, Private – that much is clear. But, I am ordering you to reconsider and volunteer for further training."

"Volunteer, sir?"

"Why, yes, it always looks better if you are ordered to consider volunteering."

I was thoroughly confused. All I knew was that I wanted out of the I.T.C. "With respect, sir, I would like to volunteer to accept a posting and do my bit."

The major stood, and his volume rose with him: "Private Thryke, you gave orders in the field which superseded those given by an experienced platoon sergeant. Lieutenant Finlay tells me that no other man in his platoon would behave in such a way. Further training is what you require, and further training is what you shall volunteer for. Explain it to him, Finlay."

Finlay stepped out of the corner and leant against a filing cabinet. "Yes, sir. Maybe there's a different way of putting this, Thryke. What you did last night jolly well saved the scheme for our platoon; you showed a clear head and innovative thinking. But, that needs developing further. Don't get us all wrong, Thryke: we don't want you to stay and undertake *repeat* training; we want you to go elsewhere and take part in *further* training."

I was still not entirely aware of what was going on. But, I was experiencing the strangest of feelings. I wanted to get out there, to test my mettle for king and country. Most importantly, I wanted to tug at the heartstrings of Luciana; to have her think that I was in peril; that I was out there, doing my bit.

Ah! So, that was what was really going on!

Lieutenant Finlay had stepped across to me, by then. "I know you want to get stuck into Jerry, Thryke – I can see it in your eyes. But, you'll see action, I promise you. You'll see more of it than the rest of those chaps put together!"

Ah! I had thrown myself in and embraced the army life with zeal – now it appeared that my reward was to be slightly more jeopardy than I had initially planned.

"Get to the detail, Finlay."

"Certainly, sir. Thryke, we would like you to volunteer for

reconnaissance duties."

"Reconnaissance duties, sir?"

The major, itching to get into the officers' mess, no doubt, took up the baton once more: "It's very simple, Thryke. As a volunteer for the Recce Unit, you'll need additional specialist training. You'll be attached to a regiment to begin with, but I am aware of plans to make Reconnaissance its own corps, at some point in the future."

He stood up and marched to the door; Finlay followed him. As Major Inskip reached the exit, he turned and left me with these words: "Well done, Thryke; the Army thanks you. Now, be on your way; you must be wanting dinner."

VIII

In November of 1942, I was in Scotland. It was snowing and absolutely freezing. All around me, men were attempting to light cigarettes, huddled in groups, trying to form windbreaks; all the gusts did was swerve around corners.

"I think something's trying to tell me to give up," snarled Thornton, putting his roll-up back into his tin. Thornton was another hardened Londoner. He put me in mind of Bristow in a way, only he was sharper – which, in fairness to Jack, was not supremely tricky.

I had been made corporal the previous week, and Jim Thornton had been amongst the first to congratulate me. Our section had gone out for a few drinks and made the most of it. I was the leader, then there was Jim Thornton, Barry Innes, Clive Banks, Big Davey Williams, Taffy Johns, Leighton Stewart and Freddie Blair. All of us had gone through the tough reconnaissance training, and we were a real unit.

The platoon sergeant was another beast of a man; he was one of the fittest and toughest chaps that I ever met. The lads loved him, and there was not one of us that wasn't proud to go into battle with him. His name was William "Billy" Clough and, as he marched along the jetty, we all stood to attention.

"At ease, lads, at ease," he said. "Here, tell you what, though: remember those Highlanders we had a scrap with, a couple of weeks ago? Well, they're down there. I shook them all by the hand;

they're good lads."

My mind went back to the incident in question. I know that "fiery Welshman" is one of those appalling clichés, but in my section there were two, and they loved a punch-up. On that particular night, you could see it coming. Taffy Johns had been winding up this group of Highlanders all night, saying that Recce men were tougher – that sort of thing – but when he started saying how terrible Scotland was, and how Wales was much better, we all looked at each other and sighed. Big Davey wasn't helping the situation by plying Taffy Johns with booze or, as I saw it, adding the powder to the keg. I tried to intercede, to get Taff to quieten down, but it was no good: he had gone in for a ruckus and a ruckus he was going to have. It was almost a relief when one of their lads threw the first punch.

Then, it went up like a grenade. Johns and Williams waded in first – Johns low and scrappy; Williams bundling men around like ragdolls – then, everyone went in. I took a few decent shots and imparted a few of my own. We all knew that we were disciplined men, and that we should have all just walked away but, once it started, it had a momentum of its own. We began to get on top, knowing the military police would soon be on their way.

At the sound of the first response bells, it all just stopped. Hands were shaken and we tidied the bar, in double-quick time; there was even a whip-round for damages. How we didn't get our collars felt, I do not know.

"We were all lucky that night, Sarge," I said.

"Luck? Luck doesn't come into it, Thryke. We're trained to evade. And, to be fair, I don't really think the police were too upset to find the bar empty. Now, come on: it's time to board."

Within half an hour, 57th Recce, plus I don't know how many other regiments, were climbing the gangplanks onto the waiting vessels, around the dockyard. Ours was a stately old liner which had been hurriedly converted into a troop carrier; anything which didn't move had been painted grey. The dockyard clankies were still coming off while we were waiting.

Our platoon, under Lieutenant Windemere, was allocated space on 2-deck. We stowed our equipment and carried out a roll-call – all, thankfully, were present and correct. The ship began to rumble, then calmed into a vibrato-drone.

We were all keen to get back out onto the main deck, to wave the Firth of Clyde a fond goodbye and too-da-loo. I went back out into the daylight.

The floor was thick with men, huddled in groups, on grey beneath grey. The last flurries of snow still blasted the cold metal, but all pretended not to mind. I raised the lapels of my coat and weaved a path toward the port rail. A few, who were already green of gill, had gathered in pockets of pale-faced arachnids, eyes sunken at the thought of the lengthy voyage ahead.

There was only so much of oneself that one could return to the sea. By the time the Straits of Gibraltar appeared on the horizon, these men would have to be disembarked by dustpan and brush.

For the time being, I counted myself lucky that I was not amongst their number and, if I let you into my confidence, this was the first time that Corporal Cornelius Thryke had been on a boat of any nature. Yes, I had seen fellows and their beaus rowing around the countryside rivers of home, but I had never joined them; I was always content to fish from the bank. Water – large bodies of it, at least – had been fashioned by the good Lord to provide a scenery; a backdrop to the essential, land-based tribulations of man. I had not even come remotely close to choosing the Navy, yet here I was. Whilst training, the notion of how I would reach my posting had not remotely crossed my mind. Now, as I saw the coast of Scotland slowly drifting by, I understood that the decision had been made for me. I also appreciated that I was heading for an entirely different continent to the one I had imagined.

I found an unpopulated length of the rail and placed my hands upon it, as a show of ownership. The steel was brutally cold and, even with gloved hands, it felt like I was sticking to it. I lifted them away, leaving some fine, woollen threads in the paint.

"Howdy. I should warn ya, that paint's still tacky."

"So I see," I said, looking at my gloves.

"Don't worry, man; you'll not need them where we're going."

A clean, gloved hand reached over; "I'm Jed: Jed Wildly, 34th Infantry Division."

"Cornelius Thryke, 57th Reconnaissance Regiment." I shook his hand, not bothered if it transferred some paint residue. "Pleased to meet you."

"Reconnaissance? Well, I'll be glad to have you in front of me when the bullets start flying! Let me shake your hand again. So, where are you from, Cornelius?"

"A small village called Little Sodbury-on-the-Wode, about four-hundred miles south of here. You'd hardly know there was a war on there, save for the rationing. How about you?"

"Well, now, I've come a long, long way. You know much of America?"

I shook my head. I didn't even know that much of Britain.

"I'm from Pine Bluff, Arkansas. If you think of America as being a big rectangle, I'm in the middle, but near the bottom. You get me?"

I told him that I did. I didn't inform him that many of the masters at Greyowls refused to teach anything about our trans-Atlantic cousins, considering it vulgar. I could, however, find my way around India without asking for directions.

"Yep," he continued, "it used to be a quiet place, then the Army came and got me; built an ammunition store right in the town. One day I'm working for the Union Pacific Railroad then, next time I look, I'm here talking to you. I'm just a boy from Arkansas."

I was just a boy from Little Sodbury. I looked at him. I had encountered Americans before, but they always seemed exotic and otherworldly; Algie used to read comic books, filled with Wild West characters. But, this chap seemed like he would be happy being a simple ranch-hand, while others galloped around and fought duels on the dusty streets.

"I mean, do you know how far it is from Pine Bluff to Tunis?

SIMON GARY

Fifty-five-hundred miles. Fifty-five-hundred! As far as I know, I am the first person in my family to leave the United States. What right has a boy like me to go toting a gun fifty-five-hundred miles from home?"

What right did a boy from Little Sodbury have to place boots on foreign soil? I shook myself. Was I being tempted by the Devil himself?

"I'd be very careful who you repeat that opinion to. You know why this mission is vital, Private."

Even as my reply tumbled out, I was conflicted. This soldier was confused; like most of us, he was just swept up in the momentum. But, momentum was good; momentum did not afford you the time to think. What if everyone on the ground just simultaneously agreed to go home? But, had this soldier, this Arkansas boy, not merely been extending the hand of friendship? Had he not just opened a small window into his own fear and uncertainty? He looked at my arm.

"I'm sorry, Corporal; you're right." He turned and gazed upon all the men on deck. "I'll see you around."

And with that, he disappeared. Strange that I remember his name, even all these years later, yet I never spoke to him again. I went back down below and rejoined the platoon.

We began to sweep south, as we passed Greenock and threaded past Arran and Ayr. We rumbled by the Isle of Man and into the Irish Sea. We tipped our hats to Dublin and Holyhead, as the Celtic amongst us felt the pull of home. While our vessel juddered by Wexford and Fishguard and into St. George's Channel, life onboard was finding a pulse and routine.

Lieutenant Windemere was nothing if not imaginative, in finding new ways to keep us sharp; we were often to be seen partaking in push-ups, squats or dangling from any available bulkhead, in full battle kit. I, and a few of the others, had hit upon using the engine room for acclimatization: it was hot, smoky and loud down there – much as we imagined a desert battleground. The stokers were more than happy to take a rest, feeling that we were slightly on the wrong side of gentle insanity. But, it helped to pass the time.

While others slept, smoked or swapped battered paperbacks, we pored over maps or thumbed through phrasebooks.

"I reckon I should be fluent in the lingo by the time I get there," said Jim Thornton. "D'you reckon we'll need it?"

"Hard to tell how the Vichy lads will react," I said. "How's your Arabic coming along?"

"Now, that's a bit slower, *habibi*." A few of the other chaps laughed at Jim's joke.

"Alright, alright," I said, "let's get back to it; there's a lot to learn."

Lieutenant Windemere happened upon the scene. "Ah, gentlemen – no, no, that's alright; don't get up. Good, I see you're employing your time usefully: the ability to draw out a little local knowledge could make all the difference. Good, good."

We all mumbled a collective reply.

"Everybody got their sea legs yet?" asked the lieutenant, cheerfully. "It was a bit hairy going past Ireland."

Complacency is not a quality that is respected by the ocean. She is undoubtedly feminine in her sudden bouts of turbulence; when we hit the North Atlantic, she was the mistress of all men. Our ship was huge, heavy and two inches thick in paint, but those wind-gusted, rain-filled swells tossed us around like a child's toy. Sleet rat-tatted onto the portholes, then was blasted away by the talons of a wrathful sea.

In the worst of it, buckets, bowls and any water-tight receptacle available were being commandeered and grasped by men, white of knuckle and queasy-eyed. Let me tell you, if you think a man can't turn green, then let me dash that notion: our deck looked like a spilt box of plastic soldiers. Some panicked and sought the air of the open deck, but it was foolhardy indeed. When morning roll-call came, we learnt exactly how foolhardy it was.

"All present and correct, sir," reported Sergeant Clough.

"Very good, Sergeant. Gather the men together for a moment, please."

If we thought this was a talk on the importance of eating breakfast, we were soon put right.

"Now, men, I want to address a matter, quickly and succinctly, before it becomes the stuff of rumour. During the storms of last night, a couple of men were lost overboard. There will be a brief remembrance service for our deck at eleven-hundred hours. All are to attend.

"Now, I have decided not to make the open deck out of bounds for the time being but, from this moment, all men must go up in pairs. If any storms of the nature that we experienced last night reoccur, the upper deck must be cleared immediately. Is that clear?"

"Yes, sir," came the resounding response.

"And remember, we are still passing the Bay of Biscay. The bay is a known area for enemy U-boats. Therefore, in the event of any naval engagement, all men are to report here immediately. Is that understood?"

"Yes, sir!"

"Very good. Now, carry on with your studies; I want us all able to get by in the local lingo, and know the landmarks before we get there. Okay? Thank you, Sergeant; take over."

"Sir!" A sharp salute was given and returned. "You heard the officer: get those books out! I want them read front ways, back ways and hinside out!"

A day or two later, I was standing on the upper deck – I had taken Big Davey Williams with me.

"Here we are then, Williams: the Strait of Gibraltar; gateway to the Mediterranean."

I was reminded of my conversation with the American infantryman, as we left Scotland. It seemed an age ago now. Blue skies and sun had replaced squalling sleet and snow.

We crossed to the starboard rail – the good thing about being on deck with Williams was that he guaranteed clearing a path to anywhere. In the distance, citadels glinted.

"Tangier, Williams," I stated; "Spanish Morocco."

Morocco. The word even tasted exotic, as I rolled it off my tongue. It came from boyhood adventure stories, of explorers, treasure hunters and pirates.

"Did you ever think you'd see Africa, Davey?"

"Do you know what, Corny? Until now, I didn't know it existed. Well, I knew, but it was something remote; far off – a place in a book. I look at Africa now and I think: *Is that it?* It's just a bit of coast – I could have seen that on a trip to Southsea."

I looked up at Williams in a state of bewilderment. He had just written off the wonders of an entire alluring continent as "just a bit of coast".

As it turned out, he wasn't finished. "Take Henry the eighth, for instance: now, I know he existed; I learned about all his wives in school: beheaded, divorced— no, divorced, beheaded, died, then divorced, beheaded, survived…"

"Catherine of Aragon, Anne Boleyn, Jane Seymour…" I offered.

"Spare me this history lesson, Corny! But, King Henry – to me, he's just a painting. I know he existed, but he almost seems fictional. You see? But, if he were stood there, between you and I, for all his history and kingyness, he'd still just be a man. And, he'd probably be a right disappointing pain."

I took a step to the right and surveyed the space. I tried to picture the rotund king standing there, wearing the same battle dress as we wore. He would be wheezing, sweating and probably emitting breath which was less than pleasant. But, there was no doubting that he was just a man.

"Besides, if I lived over there, in Tangier, Tangier wouldn't be special; it would just be home. But, if I were suddenly transported to Bridlington, maybe I'd find that exotic."

I sighed and pulled my phrasebook from my top pocket. I had to be sure that Williams's mundane take on existentialism hadn't forced out anything important.

On 8th November 1942, we boarded the landing craft.

"This is it, men; your patience is about to be rewarded. All of your training and expertise is about to be called upon. I am proud to serve alongside you all; you are a credit to your regiment. Now, let's get ashore and be a credit for ourselves."

That was when the war became real for me.

The craft began to bob and surf the waves to a golden, sandy shore: it was the coast of Algeria. Three task forces were landing simultaneously, and we were the farthest east.

"Do you think Old Giraud has managed to roll the red carpet out for us?" said Thornton, never short of a boosting quip or jape.

He didn't have to wait for his answer: the unmistakable *crack-crack* of rifles started to rent the air, then came the deep, rumbling *boom-fizz* of the cannon.

I looked back to see great plumes of water leaping angrily into the air. My heart quickened. At any moment, I could be snuffed out!

But, I felt superhuman; full of strength and vigour! In the face of death, I felt truly alive.

"They're missing by miles," I shouted, above the din. "Either they're terrible shots, or this is just a token resistance, to let us know they're here."

"I think Thryke is right, men: it's just a bit of a Vichy bark. Let's go tickle its tummy," said Windemere, who always enjoyed a ridiculous cliché.

"Okay, men. Now." It was Sergeant Clough who gave the order to lower the front of the boat. The gangplank dropped with a crash and white-tipped waves boiled into the craft. "Let's go!"

Lieutenant Windemere strode forward and jumped, thigh-deep, into the azure sea. Sergeant Clough, then I and the other corporals, then the men, followed.

The sun was beating down, but the sea was still cold. I gulped a large lungful of Algerian air, as my boots made contact with the sub-aqua sands and my organs retreated north. The weight of the water dragged me forward, and I strained all of my muscles to retain control; I did not want to be the first man to topple headfirst into the water – under the bulk of my pack, I may not make it back up. Ahead, Lt. Windemere was nearing dry land. The sea began to decrease in depth as I paced laboriously to shore, where he was waiting.

"Well done, Thryke. Welcome to Africa. Now, over there; wait with the sergeant. Keep low."

It was the first time since that cold Scottish morning that my boots had touched dry land. Back over previous scorching Algerian summers, lithe, tanned lotharios had walked these beaches with their lovers, while children dashed in and out of the waves. Now, it was slowly filling with men from across the seas – men in green, carrying the weapons of death and war.

It took the rest of the day to get everyone and their equipment ashore. Watching jeeps and tanks driving up the beach was a surreal experience, like seething metallic monsters evolving from the sea, with fierce, steaming mouths.

"We move out at sixteen-hundred hours," said Windemere, as he eventually gathered the men together. Roll-call showed that we had all made it – from our regiment, at least.

"Thryke, take some men and give the L.R.C.s a going over, will you? Make sure they're fully operational."

Soon, we had crossed the border into Tunisia and seeped farther east. Our objective was Tunis. We were coming from the west, as Montgomery chased from the south and east; in the middle was Rommel and the 5th Panzer Division. I would say it was a powder keg, but then the rain started.

"When they said we were going to Africa, I thought I'd catch a bit of sun. How long has this been now?" asked Freddie Blair, driving the Humber as best he could, in the reduced visibility.

"Four days," I replied. "It's almost biblical."

"It's a judgement, alright. This road will be impassable soon."

We rumbled on, slowly. The order had been changed a day or two before, to proceed at amber.

"Stop!"

The shout went up from Jim Thornton, who was behind us in the gun turret. "There's something up ahead."

We halted, bringing the rest of the column to a standstill.

"Out," I commanded, "and off the road."

Before I knew it, the sergeant was on me: "What is it, Corporal?"

"Thornton has reported something up ahead."

We ducked down in a ditch, by the side of the road. It was filling with water, but it hardly mattered; we were all soaked through to the skin. Rain was streaming off the end of my helmet and *plinking* between the netting. The red earth, sodden and thick with clay, moulded around us and began to suck us in.

"Thornton," hissed the sergeant, "give me those field glasses."

The lieutenant arrived and slid down into the mire with us, spraying us with mud and debris.

"What is it, Corporal?"

"A sighting of something up the road, sir. We're just investigating now."

Sergeant Clough handed me the binoculars. I wiped the rain from the lenses, which was pointless, and had a look.

"Looks like there's a couple of trees down, sir, across the road. Hang on… yes, there's another one stacked on top."

"That's a roadblock, son; there's no way they fell like that," said the sergeant, grimly.

"Banks," called Lieutenant Windermere, back down the track, "have there been any reports of enemy activity in this area?"

Clive Banks, a red-haired Midlander, who doubled as our radio operator, shook his head: "Negative, sir."

"Well," considered the boss, "I don't want to send for the sappers. We're Recce men; we'll have to check it out ourselves."

"I'll go, sir." I looked around, and was surprised to find that the voice had been mine.

"Good man, Thryke," cried the sergeant. "I'll go with him. And, one more?"

His eyes fell on Thornton, who was conveniently close.

"And Thornton. Good," said Lieutenant Windemere. "Go and have a scout about and report back. We must get this road open."

Clough, Thornton and I got our kit together and began to make our way up the streaming, red track.

"Try and stick to the undergrowth," ordered Clough. "Follow me."

It was farther than it looked. The rain continued to drive into our faces; our boots squelched and squealed in the mud.

"There it is," said Clough, presently. It was just as we had seen from farther back up the road.

"Looks like the first one fell, but the others have been placed there," I said.

"Yeah, but by who?" asked Thornton.

"Come on, there's nothing for it," said the sergeant. "Thryke, you cross over to the far side; Thornton, go right of centre and work left; I'll start this side and work toward you. Move slowly. If anything underfoot looks disturbed, use your feeler rod. Got it?"

I began to slowly cross the road, to the far side, where the tops of the fallen trees lay. The road was relatively smooth and compacted. I pushed my rod into the surface, but it would only go a few inches, before it stuck fast in the glue. Pulling it back out was even more draining; small rivulets would drain into the holes and bubble up in a gurgle. I was terrified.

"I'm pretty sure there are no mines in the road: you'd struggle to get a shovel in there," I said, pulling my rod from the ground.

"I think you're right," replied the sarge, "but, carry on with caution." He was already feeling around the trunks for booby traps.

"There are tyre-tracks on the other side," exclaimed Thornton.

My heart sank, and my eyes began to survey the horizon. Were they out there, watching us? It was the first time in my life that I had felt that kind of fear. "Stop thinking about it; just follow your training," I whispered to myself. I looked across at Clough and Thornton, whose faces were the concentrated picture of focus. Surely it wasn't just me? They must feel it, too? That's the difficulty with people: you look at them and they look fine – then you think you're the only one who must be scared. In the rain, everyone else always looks dry.

I moved in closer and began to probe within the fronds, gently.

"Thornton, get back down the road and tell them to bring up a Humber; they'll have to push or drag these off. Thryke and I will scout ahead, see what's about; someone put these here. Come on, Corny."

I climbed over the treefall, making myself a target on the horizon. Any second... Any second, it could all go black.

"We'll make our way over to that bluff," said Clough. "Whoever was here, I suspect they're long gone. But, I'd just like to make sure."

"Do you think it was the enemy?"

"Hard to tell. They shouldn't be here, but it might be a small recce force, like us."

I nodded. We began to make our way cautiously forward.

"I was impressed back there," said Clough, "when you volunteered."

"I had to: it was my first chance to set a real example to the men, you know, since I got promoted."

Clough grinned. "You've got it, Thryke, you know? You're a leader. They'll follow you anywhere now. That's why I sent Thornton back; it had to be us that went on. Do you get it?"

"Yes, Sarge."

He clapped a hand onto my arm. "Call me Billy when we're alone – I reckon you've earnt it. Now, come on, let's get a squizz on the terrain."

We eventually scrambled to the top of the ridge, which was in danger of being washed away. Clough scanned the horizon through his binoculars.

"Well, if there was a German recce unit here, they're long gone by now." He passed me the glasses.

"What do you think that is? Right over there, in those trees?" I pointed.

He grabbed the bins back and trained them in the direction indicated. "Cor, yes. Good spot, Thryke." A thin column of smoke was rising from between the distant trees.

"Could just be the locals."

"It could be, yes," said Sergeant Clough, from behind the glasses. "Something tells me it's them though, Thryke. Wow, can you feel the buzz? Record the position, Thryke. Let's get back."

We slid down the hill on our behinds, sending up waves of filth as we went.

"Do you think they saw us, Sarge?"

"Can't be sure, Thryke. Though, do you think they'd be stopping for a brew if they had?"

When we got back to the roadblock, the first tree had already been heaved away.

"Sir!" Sergeant Clough gave the lieutenant a neat salute.

"Welcome back, Sergeant. Anything to report?"

"Possible enemy position, sir."

Windemere and Clough marched off to corroborate, in a hastily pitched command tent. Then Banks, the radioman, was sent for. Thornton, Johns, Stewart and I clambered back into the Humber for a moment of shelter.

It was relatively dry inside the vehicle, until four sopping troopers climbed inside. With the engine running, it was loud but, with its six cylinders at rest, it merely became an echo chamber for the biblical pelting we had endured for days. The men looked at me.

"Stewart, Johns, disengage the Bren gun; we'll strip and clean it here, as best we can."

"Corporal." They both jumped to it. I think they were relieved that I had given them something to do.

"Did you see the enemy then?" asked Thornton.

"No, not as such," I replied, "but there was a column of smoke on the horizon – you could see it from the top of the ridge."

Stewart and Johns, both sons of the Valleys, returned with the Bren gun, which we had quickly dismantled into three sections.

"Do you think it was Jerry, then?" asked Johns.

"I almost want it to be," said Stewart.

Stewart's words, pricked by ping upon ping, hung in the petrol-stained air of the L.R.C.

You soon realized that, in the Army, all equipment had a variety of names, all designed to confuse and delight. L.R.C. stood for "Light Reconnaissance Vehicle", though I always felt there was nothing light about it; you wouldn't want one to rumble over your foot.

Of the four of us, Stewart was taking up the most space. He was not much smaller than Davey Williams, and the two of them would treat us to marvellous feats of strength, on an almost-daily basis. They were like bears: both had thick, black hair which covered their bodies. We joked that they could be brothers, had hundreds of miles not separated their respective places of birth.

"You know what I mean, though?" added Stewart.

"Aye," said Johns, "we trained for action, not to be chasing ghosts around mudflats. When are we going to get stuck in?"

Thornton, Johns and Stewart all looked at me. In the time that the conversation had unravelled, we were all cleaning the same gun components for a second time.

"We're here to follow orders and make safe the journey into Tunis," I said, firmly.

"Yes, Corporal." The response came from all three, in unison. They were good men.

The gun was rattled back together and re-installed in the turret. Soon after, the lid went up, sending rivulets of water dripping into the cabin, mainly over Johns.

"Here, what are you playing at? Put the metal back on the hole. Can't a man keep dry in this godforsaken country?"

The face of Banks, the radio operator, appeared, morbidly silhouetted against the judgemental sky. "The boss wants to see you, Corporal."

"Right-ho; I'll be there now."

Johns grinned; "Did you hear that, Stewart? We've got him speaking like a Welshman already. He'll be cheering for Cyril Challinor by the end of the week."

I began to clamber out. "Last I saw, we beat you three-nil, in 1939," I called back, as my torso disappeared into the murk. I cannot possibly share the responses that I got to that one.

Captain Welly and Major Even-More-Welly had joined

Lieutenant Windemere. "Sir!" I snapped a slick salute.

The three officers saluted back. As commissioned men, the rain did not dare to sully their uniforms; each looked brushed up and bone dry. I became incredibly aware of my muddy gaiters.

The major nodded to the captain; the captain turned to the lieutenant. "Carry on, Lieutenant," said the captain.

"Thank you, sir."

Lieutenant Windemere turned to me, just as Sergeant Clough arrived on the scene. Clough gave a salute so smart you could have decorated your house with it.

"Thank you, Sergeant," said Windemere. "Okay, Corporal, it has been decided to send a section ahead, to recce for the Recce, as it were – your section has been selected."

"Yes, sir."

"Now, Sergeant Clough here will lead the section; you will move at speed and be the forward eyes for the regiment. You will engage the enemy, should it become necessary, but your first objective is to return with actionable intelligence for air support. Is that understood?"

"Sir."

"Excellent. Be ready to move out within the hour. Carry on, Sergeant."

The gloom of day had progressed into the gloom of night, as our section slipped away from the rest of the troop, packed tight into a Bedford M.W. The sergeant and I sat up front, with Trooper Barry Innes, who was the section driver. With the screen folded up and the tarp set up, we were at least assured some warmth from the engine, and a little respite from the rain. The others, in the back, were not so lucky, but they were the eyes of this mechanical beast, staring off into all directions, omnipotent and sharp.

To the untrained eye, we looked nothing like an advancing army, but a German spotter would know what we were immediately. If you could take out a forward reconnaissance unit, you could be buying time and surprise. An army that did not know you were there were not an army; they were a sitting duck. If you were dug in, you could deliver a devastating blow before your opponent knew what was happening. It was our job to prevent this – ours alone.

A direct strike from a Moaning Minnie could come now.

Or now.

Threat was in the murk, and the murk was our watery cloak.

"Stop here," commanded Sergeant Clough. "Get in close to that clump of trees. Corporal, get some netting over it, then bring the men together."

"Sarge." I was climbing out of my seat, just as the truck was coming to a halt. I dropped down lightly, like a cat; a busted ankle here could mean death.

"Get this thing covered up," I looked around, "then gather over there." I pointed to what looked like a depression in the ground. "Looks like we're on foot from here."

The men leapt down and began to unload equipment. I stood at the head of the line, as Banks and Williams passed down the Bren guns and our only anti-tank rifle.

Sergeant Clough walked around from the front. "Okay, men, gather in. Our objective is to carry out a sweep of that wooded area to the southeast – that's where Thryke saw the smoke this afternoon. Keep to the edges of the road right now, and use what natural cover you can. We move at amber in five."

It was probably a half-hour later when we dropped down from the road and began to swing toward the trees.

It was Taffy Johns who halted the column. Instinctively, we all hunched down. But, there was no need: we had all seen it.

An Sd.Kfz.10 was sitting, abandoned, just short of the tree-line; it was tilting at a strange angle. It was definitely empty and had been stripped of anything useful.

"They could be watching us right now!" said Big Davey Williams.

It was the first time that I had sighted anything resembling the enemy. My heart was beating fast; I felt hyper-sensitive. If a desert squirrel had moved out there, I would have seen it.

"What do you think, Thryke?" It was the sergeant. In a short while, I had become his confidante.

"Looks like the front axle has snapped, Sarge. I reckon it's been here a while; occupants are long gone. Could be booby-trapped, though; no point us going through it."

"Agreed. Banks, Blair, record the position and radio it in. Thryke, get the men ready to go into the wood."

There is something even more sinister about entering a forest at night: death lurks behind every tree, up every tree and between every tree.

"Keep a five-yard spread, lads. Move slowly," I commanded.

We edged deeper into the darkness, lunate and silent. The canopy offered some protection from the rain, but those drops which flopped down, rolling from leaf to leaf, had built to the size of golf-balls; they sploshed with plinking delight onto our tin helmets, and always swerved and ricocheted with an accuracy which left a serpentine trickle tracing the tensing muscles of the spine. At least, you hoped it was water.

I surveyed my sector with, what I wished, was the accuracy of a Native American tracker. I had seen them at the pictures, picking up a blade of grass and discerning that twelve men, all named Hoss, had passed there approximately eighty-seven minutes ago. The truth was that I was looking for wires and boot-prints, and that was about it – much more was beyond me, at that time. My primary thinking was not of vigilance; it was of fear. At least with your nearest man five yards away, we could all pretend that we weren't shaking.

We approached a clearing. A signal went along the line to halt, and a cold sweat broke out on my brow. I crept from my position and began to move toward the centre of the crescent. The sergeant was waiting.

"Sweep the perimeter for wires." He pointed to a scorched circle of earth: "They were here, alright."

We fanned out, once more, though it was not more than ten minutes later that the section was back together, huddled in some scrub. The sergeant had a scrap of paper, and was sketching the clearing.

"Right, so how many wires did we find?"

"Three, Sarge" I confirmed.

"Okay, mark them and make them safe."

"Or?" There was a thought percolating in my mind.

"What, Thryke?" rasped the sergeant.

"What if we triggered them? From a safe distance, of course?"

Big Davey Williams scratched his head. "Why would we do that? We'll give away our position."

"They know we're here, anyway; can't you feel them watching?" chimed Blair, who was always prone to over-exaggeration.

"I just figure that if they are out there, let's draw them out. If they think they've got the upper hand, they might get sloppy. If they're already miles away, they won't know anyway, and we will have cleared the explosives, at least."

As I was speaking, I realized what I was saying. No longer the chaser, hunting on their terms. "Well, Sergeant?"

"Sod it; let's do it! Williams, Johns, find a good line of sight into that clearing and set up the Bren. Thornton, Innes, you take this wire; Stewart and Blair, you set up this wire; Thryke and I will take this one. Banks, you find a position and set the radio, just in case."

The sergeant nodded to me.

"Okay, men, you heard the sergeant. Check watches; we'll blow the place in exactly ten minutes. Got it?"

The men all nodded and dissipated into the trees. Even Big Davey Williams moved silently, like a spectre.

"Come on." I scurried off, in pursuit of the sergeant.

We quickly found the wire.

"Got that twine, Sarge?"

Carefully and breathlessly, I tied the end of the thick cord around the tripwire. Clough then began to scoot backward, unravelling the string from the spool.

Suddenly, the sergeant grimaced and began to topple over. I watched in horror, as tension quickly whipped into the twine; I was still crouching at the business end! The wire vibrated as Clough threw the spool clear, just in time. I exhaled and blew out my cheeks. The booby trap remained intact, for now.

I moved, picked up the spool and quickly ran it out to the rear of the tree, where the sarge was waiting. He grinned. His teeth were glowing white, against the night and the camouflage of his face.

"Admit it, Corny: you shit yourself!"

"I always had faith."

"Well, let's hope none of the other lads does similar."

They would all be in position by now, crouching behind trees, ready to trigger the devices.

"Just a few more minutes," I said.

The world fell silent, sleeping just like the natural countryside should. It was men who were about to scar and defile it; to burn and destroy. How far had I come from the harmony of that simple country boy?

"Here, I'll have a shilling with you," whispered Sergeant Clough.

"Go on."

"One bob says that Thornton goes early."

"Alright, Billy, you're on." I shook Clough's hand. I was glad to feel that his hand was cold and clammy as well. Perhaps blood flowed in his veins, too? I also knew that Clough was onto a surefire winner: Thornton would undoubtedly set the pace.

Billy looked at his watch: "Thirty seconds..."

Booommmffffffff.

A low, rumbling explosion sent a tremor through our position.

Booommmffffffff.

Booommmffffffff.

Booommmffffffff; the fourth explosion ripped up the floor of the clearing, sending sods of earth high into the bristling trees. A high-pitched wave tore into my ears and rattled my eyes around in their sockets, like a couple of billiard balls. The smoke and debris bent around the clearing, as the aftershocks rumbled on.

Then, the second wave of noise began; the unmistakable repetition of machine-gunfire began to rake the clearing. Bullets were thudding into the trees all around; I watched the trunk behind me, as three rounds tore into it, ripping the bark belly open with ease. Other boughs burst apart, as bullets pinged off of them.

But, we Recce men remained firm, as I gave the signal to hold. The enemy still did not know we were there; as long as nobody caught a stray round, there was a chance we could get out of this alive.

Hold.

The gunfire continued for what felt like minutes, but it was probably not even thirty seconds. Whilst under fire, Sergeant Clough reeled in the telltale string – I hoped that the other teams had done similarly.

Hold.

The gunfire stopped, and the angered forest began to fall back into night.

Clough raised a thumb and looked questioningly toward me. I nodded; there were no new holes in my torso. I prayed the others had fared as well – after all, this course of action had been my idea.

We waited. My hand still conveyed the same message:

Hold.

The smoke dazzled, as droplets of water fell, leaving trails like ladders in dernier. In the distance, I could see figures slowly emerging from the murk: men crawling forward on their stomachs. They expected to see a pile of discarded and mangled bodies, but there were none – not of men, at least; the mortal remains of several plump ravens littered the outer circle of the clearing.

"Niemand."

"Bist du sicher?"

"Tiere vielleicht."

They were just normal men, as confused and as afraid as I was.

Hold.

A few more came forward, slowly at first. One even removed his helmet and scratched his head. There was no jagged line of slathering shark teeth; no feline pupils, like slick oil in the night; he looked like Jethro, a man I occasionally saw in the village pub.

Soon, I counted six – perhaps the number of men who might have travelled in the vehicle we had passed.

Hold.

One or two more ventured forward. Getting sloppy. They were convinced that it was a false alarm. I could almost smell their relief.

Just a moment longer.

A couple of the soldiers skipped around the clearing, picking up some of the dead birds. I allowed my hand to fall.

The return of fire wreaked havoc among the enemy. Four were mown down before they knew what had happened. I heard their screams, as their fit, young bodies were shredded by the barrage.

I saw one, crouched down behind a tree, panicking with the bolt of his rifle. I lined him up and squeezed. Instantaneously, his hand went to this throat and he dropped.

I heard as their machine-gun started up again, but there could not be that much ammunition left. Billy Clough left my side and plummeted away to the right. I spotted a muzzle flash that looked like it was following the sergeant; I pulled the trigger again.

It was then that I caught sight of Sergeant Clough. He had swerved around in an arc and, on the move, he removed the pin from a grenade. In a single motion, Clough launched the projectile and dived behind a tree. Seconds later came the explosion, and more terrified screams. The black smoke and the trail of pops told of ammunition searing in the flames.

I raised my hand.

All fell silent.

We waited… all of us contemplating what we had done.

My instinct was to dash around and see if any of my section had been injured, or worse, but something held me in check. I sat, with my back against the bullet-ridden tree. I knew what I had done.

A hand came and grabbed me by the chest, shaking me to.

"Well done, Thryke; I think we've got them all." It was Sergeant Billy Clough, back from launching his grenade. "Have the men fall back, then we'll scout the area."

Another hour probably passed, as we fanned out, searched the area and approached the clearing from the other side. I will never forget what I saw.

Instinctively, I knew where they were, the men that I had killed. The first body I saw was the man I shot in the throat; he lay there, his head cocked to one side, looking at the stars – his once-bright eyes had faded into glassy fear. His helmet lay at his side, pocked with spotlets of blood. He was no older than I, yet I had seen fit to end his life. His left hand lay across his chest – in it was a crumpled photograph, now stained black with midnight blood. I left him holding his memories.

The second I found slumped over his gun, as if he were preparing to fire. There was an entry wound right between his eyes. I crouched down.

"Don't do it, Corporal!" It was Billy Clough. "He would have done the same to you. This is war."

I knew he was right. "He had his gun trained on you – just before you threw the grenade," I told him.

The sergeant clapped me on the back. "You did good tonight."

Banks was on the radio when we all gathered back. Through some sort of miracle, all nine of us had escaped unscathed.

"We're to wait here; the troop will catch us up. They're moving now." The sergeant nodded and looked at me.

I went and posted myself on lookout, but I don't think I saw anything. Just those two faces… night after night, after night…

In the morning, we buried the German dead in that clearing. I dug until my hands blistered, and reflected until ordered to leave.

IX

By February of 1943, 57th Recce had built up quite a reputation, and our section had picked up a number of battle honours.

Lieutenant Colonel Cheuvaux-Bruin briefed us as to our next mission. He was a fighting officer, who led from the front – another who had been born into the officer corps; I don't know what he would have done, had he not had the distraction of war. He would have been a big-game hunter, fearless mountaineer or polar explorer, probably; boys would have grown up reading about his exploits in comic books. In fact, they probably still would, as commanding officer of the fearless 57th Recce. The Bear, as we called him, was the stuff of swashbuckling fiction. I would have followed him anywhere.

I was proud that my section was still intact. We all hated it when we lost men. There was something so final about singing "Jerusalem" on an African field.

And did those boots, in modern times,
traipse among sodden wadis red?
And did those men, so far from home,
in bloodied tunics, bury dead?

"We're off to Kasserine, to support the U.S. Army and our 78th Division," said The Bear, to the massed ranks of the regiment. "We must hold the pass and push back the 5th Panzer and their Tigers. Our role will be vital. I know you will all do your bit."

We ended up in El Aroussa.

Our motto was "only the enemy in front", and El Aroussa certainly lived up to that; we did not have to go far to reconnoitre the enemy positions. We held the railway station, but Jerry held some farm buildings, not too far away.

"We're going to assault the farm," said the sergeant, one afternoon, as we were tucking into a bit of food. I remember it as clear as day – not because we were not used to attacking things by now; no, we were as grizzled as our foe in the Afrika Korps – but because today the sunshine was streaming in through the station-house windows, and the food was uncommonly good.

"Can we finish this first, Sarge?" joshed Big Davey Williams. "I wouldn't mind another dose of that." Williams mopped at his gravy with a hunk of bread. We hadn't had fresh meat like this in a long time.

"We go tonight," said Clough.

We had recced the site a couple of times, and were aware that it was well defended but, in our hearts, we all knew it had to go: the Germans had used it to launch sorties more than once, and our Hurricanes were busy elsewhere. The railway line passed to the west of the farm, and that was where my section was to attack.

The lieutenant continued the briefing:

"Mortimer, your section will come in from the southeast, like so, and Beattie – sorry, Beattie – you lot will cover the extra ground and join the party from the north. When we can take the farm, it will give us a firm base to recce further territory and push the Germans back, toward the hills."

We went at dusk; night is good, but twilight is better. As we moved out, the mortars started to fly overhead: cover from our side; offensive from theirs. We were in a shrinking peninsula of Allied territory and were in increasing danger of being cut off.

"Wait for me!" The C.O. himself was dashing up behind us, strapping a pack to his back.

"Sir?" Poor Billy Clough looked astonished. I think I was wearing the same, guppy look.

"Well, don't just stand there, gawping; lead the way, Sergeant Clough. I plan to be eating supper at that farmhouse table with the greatest of alacrity!"

The sergeant looked at me.

"He means to get a move on, Sarge; the boss is hungry."

Lt. Col. The Bear Cheuvaux-Bruin guffawed: "Thank you, Corporal. At least one man in this unit understands me! Tally ho!"

We crossed the railway track and moved across the open field, until we came to the tree-line. We followed the woodland for almost a mile. I looked across to the right: black smoke was rising from the farm outbuildings.

"Looks like our chaps have scored a direct hit on their ammunition dump. That should make things interesting," said The Bear.

We all looked at each other. The presence of The Bear had

disrupted our natural equilibrium. We didn't mind Cloughy coming along – he was on the same wavelength – but this was different: The Bear was a senior officer.

"Sergeant, Corporal, with me," he ordered.

Dutifully, we both made our way to him.

"So, chaps, how do we cross this open ground?"

I exchanged a look with Clough. "That's easy, sir. Just up ahead – you see there, look – there are a couple of old railway carriages on the line. We recced it a couple of nights ago," I said, proudly.

"Good, chaps. Okay, Sergeant, seems to me that you should take it from here."

"Sir?"

"Tell the men what to do, Sergeant Clough."

"Roger that, sir. Corporal, get the two-pounders and the Bren set up; give us covering fire as we nip across."

The mortars continued to rain in. There was another explosion in the compound, as further cases of ammunition caught fire.

A few seconds later, our portee was in position. Stewart and Blair got to work and soon began to pump the two-pound shells into the farm buildings.

The Bear sighed: "I hope they leave me somewhere suitable to set up as an office."

As he said it, Williams and Thornton opened up with the Bren gun. The enemy was returning fire, but I could not tell from where or at whom. I suspected that all of our sections were experiencing heavy resistance, but the moment had come to cover the ground between us and the railway carriages; we had to make a dash for it.

"Are you ready?" asked The Bear, gulping oxygen, greedily.

"On three," gasped the sergeant. "Three!"

We dashed out into the confused field, with its soft grasses caressing our boots. The Bear, Clough and I went for the right-hand carriage, Innes and Johns, the left. But, it felt like we were running through treacle. It comes back in dreams, sometimes: that feeling of running, but expelling energy without traction.

Out of nowhere, a high-pitched, mechanical scream caught us from the right. Two Stukas swished into the field, like a pair of banshees, not twenty feet from the ground. They opened up their machine-guns and strafed the grassland.

Somehow, Stewart and Blair had seen them coming and managed to take out the tail of one, but it was not enough; both Stukas screeched toward us, in a frame of smog and flame. The rapid punching cadence and muzzle flash caught us all dry-throated and open-mouthed. All I could think to do was dash and dive but, in my heart, I was preparing to die. Any second now, the rounds would rip through me – any second. I scrunched my eyes shut and flew.

The Stukas had passed overhead, as I scrambled the last few yards, to the relative shelter of the carriage running gear. The Bear came and crashed next to me. One of the planes peeled off and up to the right, no doubt looking to get our boys coming from the north. The other hurtled and exploded into a barn, sending shards of shattered timber and goatshit tumbling into the orange sky. Against the fiery backdrop, I saw the devastation.

Back in the trees, our Bren had stopped. Thornton was dragging a huge carcass away from the gun position: Big Davey Williams was dead.

With my back against the bullet-torn carriage, I looked to the right, where another body was lying motionless in the grass. I saw Innes staring back at our fallen comrade: Taffy Johns who, not seconds before, had crouched with us in the woodland, had been ripped apart by the gunfire, too.

Then I realized: where was Clough?

I scanned the pasture and saw him, as he was trying to pull himself up, clutching at his torso. His face was contorted and thick, ruby syrup oozed from between his fingers. Billy pulled himself forward, then toppled, collapsing back into the long grass. I didn't think; I stooped low as I dashed back into the field.

"Corporal!" cried Cheuvaux-Bruin. "Come back! That's an order!"

But, I didn't hear. I grabbed the collar of Sergeant Clough's uniform and dragged him, one-handed, across to the carriage, where I propped him up against a rusted steel wheel.

"Keep pressing on the wound, Sergeant. We'll get you out of here."

The lieutenant colonel looked at me and scurried to the buffers between the carriages, with pistol drawn. To his left, Innes was still staring towards Johns, not comprehending the situation at hand.

Our Bren gun started back up, while Afrika Korps men were leaving by all exits, discharging Lugers in retreat. I moved to the end of the carriage and dropped a couple, with shots from my rifle. Then, I saw a face in the window, topped with a Recce cap badge. We had taken the farm. This battle, at least, was over – though, another was just about to begin.

Stewart and Blair had dismounted from the two-pounder and, firing pin in hand, were dashing through the grass to my position.

"Stewart! Blair! Get the sarge inside. Get a medic to him. I ran back over to the portee, knowing that there were some stretchers on board – I dropped one by Thornton.

"It's too late, Corny," he said, choking on his words: "he's gone"

"Well, let's get him inside."

By the time we had managed to carry Big Davey Williams into the farm, the courtyard was being used as a makeshift morgue, Axis to the left, Allied to the right. I looked down into the face of Johns. He looked peaceful; there would be no more fighting for him. But, Sergeant Clough? Sergeant Clough was not there.

I helped Thornton place down Williams and dashed inside. I came into a large, open kitchen area, which was now doubling as a theatre. I saw the chevrons of a sergeant, on an arm which dangled over the side of the large, wooden table.

"Where's Corporal Thryke?" a voice, weak yet optimistic, was calling for me.

"Here, Sergeant!"

"Where the bloody hell have you been?" He coughed, wheezing heavily as he inhaled. Men moved aside, like tides, and let me through. I picked up his left hand and held it between my own. It was sticky with blood, but growing clammy and cold.

"Those planes were a bit of a turn-up for the books, eh?" he stuttered, from crimson lips. "Got me good and proper."

"We'll get you fixed up. Don't worry."

The medical orderly shot me a withering look, but I just grasped the sergeant's hand all the more tightly.

"I was hoping to get home one day, Thryke; get back and maybe find myself a wife."

This time, I did not answer. Lt. Col. Cheuvaux-Bruin removed his cap.

"Say, Thryke, you've got a girl, haven't you?" spluttered Billy.

I nodded.

"Let me see her, one last time."

I fished into my tunic and withdrew the photograph of Luciana. It was far less pristine than when I had received it, back when I was a boy. I passed it to him.

"Yes. Yes, that's her." He winced, swallowed and gasped. "I'd have got back and beaten you to it, believe you me."

Even torn and riddled by Stuka rounds, Billy Clough still managed to raise a laugh, muted though it was. He handed me back the picture, leaving a single, bloody thumbprint in the bottom, right-hand corner. As I took it, he shot his arm across and grabbed my wrist.

"Cornelius," he turned his head and looked me square in the eye, "thank you for not leaving me to die out there."

As his grip loosened, I knew that Sergeant William Charles

Clough, hero of the 57th, had passed.

It was a black day.

Now a decorated sergeant myself, I and the corps followed Lieutenant Colonel Cheuvaux-Bruin back toward home. As the months turned into years, we slogged up through Sicily, over to Taranto, Foggia, Termoli and from Orvieto onto Lake Trasimene.

We held up in a ruined church for a couple of days, enjoying the silence which came with the temporary absence of Panzers. I leant up against the thick, cool buttress and let my eyes drift closed. The sun warmed my weathered face and the inside of my lids shone, with a satisfying candy-apple red.

I took a swig from my canteen of water and allowed myself to trace the chilled path, as it slalomed into my stomach. The locals had said that the spring had healing qualities: *sanctus aquam; sanctus est*. I wondered if it would seep into my soul and offer me redemption.

I began to drift toward sleep, as far as my body would now let me. It was without thought and dreamless – that was now my real definition of peace. For the first time in months…

"Sergeant Thryke."

…I listened to a pipit, singing in the cedars.

"Sergeant Thryke."

"What is it?" I said, gently.

"It's the C.O., Sarge: he wants to see you."

I shifted slowly in my spot. "I'll be along soon."

When I opened my eyes, he was still there.

"Well?"

The young trooper shifted nervously, from foot to foot. The disturbance wasn't his fault, but this trial was character building.

"The officer suggested that you should come at once, Sarge."

I arched an eyebrow; "Suggested? Or, did you infer it?"

Trooper Harris tilted his head in recall. "No, he definitely sounded agitated, Sarge – as agitated as he gets."

I began to slide my back up the slope of the buttress, until it eased me into the upright. I pulled my beret from my epaulette and placed it smartly on my head.

"Thank you, Harris. I shall go now."

The bulk of the damage had been done in the nave, or more accurately the roof which used to enclose it. Nature had taken root at a surprising tempo. A single mallard could often be found sitting in the font, though the villagers had strictly forbidden us from eating him. A rather officious notice, reading "Do not consume ducks" had been hung from the pulpit, in support of this topic. Monty had remained safe, up to now.

I clambered over some rubble and timbers, and dodged the wildflowers growing between the tiles. I made my way to the South Transept, where it was widely known that Lieutenant Colonel Cheuvaux Bruin had made his office, and was catching up on the paperwork side of the war. I knocked on the heavy, oak door.

"Enter."

I unlatched the door and pushed it open, into the room.

The Bear had finally found a desk and was seated behind it. He glanced to either side, where a major and captain were standing, each smoking a cigarette.

I saluted. "You sent for me, sir?" Perhaps it was about the medal he had promised me.

"Ah yes, Sergeant Thryke, please come in. Gentlemen, would you leave us?"

The major and captain both looked at The Bear, then dropped their eyes after they passed me. I examined them at that moment and felt unease. As I stepped into the room and stood to attention, the door was closed behind me.

"Perhaps you had better sit down," said The Bear.

There was something in his tone that made me pull up a chair. I had followed this man into countless bloody engagements, and now he couldn't look me in the eye.

"It is my duty," he began, "my solemn duty, to inform you that your brother, Henry, has been killed in combat, while serving in France. I'm sorry."

The C.O. continued to look down at his desk.

"There must be some mistake, sir. My brother is not in the Army; he is at home, in a reserved occupation."

"He succumbed to shrapnel wounds, after an enemy shell hit the tank in which he was travelling."

"But, Henry is at home, sir, working on a farm; feeding the country."

The Bear continued to read from his papers: "*'Henry Bartholomew Thryke; 17 – 3 – 12, Little Sodbury-on-the-Wode.'* He asked that you be informed, in the event of his death."

"But…"

"I am so sorry, Sergeant."

I could not comprehend it; I was frozen.

The lieutenant colonel rose and walked toward the door. "Take some time; stay there a while. Help yourself to anything you want. There's even a bottle of communion wine in the drawer. I'll see that you're not disturbed."

And, for many hours, I was not, but they found me sitting in precisely the same way as they had left me. Catatonic. Disbelieving. The dream of home I had been carrying had been ripped into shreds.

My brother – my beloved brother, Henry, skipper of our troop – was dead? It could not be true, surely. Had he gone and joined up? Why had he not told me?

They said I became braver from that point, but it is not bravery if you are numb; it is recklessness: the recklessness of the man with nothing left to fight for. I killed in the fire of that rage. I killed without discrimination, and I forgot the fear I saw in their eyes.

The war had finally killed me, too.

Part Four:
Film

EDITOR'S NARRATIVE
Quentin Prowler

Cornelius Thryke demobilized in late-1945, first arriving at Shorncliffe, then heading for the No.5 Military Dispersal Unit, at Queen's Camp, Guildford. Along with so many others, he received a suit, shoes, hat and a raincoat, amongst other essentials, along with a small financial grant. It is clad in these simple garments that Cornelius once again takes up the tale…

THE MEMOIRS OF CORNELIUS THRYKE.

X

The platforms and the stations were abuzz with men, milling this way and that, like bees. We all looked the same; you could not tell one from the other.

I sat on a bench and watched them drift away. I was once Sergeant Cornelius Thryke, a decorated hero of the 57th Reconnaissance Regiment; now, I was just another fellow sitting on a station platform, with no idea where to go. I was thirty years old, and had no inclination of who I was.

Perhaps I should go home. But, I scarcely remembered where that was any more. I thought of Henry. He would not be there to welcome me, with a foaming pint of ale. He was dead, lying in some unvisited grave in France.

Back at home, I knew Mother blamed me for Henry's loss. He had struggled with the guilt of being left behind; he had heard the comments as he passed by; he had seen the stares. In the end, it all got too much for him to bear.

It was with a crashing realization that I thought of him again. I felt ashamed: I was so busy looking after myself that I had not grieved for my brother. No wonder I could not look our mother in the eye. So many others had died, yet here I was, having the temerity to be passing life sitting on a railway station bench.

But, I still couldn't move. I tried to motivate myself with the thought of a clean, soft bed and a fried breakfast in the kitchen, but I kept seeing the empty place my mother had laid for him; I smelled the bacon – my own and that which would go uneaten. Cold, limp, pink flesh, buried alone, his mouth full of ash and soil.

I had seen many die, and I had seen those who had called out for their mother; for that familiar hand to soothe a body torn. But, who would fix a torn mother? Her eldest son was gone, because he could not bear the shame of not following his little brother. If only I had stood up and played the conchy! I was no hero.

I had asked for a warrant for home; I didn't know what else to ask for. For years I had been certain about everything, I'd had to be. Even though I had faced the uncertainty of death, I met it in the way which I had learnt. Then, I asked for that ticket. But, I knew I would not use it. Not today.

What if I went and holed up in a B-and-B for a few days? And, then what? Climb into a beer bottle? The idea appealed on a certain level, but once you were rooted in the drink, was there ever really a reason to haul yourself out? Many did but, no, I would not do that.

Some of my men had said that I was welcome to visit them. Any time you are in the area, they had all said; you've been good to us, Sarge, they said; come and meet the wife, the mother, the sister, the neighbour's Persian cat. Perhaps I could do that. But, you know how it is when someone says come round or stay in touch: it is seldom meant and more rarely taken up; it is a meaningless platitude. A bit like "sergeant". *Sergeant* Cornelius Thryke. Mister Cornelius

Thryke. I hadn't taken any of their addresses, anyway. No, I could not do that.

Addresses.

With a jolt, I sat up and picked up my (light) case, from the ground. Resting it on my raincoated lap, I released the clasps with two deft thumb swipes, lifted the lid and began to rummage. There was a letter – yes, one of a few which had found their way to Italy. Here it was. I took it from the case, regarding the jagged tears that I had excitedly made along the envelope. It was from Luciana. I reread the letter, though it now felt fresh and new.

Yes, she had taken a flat in London. Could I go there? Would she still be there? Could I?

In my mind, I was still undecided, yet I found myself chattering to a guard.

"Excuse me, when is the next train to London?"

"This is it, sir."

I began to dash off.

"Where are you going, sir?" called the guard after me. "It leaves in one minute."

"Ticket," I shouted back.

The guard motioned me back: "Don't you worry about that, sir. This is my train; I'll see you alright. It's the least I can do. Not far to London, anyway."

So, in a way, it was the guard that decided for me. I was on my way to London, to see the only woman I had ever loved.

I had only been to London a handful of times, all on my way to somewhere else, but even I felt the relief there. The scars were deep, however; bomb damage everywhere.

The natty cut of my demob gear drew the odd smile, the odd tip of the rim, or eyes to avert from my weathered, leathery face.

"Who were you with?" asked a chap on the tube.

"57th Reconnaissance."

The carriage looked on in silence, as the man shook my hand. Sadly, it wouldn't last.

My route was circuitous and oscillated past the correct tube stop, until my directions brought me to a halt in front of a grand, Victorian structure. I stood at the gate and scanned the full height of the whitewashed building, searching for traps and sniper positions. All appeared safe, so I pushed at the gate, traversed the patterned path and moved slowly into the lobby.

I climbed the plush, carpeted stairway to the second-floor flat Luciana had taken when posted to the War Office. I thought that I had become numb to fear, but there is nothing more stirring than approaching the door of a woman, believe you me.

I removed my hat, smoothed my hair, straightened my tie and knocked. I listened; I could hear music. It sounded strange to me; something otherworldly. I listened intently for footsteps. A male voice?

"Whoever it is, send them away, darling."

My body tensed. I turned away, head bowed, rehatting as the

door opened.

"Yes?"

My eyes closed. I didn't ask them to. Her voice was like balm to every scar, tear and aching muscle.

"Can I help you? I'm afraid I don't have any coins?"

I turned.

We both stood in silence. Her mouth, plump-lipped and moist, fell open and slowly rose into a smile. Her eyes flicked, drawing in the picture she saw; comparing; contrasting. A single tear betrayed her knowing, and it traced her cognizance from cheek to lip. Instinctively, her tongue flicked saline to lip. Another tear fell. And, another.

"Who is it, darling?"

She made no response. I again removed my hat and began to revolve the brim sheepishly, in sweating fingertips.

"Look at me."

I raised my old eyes and tanned, lined face.

"It is! It is you!"

She leapt forward and flung her arms around me.

I reciprocated and inhaled, deeply. Perfume – the dizzying scent of a woman.

"Cornelius!" She wept freely now. "So many days I feared this moment would never come."

"I shouldn't have come. I'm sorry."

"Nonsense! Nonsense! Come in. Come in, please!" She reached down and picked up my case. As she felt it in her hand, she looked at me; "Please come in, if only to retrieve your case."

And so, I found myself in a spacious front room, tastefully lit, curtains drawn across what I assumed was a smart bay window. A man looked up from a sofa, swirling a brandy balloon.

"Who is your friend?" he asked. I could snap him. Snap him right now.

"This is Cornelius. Isn't it wonderful? We've been friends since school. Cornelius, this is Alan: a... er, a friend of mine."

I nodded at the interloper. His skin was pale and he had long, wavy hair.

"You look dead beat, old boy. Come and take your weight off," he said. *He* was inviting *me* to sit down?

Luciana took my coat and hat out, and I sat down on the sofa opposite him. Silence.

"So," said Luciana, bustling back into the room, "when did you get back?"

"Yesterday," I answered, still studying my rival. "I got released from Guildford this morning."

I was delighted when Luciana came and sat next to me. She lifted a glass from the small, chic table. "Can I get you one? It's just brandy, I'm afraid."

I nodded: "Thank you."

My eyes followed Luciana as she crossed the room. I inhaled the air as she passed, though I was aware that I was being watched. Weighed.

"I thought you went to an all-girls' school, Luciana?" called Alan.

Glass chinked on glass. "I did. Corny's school was nearby. We used to put on plays and such like for each other." She glided back, drink in hand, and handed it to me with a smile. She sat next to me again, closer this time, and squeezed my arm.

"I still remember your Snug." She looked across at the third: "He was magnificent, Alan!"

"Oh, an actor!" he exclaimed. "How wonderful."

"It was many years ago now," I said.

"Don't be so humble, Cornelius," said Luciana, pressing into me again. "Alan is down here making a film, over at Borehamwood. He's got me a part: a few speaking lines. Isn't it exciting?"

"Well, it's not my film – not really; my father is directing. But, I am heavily involved – behind the camera, of course. I'm so looking forward to seeing your rushes, Luci. I think you will shine! Don't you, Cornelius? Don't you think she will shine?"

I took a sip of brandy. I was beginning to sink into the sofa. It was ridiculously comfortable. It was like a cloud. "I think she shines in everything she does."

Luciana struck me lightly on the knee. "Oh, you're both incorrigible, but flattery will get you everywhere! Imagine, me a film star!" She threw her head back and laughed. Immediately, I was a boy again.

"Well, I shall certainly go along to the picture house, when the film comes out," I said, encouragingly.

Luciana looked at me; "Come to the premiere, darling!"

I smiled. I couldn't see myself all dressed up like a dog's dinner.

For a moment, I longed for the surety of my battle dress. It felt like I was swimming – swimming with no sight of land. Each direction was the same; it mattered not. Every so often, the water dragged me down or engulfed me with a wave. It was so cold. So silent. Without the constriction of fear, I was expanding, losing sight of my edges, unable to recognize who I was. I drained my glass and stood.

"Well, I really must be going. It was lovely to see you, Luciana. Nice to meet you, Alan. Good luck both with your film."

Luciana looked up. I knew I shouldn't look, but I did, like a fool. It was all in those eyes, you see – it always was.

"You've only just got here."

"Yes, but…"

"Where are you going?"

I had received training in how to stand up to interrogation. Either I had not listened, or it was useless.

"You can't be going home: it's eight o'clock now; there won't be any trains that will take you there."

I checked the floor to see if the rings she was running around me were visible. Not yet.

"I thought I might check in somewhere."

"Sit down."

I felt the fight leaving me. I sat back down.

"Look," she said, "I'd offer you a bed, but Alan has the spare room."

"Yes," Alan confirmed, "Luci's kindly putting me up, until my digs become available near the studio. The film industry is full of waifs and strays like me, I'm afraid. Lucy is such an angel."

"Alan's in the...?"

Luciana hugged herself and laughed again. "Oh, wait, I know what you thought! Alan, do you know what Cornelius thought? He's no more my love interest than you are!"

I looked at Alan, and Alan looked at me. At that moment, we were kindred spirits; we understood each other. There was pain etched in his face, and he probably saw it in mine. Love was the great leveller: the film director and the war hero. Our tragi-comic understanding fell into Luciana's next words.

"I can offer you a sofa for a night or two, until you decide what you want to do. I can only imagine how lost you are feeling."

The empathy washed over me. I already knew how fantastically comfortable the sofa was. Luciana grabbed my fingers, one soft hand over, one smooth under.

"I don't want to be a burden."

"No burden. Stay, please. For me."

I was routed. I pushed back into the chair and felt its warmth.

"Thank you. Now, that wasn't difficult, was it?" declared Luciana. "Here, let me refresh your glass."

My mouth bobbed up and down, but no words came out. But, that sofa...

"You'll have to go to the off-licence tomorrow, Alan: I can't see this lasting the night," she said. "Say, we could all go. Take Cornelius to the café first; give him a good old English breakfast. A real taste of home."

I was supposed to have painted her outside of Parisienne cafés.

"That's if you're not busy of course, Corny," she added, archly. "Have you given any thought to what you might do, now you're out of the Army?"

I had zero ideas. "I only know how to do one thing," I offered.

"Nonsense." She was back on the settee now, handing me another drink – large measure. "Your lot were some of the best trained in the Army."

"May I ask?" Alan directed the vagary towards me.

"57th Reconnaissance Regiment. When I wasn't fighting, I was driving or being a mechanic, or a radio operator."

Alan's eyes widened a little: "Recce, eh? I read about you chaps. I... er..."

I could see he wanted to carry on and elaborate, but I offered him nothing. Then, his face lit up. "I say, I have the most capital idea!" He sat forward, looking directly at Luciana; "Why doesn't Cornelius come with us? Come and work on the film, when shooting starts?"

"Do you think...?" asked Luciana.

"I'm sure I can swing you some work, Corny. May I call you Corny? There's always bits of electrical work, or maintenance, or driving, or..." He stopped, suddenly. "I don't know, though."

"Why?" asked Luciana.

Alan looked uncomfortable: "Well, it's... I do hope you won't be offended, Cornelius."

"Offended?" I wasn't quite sure what he was driving at.

"Well, it's a war film, you see. Cornelius, please don't think we're trying to profit by what you went through, but there's an appetite for your type of story; it is what the public want. They'll watch them as quick as we can write them."

I looked at him. I looked at Luciana. I had thrown myself wholly into army life and made it a success: there would be darker days – I knew this. But, what if I threw myself entirely into this? "I do need some work... if you think you could find me some."

Luciana was now bubbling over with excitement: "He could advise, too... on authenticity; on the way things are done."

Alan didn't look convinced, but he went with it. Of course he would. "Perhaps, yes. We've got an advisor or two, but another pair of eyes is always welcome."

He looked back at me, now. "Perhaps we could get him some extra work."

"As many hours as you need," I said, trying to look keen.

Luciana giggled: "No, not extra work, silly; *extra* work!"

"I don't understand."

"He would be rather useful for that," said Alan. "Extras are those people who work in the background of the film. You know, if there is a crowd, or a mob, or a marching troop of men. Yes. That you could do, perfectly."

I scratched my head. "You mean me, be in the film? In the background somewhere?"

I was back on the cricket square again, looking down at a pole-axed Latimer, blood pooling from a head wound (had there been that much?). My decision then led to such boyhood joys. *Throw yourself in, Thryke! Throw yourself in!*

"Well, if you think you can square it for me, Alan."

He smiled and offered his hand. "Given what you have done for us, it would be my pleasure. I'm sure Father will see it that way, too."

I shook his hand, warmly.

I was going to be working in the movies.

The sofa, it turned out, was too comfortable for sleeping; I just lay and stared at the ceiling. It was deathly quiet; only the ticking of a carriage clock, or the odd noise from the street, could be heard. I wasn't sure what time it was – maybe one or two in the morning – but there was no need to keep watch. I knew I could only sleep in short bursts: I hadn't slept deeply for years.

I pulled the blanket up to my nose, hoping to capture the essence of her scent, but I could only discern the faint memory of a distant laundry day. The clock continued ticking.

It was then that I heard a door open, behind my head, out in the short hallway. My body tensed, even though I told it not to, and I strained to listen for footsteps: bare feet upon carpet. Impossible. Then, a voice whispered from the doorway: "Are you awake?"

It was her! It was Luciana. I began to move. "Yes."

"No, don't get up." She came and sat on the floor, her perfect spine against the drop of the settee. I looked at the back of her head: her blonde locks had been cut short – a legacy of her time in the service. I picked up the slight fragrance of apples.

"You can't sleep either?" she asked.

"No."

"I guess this must all feel so terribly strange to you."

It did. "Yes."

She turned her head. Her eyes flashed in the darkness. "I'm so glad you came."

"Me, too." I dropped an arm down and brushed the cool slickness of her robe.

She reached up and took my hand. "Tell me, why did you come?"

I let her question hang for a moment. I wasn't sure if I could give an adequate answer – one she wouldn't hunt down. "I wanted to see you. It made sense, as I was already near."

She squeezed my hand. "You didn't want to go home?"

I gently pulled my hand away.

Luciana turned, shifting onto her thigh, her legs under her in a V. Shamefully, I began to trace the line of her calf... Higher...

"Have I said something wrong?" she asked.

"Henry."

Her eyes looked away, as she sought to place the name. "Your brother? Why would he not want you back?"

I hadn't told her. There had been no reason to.

"He... he couldn't accept the guilt of staying behind, working out the war in a reserved role, while I was out fighting."

"Oh."

"He joined up. He didn't make it back."

"When?" There was a tenderness in the question. We both knew what she was asking.

"Last summer. In France."

"I'm sorry. I'm so sorry."

I didn't say anything for a minute. People always said they were sorry, but I was the one who had reason to be.

"Mother... I... She will never get over it. I think she blames me. I don't think I can go back there, Luciana. At least, not right now."

"Perhaps she needs you there, more than ever; that might be true. Cornelius, please. What you did – what you *both* did, and all those others... You answered your nation's call. You're a hero."

She was probably right. But, deep down, I knew I didn't fit in Little Sodbury anymore. To go back would be to shrink, and that was not possible. Not after everything. To go back meant never leaving again.

We sat in silence for a good while, each of us caught in the *tick, tick, ticking* of the clock. Presently, Luciana spoke again:

"I often thought of you, you know."

I offered my hand again. She took it, gratefully.

"Every day," she continued, "I checked where your regiment was; what they were doing. Every day I scanned the list for you. I'm so glad you were never there."

"Pass me my jacket, please."

Luciana looked at me, puzzled, but scooted across and unhooked my jacket from the back of a wooden chair.

"This one?"

I nodded and extended my hand, grasping the demob coat by its scruff. I began to search for the inside pocket. Luciana flicked on a small lamp and eased my task.

"Thank you," I said, softly. "Here."

I passed her the photograph: the same picture that Luciana had sent me, five years before. It was a bit creased and tatty now, but it was still recognizably her. She looked at it in the pale lamplight.

"You still have it?"

I nodded. "You came with me, through Tunisia, Sicily and Italy. You were always close."

Luciana climbed onto the sofa beside me, and flung her arms around my neck. I turned my face toward her, leant in and our lips brushed together.

She pulled back: "No."

"But, don't you want—"

"I'm sorry, Cornelius. I'm tired; I need to think." She pushed herself upright. "We'll talk properly. Maybe tomorrow."

She placed the photograph on the coffee table, dabbed at her eyes and walked back out of the room, without another word. I heard her bedroom door close, and a key turn in the lock. Surely, she didn't believe that I would…?

I stood up, thinking that I might dress and let myself out, into the night. If I walked back to Waterloo, there might be a train, soon after I got there. Perhaps Luciana was right: my duty was back in

Little Sodbury, to provide for my mother and sister; to help them through their loss. Maybe I could pick up my old life as a painter and handyman.

But, with each passing day, that option became more distant.

I spent a couple of days in the flat, with Alan and Luciana, but each day I found myself out wandering the streets. The signs of war were everywhere: there were boarded shopfronts, piles of rubble, shattered glass and shattered lives – I was not the only one. It had truly been a world war.

I walked past churches and old servicemen's hostels, and began to think of the last time I had seen Uncle Biggles. How old would he be now? Why, he must be in his mid-seventies. I hoped that he had found somewhere quiet to retire, though I was not sure if he had any money. He was the wandering ex-soldier, but at least God kept pace with his stride.

I stopped outside another church. This time, I decided to go in. I pushed back the door – they were always unlocked in those days, when there was decency and respect.

It was cold inside. I removed my hat and walked slowly up the aisle, selecting a pew near the back. There, I sat and reflected.

About twenty minutes had passed, before the priest appeared from the vestry. He busied himself around the altar for a while, then bent his head in prayer. Above his black, kneeling figure, the sun performed kaleidoscopic contortions, anointing the old man's shoulders in reds, blues and yellows. In my observation, I began to breathe deeper, and I gently closed my eyes.

When I opened them again, the reverend was clip-clopping down the aisle, toward me. He chose the pew in front of me, but shuffled along, so that he could look at me along the hypotenuse.

"I'm sorry; I hadn't meant to doze," I said.

"Reflection takes many forms. I just came to see if you were okay."

"I'm fine. Thank you."

We sat in silence for a while, but the priest did not take his eyes from me. "You served abroad?" He was studying my face.

"Yes."

"I thought so. The change of life must be difficult for you."

"It is. And, some of my old life will stay with me forever. Reverend, how do you think God will judge me?"

The reverend continued his exploration of my face. "How do you judge yourself?"

I shrugged.

"You see, how I see it is like this," continued the reverend: "your objective was to restore peace, was it not? Your wish was to see a return of love, and to return to the arms of those you love."

"It was, Reverend." Involuntarily, my hand went to my inside jacket pocket. "But, now it is over, I am torn between love and duty."

"Ah," sighed the reverend. "Must they be exclusive? Each one should use whatever gift he has received to serve others, faithfully administering God's grace in its various forms. This is our Christian duty, which is always delivered with love."

I nodded.

"I must say, I have not seen you in our congregation before?" said the reverend. "Perhaps you will join us this Sunday, for Holy Communion?"

"I am only staying in London briefly, I am afraid. I am not from around here."

"Ah, well." He touched my hand, which was on the back of his pew. "You'll find God will be exactly where you are, when you are ready for Him. Where is home, young man?"

"I'm from Little Sodbury-on-the-Wode. I'm just staying with a... er, friend, while I get myself together."

The old reverend smiled, broadly: "Ah, I see. Torn between love and duty – I see. When did you return from the Army?"

"A few days ago."

He nodded a snow-capped head. "And you have not been home yet? And, that makes you feel guilt?"

"It does."

"And here, you say, you are staying with a friend?"

"Yes."

"The love side of the equation?"

I nodded. "Plus, I have the potential for some work hereabouts. When I go home, I don't have a job to go to."

"And, wherever it was you said, am I to understand that it is not the bustling metropolis, with situations around every corner?"

"No, Reverend."

"Ah."

"But, there is more." It felt good to talk to this complete, though serene, stranger. "If you would hear it?"

"I would," said the vicar. "But, why not come to the rectory? It is just next door, so still within reach for my flock, only it does have the added attraction of tea, and I am gasping. Come on; this way!"

By the time I had left the vicarage, I had explained all about Henry, my mother, Luciana and the offer of work in the movie studio. I had also seen the promise in my life. Yes, the reverend had said, it would take time to reconcile the war, and all I had seen, but had I not been delivered, to carry on toward God's purpose for me? Perhaps the gift of work that I had been given was still to reveal its full light.

We sat together in his small study, drinking tea and eating a slither of cake – rationed in all things but joy – and he helped me write a letter home. I remember feeling so much better as I signed it.

"I'll post it with my correspondence," the reverend said, cheerfully. "Now, go in peace, and good luck, young man.

As I write this now, I recollect that I had never even asked his name, this wonderful vicar of mine. And, though I promised to find my way back to his church, I must report that I never did. Sadly, he will be gone now, but a part of his ministry still lives, in each day I grasp as my own.

XI

It was only a few days later when I walked onto the set of my first feature film. Alan had travelled ahead, leaving Luciana and myself the luxury of the trundle out on the train, together. It was a sunny September morning, and autumn had long since elbowed summer into the amber shrubbery.

"Stop!" I cried, as we walked in the direction of the studios.

"What?"

"I want to capture this image, just now. The sunlight is striking you so beautifully. I want to remember the moment you become a big star!"

She giggled and grabbed my arm. "Now, don't be silly. I've only got a few lines."

"Ah, but that's how they all started: with a few lines." We were back on the move again. "But seriously, Luciana, how are you feeling?"

"Like I've eaten a bag of swans, and they're in there fighting to get out."

I chuckled. Luciana had always been an example of confidence and poise. But, swans? Maybe that was what a baronet served up on his wartime table, with special permission of the king. "You'll be brilliant."

She squeezed herself against me. "But here I am, being all self-centred again. How are you feeling?"

"Oh, I am okay." I was lying, of course; there was a small part of me that was a little unsure about the whole thing. "I'm used to being the new boy in a strange situation."

"But, don't you think this is wildly different?" Luciana said.

I didn't, until then. "When we were at school, or in the service, it was something we did, yes, but we knew there would be an end. Sometimes, we longed for it to finish – there was always the hope of that. But, not with this. We're coming along today with the hope that life in the films doesn't come to a halt. We hope that it blossoms and grows and... well, you know. I feel that, for the first time in my life, the journey isn't set, and there's a whole future out there. I don't want to mess it up on the first day."

It had never struck me just how much Luciana Fortescue-Ripley-Jones cared about the stage, films and acting. Perhaps that's why our eventual careers took such different trajectories. Or, it could be that she simply grew more beautiful over the years, and I had a face for radio.

When Luciana's protestations had finally got me through security, we both made our way to the studio to which we had been gruffly directed.

"Luciana! Cornelius! I'm so glad you got here okay!" It was Alan.

"Alan," said Luciana, fiercely, "you forgot to put Cornelius's name at the gate. I only just managed to get him in!"

"Did I?" Alan looked directly at me. "I'm sorry, darling; everything's been so busy. But, he's here now. Come, I'll take you to meet my father. Cornelius, if you go round the back there, where that van's coming out, and ask for Maintenance Bob, he's expecting a new man."

Alan steered Luciana away, into the commotion. She looked back over her shoulder, mouthing the word "sorry", then disappeared.

Maintenance Bob was not an easy man to find. It appeared that he and his men were dug in somewhere, in the far reaches of the set.

"I'm looking for Maintenance Bob."

"Aren't we all, dearie? Try back there, behind the catering tent."

Eventually, I came across three men playing cards on an upturned crate. They didn't seem much interested, as I approached.

"Sorry to disturb your game, fellas, but I'm trying to track down Maintenance Bob."

The older of the three looked up, and pushed his cap up his forehead. "I'm Mr. Plummer. And, who might you be, sonny?"

I took a deep breath and counted to ten.

"My name is Cornelius Thryke. I've been sent over by Alan, the director's son. I'm your new man."

Plummer stood up, removed his cap and scratched his head. "Well, what have they sent me now? What's your background? What do you know?"

I looked him straight in the eye: "Enough." I was upset with myself for feeling angry, but I wasn't prepared for a hostile welcome.

Plummer stepped around and over to me. "I'll decide what's

enough. Now tell me, where have they just got you from?" He turned and grinned back to his mates. To be fair to them, they didn't look that impressed with the way their foreman was handling the situation. "Hardly kitted out for it, is he? Turning up in a whistle."

One of the other chaps piped up: "That's obviously his demob suit, Bob – it's the same as the one they gave me. Give him a chance, eh?"

The second chap, who was probably just a bit younger than me, got up and offered me a hand. "I'm Cyril. And that," he said, pointing at a gangly teenager, "is Dodger."

I shook Cyril by the hand. "Cornelius, but chaps call me Corny."

"Now, look here, Cyril," interjected Maintenance Bob, "this is my team, and I haven't said I'll take him yet – demob suit or not. We all did our bit – Dodger excepted, of course."

It was already clear that if you wanted something done, you went to Bob; if you *really* wanted something done, you went to Cyril.

"I know, Bob: you defended the coast in the Home Guard. I did my turn in the R.A.O.C. and I'm sure this chap did his share, too."

"Well, he got that suntan from somewhere," said Bob. "Okay, I'll give you a chance, see? But, this is my team."

"Understood," I replied. "It must be tough when they send you a stranger, out of the blue."

"Well..." Bob seemed to be mellowing. He reminded me of Bristow, in that sense: once he'd had his say, he was alright.

"Who did you serve with?" It was Dodger. I reckoned he was about seventeen or eighteen.

"You don't have to answer that, lad," said Bob. "Dodger has a little game: you tell him who you were with and he gives you back their records. We sort of look after him, back here; he's the godson of the director, or something."

"Go on then, mate, for larks: test him."

I'd kind of been hoping that I wouldn't have to keep introducing myself by regiment, but I guess the war was only just over. It was a question you could be asked back then, like what football team you supported.

"57th Reconnaissance Regiment."

Dodger shot back, immediately: "Tunisia, until May 'forty-three, then Sicily and Italy."

"He's right!" I laughed. Bob looked a little sheepish.

"57th Recce, eh? Cor, you saw some action, I dare say!" Cyril turned to Bob: "Your call, Mister Plummer; what do you say?"

"See if you can sort him out some gear. Then put him to work on that generator."

I had stripped, cleaned, reassembled and brought the generator purring into life before lunch. In fact, I would go as far as to say it was the most satisfactory piece of work I had done in years. I reflected on the peace that I had drawn from the task, and how it had successfully stopped me from thinking about… Ah, I wondered how she was getting on. I was standing, wiping my hands on a rag, as the others began to filter back from one job and another.

"He's got it going, Bob," called Cyril, as the foreman came back into view, Dodger in tow.

Bob clapped his hands: "Fantastic! We'll take that back across after lunch. You coming, Corny?"

It appeared that I had been accepted into the team. In my book, deeds have always spoken louder than words; Bob needed to know that I was able, and he had allowed me the opportunity to show him. "Sure."

The catering tent was compact, but buzzing with life. The four of us joined the queue, which snaked past various trays and hotplates. As I stood there, I reminisced about that first dinner at the P.T.C., and queuing with Bristow, Ginger, Mac and Jenkins. I didn't even know which of them was still alive; I hoped they had all made it.

"Looks like a stew today, men," said Bob who, as the lead man, headed our column in the queue.

I wouldn't have minded what it was: I had the hunger that only a decent morning's work could deliver. You have to remember that food was still on ration but, however they did it, the caterers always did a sterling job – that has been true of every film set that I ever worked on. If an army marches on its stomach, a film cast acts out of delicious metallic trays.

I was just wiping my plate with a piece of bread, when I saw the look on Cyril's face change. His expression fair lit up, as his eyes were drawn away from the important business of eating.

"Cor, Bob, have a look! That's a new piece of totty, isn't it?" He dug the foreman in the ribs, causing him to spray gravy onto the sheeted trestle table.

"Will you not... Oh, yes: not bad; not bad at all, I'll give you that."

"I wonder where she sprang from?" Cyril asked, of no one in particular. I glanced in the direction that both men were looking and smiled to myself.

"I'm not too bothered where she came from," said Bob, "but I know where I like to take her, in that get-up!"

Of course, they were both talking about Luciana. Naturally, I'd heard men talk like this in the Army – it's what they do – but I wasn't about to join in this conversation to curry favour with my new pals.

Luciana had entered the tent with Alan and another man – he wore the uniform of a captain and had one of those pencil moustaches, which were all the rage at the time.

"Who's she with?" I asked, innocently.

"In the uniform?" replied Cyril. "Why, that's the leading man himself: Archibald Blythe. You must have heard of him."

Now, I shall admit this was less than good news. I watched them closely, Luciana in her Air Force blue and Blythe in his Army green: they were smiling and giggling at each other's quips. If, previously, I had believed that Alan was the competition, I was now afraid of losing my chance to Blythe. Yes, he was older, but wasn't that the attraction? The dashing movie star and the would-be movie starlet? I watched intently, as though through sandy binoculars. Perhaps Luciana sensed my distant attention, for at that moment she looked up and our eyes met. She waved and I waved back.

My stock in the maintenance department immediately went up.

They were astonished.

"You know her?" said Cyril, stowing his eating irons on a spotless plate.

"You didn't say," added Bob, completing the pincer.

"You didn't ask."

Bob scoffed: "We've got a proper dark horse here, gentlemen! Keep your ladyfolk in check; Cornelius is on the prowl!"

"It's not like that, Bob. I've just been staying at her flat for the last few nights."

Bob clutched his chest, feigning a coronary.

"Are you okay, Bob?" japed Cyril. "Do you need a doctor?"

"I'll be okay, Cyril; I should pull through, as long as laughing boy here doesn't keep dropping me into a state of shock!"

Maintenance Bob recovered sufficiently to stand and grab his plate. "Okay, men, dinner break over; let's get back to it. Dodger, close your mouth. I know Thryke here has you agog, but show him where the set designers live; see if you can't borrow some turps."

On the walk across, Dodger maintained his record of staring at me in an unsettling way. His dedication almost caused him to trip, on a couple of occasions. Enough was enough.

"Are you alright there, Dodge? You almost fell over."

"Yes."

"So, you're taking me to the set-making people?"

"Yes."

"And, you're quite sure you're alright?"

"Yes. But…"

"But what?"

"What was it like? In the desert, I mean, when you were chasing Rommel."

I stopped walking for a minute. Dodger seemed to dance on the spot, then skip back.

"It wasn't like the comic books would have you think, lad: scorching during the day and freezing in the middle of the night. The desert is a strange place: men stop thinking there; I've seen them go mad."

"And, the lady?" he asked.

"Lady?"

"Yes, in the canteen."

"Oh." It appeared that Dodger could switch subjects with speed. "Her name is Luciana. I have known her from... Say, Dodger, how old are you?"

"Eighteen."

"Well, since I was a bit younger than you; I was sixteen when I first saw her. We were both in school productions. Why, the best part of fifteen years has gone by since then."

"Will you introduce me to her?"

"Only if you promise not to steal her away."

He blushed and looked down. He fished something out of the pocket on the chest of his dungarees, and I watched as he unwrapped something small and leather-bound.

"My names book," he announced. "Mr. Plummer doesn't like me to have it, but I collect people, writing their names. Please?" He held it out to me. I noticed a small pen inserted into the spine.

"You want my autograph?"

He nodded: "Here, on this page. Sign and write your regiment."

And, this is the genuine story of the first autograph I ever gave. It is also the one I remember the most fondly. Dodger – or, Daniel, as I later found out he was named – was a lovely lad; wouldn't hurt a fly. Not like the hooligans of today. I took his book with all humility, signed it and printed underneath: *"Sergeant C.A. Thryke, 57th Reconnaissance Regiment."*

"Come on," I said; "let's go and find that turps."

It so transpired that there was no way I was going to get that turpentine! Bob, it appeared, had sent me in for his own amusement.

"What do you mean, you want to 'borrow' some turps? You're hardly going to bring it back, are you?" There was no doubt this lady was fierce, like a one-woman Panzer division. "Who sent you?"

"Maintenance Bob."

She tutted and rolled her eyes skyward. "Maintenance Bob! That man needs to learn to get his own stores. I'm sorry, love, what was your name? He'll have to get some petty cash and go out and get some; he can't keep coming over here on the earhole, you hear? Tell him to run his department properly and do an inventory, see. Coming over here on the earhole for turps! If he weren't such a dab hand with a spanner, they would have got rid of him ages ago, because he has no idea of how to run a film maintenance department – no idea at all."

I looked around. Dodger had abandoned me to face the music; he was obviously aware of what I was to encounter. But, something perverse inside me was having jolly fun.

"So, just to be clear, I cannot have any turpentine spirit?"

Another tirade was forthcoming: "Have you got cloth in your ears? Are you new? I don't know where they get these people from, I really don't. Coming in off the street with absolutely no appreciation of the fine equilibrium that must be maintained in a business of this nature. Army, were you? Just fill in a chitty and everything turned up, I suppose? Well, this is a thriving set-design department, and we don't stay that way by giving out our stock, willy-nilly. Now, if there was nothing else, I've got important jobs to be getting on with."

Defeated, I turned away with empty hands. Dodger was still nowhere to be seen, so I decided to wander back to the shed to pick up the next job card. I hadn't gone more than thirty yards, when Dodger cut across my bows and grabbed me by the sleeve.

"Come on, Sarge; let's go this way. It's longer, but it takes us past the stage."

"No wonder you scarpered!" I protested. "That set design supervisor is a terrible harridan. I've got to go back with nothing now."

Dodger produced something from behind his back: "Nah, Sarge, go back with this." It was a small tin of spirit.

I laughed: "So, that was the plan all along? You used me as a diversion!" I had to chuckle. "Won't they notice it's missing?"

"No, I go round the back and Old Charlie gives it to me – they've got loads. We just need someone to stay out the front and keep Maud busy. She has the eyes of an eagle."

"And the talons!"

"Come on."

Our production, it seemed, was filming mainly on stage three. There was one other film team in stage one, and the others were beginning to take bookings; the movie business was definitely on the up.

"So, are you staying in the trailer with us, then," asked Dodger, "or are you going back with your lady friend? There is a bunk for the fourth man."

I hadn't given any thought to the living arrangements, but it made sense to stay on the set. Everything was designed to keep the artists and supporting crew happy, within the confines of the studios: there was a shop, which sold everything you might need, meals available throughout the day, and a little post office, from where you could send correspondence home. It wouldn't take me long to settle into studio life.

"Here we are, Sarge: stage three."

We approached the large, hangar-type affair, and peered in through the giant doors. It was like a glorious world of possibility. Lights shone down, like stars on strings, and cameras traversed the sea of wires on rail tracks. Diplodocid-necked booms, with fluffy heads, dipped in and out, like a terrible lizard ducking to drink. All about, people whirred this way and that, with the hum of intent and concentration. It was simply marvellous. I knew that this is what I wanted to do.

"Hello there, young Daniel. And, who is this with you?"

I got the impression that Dodger was something of the celebrity himself, in the environs of the studios.

"This is Sergeant Thryke, of the 57th Reconnaissance Regiment."

I extended a hand. "It's just plain old Cornelius now," I said. "I say, this is all tremendous stuff."

"Sidney Mallard, electrician. Pleased to meet you." He looked around him. "Yeah, I suppose you forget how exciting it all is when you've been at it for a while. Now Daniel, how about you come in and have a closer look? But, stay hushed: they're going to be shooting the next scene in a minute."

We walked in, as invited, and made our way quietly forward. The doors closed with a *thunk* behind us.

"Quiet on set now, please. Places everyone. Okay. Cameras rolling... and, action!"

The set had been made up to look like an office. Archibald Blythe was seated. There was a knock on the door.

"Come."

The door on the set opened, and in walked Luciana Fortescue-Ripley-Jones.

"The major asks you to come immediately, sir." She delivered it faultlessly; I beamed inside. Dodger, meanwhile, dug me in the ribs.

"Oh, very well. Thank you. Oh, and one more thing."

"Sir?"

"Dinner, tonight?"

"But, sir, fraternizing is strictly—"

"I shan't take no for an answer. I know a lovely little place, well-stocked." Blythe crossed from behind the desk – a camera followed him; he grabbed her by the arms. "You don't want me to have to make it an order, do you?" he purred, like a bounder and a cad.

"No, sir."

"Good, then I'll pick you up at eight. And, for Heaven's sake, wear something pretty."

"And, cut!" roared the director. "Good work, Luciana; not bad for your first scene."

Alan was first onto the set, steering her away, an arm around her shoulder. But, it was Archibald Blythe I saw looking on; there was something more than acting in his eye.

"Come on," I said, my heart sinking in my chest, "let's get back to the maintenance shed."

A couple of days later, I was wandering around the site on my own. Either Dodger had disappeared, or I had somehow slipped him – I forget which it was, and I suppose it does not overly matter. But, there I was, on my Jack Jones, enjoying a stroll in the sunshine. I had taken to carrying a small tool roll, so it looked like I was on my way somewhere, or had just finished something urgent and was on my way back. I don't think anyone, Maintenance Bob included, was really too fussed about what I was doing. It was a definite novelty, and I allowed myself the luxury of enjoying it.

"Cornelius."

I carried on walking, with that half-feeling that someone had called my name, but not being sure enough to turn round. There could easily be another Cornelius.

"Cornelius, over here!"

It was definitely my name. I looked left, in the direction from which the call had come, and saw Luciana leaning up against a tank, elegantly smoking a cigarette. I ambled across, suppressing the desire to accelerate into a trot.

"Hullo, Luciana. How the devil are you? I've not seen you since we got here. But, marvellous, isn't it?" It was chipper, upbeat and largely nonsense.

"I know. I've missed you." She stopped short of hugging me, lightly touching my shoulders, instead. "I've been wondering how you've been getting on. I've only caught a glimpse of you in the catering tent."

"A short glimpse is usually enough for anyone."

She snorted and sent a spiral of smoke into the air. "You do make me laugh, Cornelius Thryke."

Luciana was standing in the W.A.A.F. uniform, the one I had seen her in the other day. I stood in my workman's dungarees, shirtsleeves rolled to my elbows, tanned forearms shining in the autumn sun. She looked me up and down.

"You look good in that uniform," I ventured.

She ran her hands over her tunic, as if testing it for size. They came to rest on her hips. "Yes, I might as well have kept my old one. They've found me a few more scenes to do, and a couple more lines."

"You're doing well, Luciana. I'm pleased for you."

She smiled. "Well, I must say that's a natty costume. What scene is that for?"

"Costume?" I chuckled to myself. "This is my workwear, for the maintenance department."

"Okaaay." She elongated the *"ay"*, as if figuring something out. "Well, what scene are the maintenance department in?"

"No; no scene, I'm in the actual maintenance department. You know, the chaps you call when something breaks down?"

Luciana stepped forward and ran a finger along the top of my dungarees. She hooked it behind one of the straps and gently pulled me closer. "The *actual* maintenance department?"

"Yes."

"But, I thought Alan was going to get you in the film?"

"I guess we can't all be film stars."

"But…" She seemed genuinely upset.

"It's okay. It's work, and that is more than I could have hoped for a week ago."

"It's my last day today," she said. "Will you come over to The Clapperboard tonight?"

"The what?"

"The Clapperboard, silly! Have you not been there yet? It's the bar on site. It's open to everybody – even…" her words trailed off.

"Even the maintenance department?"

"I didn't mean... I'm sorry. I've got to get back."

"I know; don't worry. Come on, I'll walk with you."

We walked in silence back to stage three. In the time it took, I knew that I had to go to the bar that evening, if only to say that I had tried; I don't think I could have looked myself in the mirror if I had just let her drift away. I wasn't sure what love really was, but surely this feeling was near enough. I thought about her when she was not there; I saw her when I closed my eyes. Her success meant more than mine. Yes, I simply had to go to The Clapperboard that evening.

Luciana and I arrived at stage three and found the hangar doors open. We both knew enough by now to know that this meant there was no filming going on, and that it was safe to enter. Luciana sauntered in, like a jaded old hand; I, still a little in awe, was a tad more reticent.

"Come on, Cornelius. Come and say hello to a few people."

I nodded and walked in, taking my place at Luciana's side. Nobody seemed to take much notice of me.

"Why, here he is now!"

I can only describe it as like one of those moments when an unexpected cowboy walks into a saloon: the chatter stops, the gambling stops, and even the pianola screeches to an unceremonious halt. Instinct told me to pause, and to stay where I was standing. Luciana hadn't received that training, and dragged me in farther.

I was drawn into the orbit of an enormous, grey-bearded man in a floppy beret; everyone and everything appeared to be revolving around him. I then understood that standing next to him, like a skinny moon, was Dodger.

"This is who I was telling you about, Uncle: this is my new friend, Sergeant Cornelius Thryke, of the 57th Reconnaissance Regiment."

The beard beamed beneath the beret, and I was offered a bear paw to shake.

"Basil Karslake. How do you do? It gives me great pleasure to welcome a genuine war hero. Plus, any friend of young Daniel is a friend of mine."

I nodded.

"Oh, and I see you've met our newest star," he continued. "I'm predicting great things for Lucy here – great things indeed."

"Mr, Karslake," I began, "she has always been a star, ever since I first met her."

"Ah, so you are long acquainted?"

Luciana saw her opportunity: "Ever since I saw him in *A Midsummer Night's Dream*, many years ago, now."

"An actor, too?" guffawed Karslake. "Well, this is fortuitous. An actor and a sergeant!"

"I know he can do it, Uncle!" cried Dodger.

"Okay, Thryke, I'm going to give you a try; if I can help a serviceman on his way, I should like to. Report to wardrobe at 0800 hours tomorrow; they'll kit you out. Now, would you mind taking Daniel for a cup of tea? The devil's work here is never done."

And, with that, my audience was over. I had met the great director – as he would become – Sir Basil Karslake. What's more, I was thoroughly confused by the whole experience.

"Wow!" exclaimed Luciana.

"Wow!" I repeated, in my puzzlement. "What just happened there?"

"I think you're going to be in the film."

Dodger crashed in and slapped me warmly across the back. "It's true! They had a sergeant major for the parade ground scenes, but he's come down with laryngitis; you're taking over. You've even got a few lines!"

"And, who is this handsome fellow?" asked Luciana.

"Ah, this," I proudly introduced, "is the one and only Daniel 'Dodger' Handy. And, very handy he's proving to be."

"Well, thank you," said Luciana, leaning in and kissing him on the cheek. "You are indeed a wonderful young man."

Cyril, Bob and Dodger, sitting outside the trailer, were cooking sausages over a small fire. As I emerged, washed, shaved and back in my suit, they all looked up, befuddled by my decision to leave them to their fun.

I had expected Bob to push back against the news of my sudden promotion to the cast, but he was surprisingly supportive: "Take what time you need, but remember there's plenty of work to do here." I had thanked him and promised that I would always wash back up on the shores of the maintenance shed. They had offered me the hand of friendship and camaraderie, after all.

"Here he is!" exclaimed Bob, as I climbed down onto the makeshift steps. "Looking sharp."

"Thanks, Bob. Though, I don't feel it."

"What, a man like you? I'd have thought this was child's play."

On the surface, Bob's comment was spot on. I had fought on some of the fiercest battlefields on Earth; there was no risk of getting shot tonight. "I was trained to deal with Germans, not women," I said, grimly.

Bob and Cyril both let out low humming sounds, in recognition. Dodger just watched.

"So, what's the plan then, skip?" asked Cyril.

I didn't know. I could only hope that I could feel my way to one; do what felt right in the moment.

When I finally got the nerve together, I pushed open the door to The Clapperboard and went in. It actually wasn't all that bad.

It was a large, square building, and a long, mahogany bar stretched across two-thirds of it. Along the top of the bar, and across most of the walls, hung signed photographs of luminaries from before the war: Albie Spintoe, Elizabeth Duckling, Frank Horsefly, Hettie McAnuff – they were all there. I even spotted a young Archie Blythe, though the same pencil moustache adorned his smooth, marble face. Where the photographs receded, strange props sprang up in their place: a prosthetic arm, a vampire duck and a full deep-sea diver's suit, with buffed bronze helm. It would have been educational to walk around, when the place was empty, but it wasn't; it was packed, and a blue fug clung permanently to the ceiling.

A violent group guffaw broke out, peaked with the high-pitched screech of a scandalized woman. Yes, I was definitely in a bar: earthy and raucous! It was time to get a drink. I walked up to the bar and waited.

"What will it be, sir?"

"I.P.A., please."

"I.P.A. Anything else?"

"Just the I.P.A."

As he disappeared to get my beer, arms were flung around my shoulders, and I received multiple kissing assaults to my cheek.

"He came! He came! My Cornelius came!" It was Luciana.

"Of course I did. Can I get you a drink? I'm in the chair."

"That's frightfully decent of you, darling! I'll have a G-and-T, Archie will have a whisky and Alan will take an ale, if that's quite alright."

The barman came back. "A shilling please, sir."

"A shilling?" I hadn't meant for it to come out, but it did. Simultaneously, I began to calculate how far the money in my pocketbook would go. It should be alright. Besides, buying a drink for Archibald Blythe could never be a bad idea.

"A shilling please, sir," repeated the barman.

"I'm sorry: could I also have a whisky, a G-and-T and another I.P.A., please?"

The barman rolled his eyes, looked less than impressed and

wandered off, chuntering to himself.

"Oh, you are a sweetheart," said Luciana. She gave me an additional squeeze; her breath was already thick with gin. I didn't think it was going to be a long evening.

"Been here long?"

"About two glasses," she replied.

"Looks like you're going to be trouble, tonight."

"I'm trouble every night," she purred.

I looked at her. Could it happen? No. Be the gentleman.

"Five and four," announced the barman, clunking my purchases onto the bar.

"And, take one for yourself," I said, gallantly.

Archibald Blythe, as far as a bounder could be, was a thoroughly spiffing gent – which is more than can be said of that director's son, Alan Karslake. At least Archie was open in his intent; Alan hid behind pith.

"Ah, here she is: the prettiest filly in the film. And, who is this? A friend?" asked Archie.

"This is Cornelius Thryke, who I told you about," stated Luciana. "Of course, Corny, you know Alan, and this, if I may present him so, is the incorrigible rogue, Archibald Blythe."

Archie stood. "A pleasure, sir. From what Lucy tells me, we are all in your debt; I shake your hand with all humility. Come, join us. There is room if we all shuffle around, but don't you dare sit between me and this gorgeous specimen!"

Blythe slapped Luciana's bottom as she sat down. I should have been raging, but it was difficult in the face of such obvious caddishness.

"So, tell me, Cornelius," said Archie, "how do you happen to know this mouthwatering creature?"

"We met at school, Mr. Blythe."

"Oh, do call me Ar-chie." He split the name, like an aristocratic sneeze. "And, it appears that I am doubly in your debt, as you have furnished me with some of Scotland's finest. You are a gentleman, sir. Cheers!"

We all raised our glasses and clinked them together.

"Saluti," I said.

"Oh, a little Italian?" observed Archie. "The language of love, my sweet!" Luciana yelped and leapt a little in her chair. Archibald Blythe's right hand returned into view – I looked straight at it. He caught me and smiled.

"So, you met at school?" enquired Archie. "Childhood sweethearts? Then, you had the pleasure of seeing her coming into flower, did you not?"

"I had the pleasure of seeing her act."

There was enough seriousness in my voice to make Archibald sit up and take notice.

"I have shared that in that gift, too. We have that in common, at least."

"Luciana is going to be a star," I said.

"No doubt," replied Blythe. We touched glasses again.

"I am here, you know," cried Luciana, bursting into the

conversation. "Kindly stop posturing around me as if I am not."

Her ire was short-lived, as she leant forward, as though communicating a secret; "I've not had the chance to tell you yet, Corny: I've got myself a part in the next film here, too. It's a much bigger role, too."

Archibald, never one to miss a trick, put his arm around her in congratulations. "Nothing more than you deserve, darling. Talent doesn't go unnoticed."

It was time for Alan to pipe up: "Well, let's not hide Cornelius's light under a bushel; he's got a few seconds as a regimental sergeant-major to film tomorrow. Although, he does have to give that simple maintenance boy fifteen percent."

"His name is Daniel," I said, slowly, "and I'd rather have one of him than ten of—"

"Gentlemen, gentlemen, this is an evening of fun and celebration! Let us not argue. Why, I have a capital idea!" interrupted Archie. His voice rose to a thunderous shout, which cut through the noise and landed at the bar: "Champagne! Two bottles of Champagne here!"

The bubbly had gone and the crowds were thinning out, by the time I next found myself at the bar. Luciana walked across behind me.

"Don't get me another."

"Are you sure?"

Luciana hiccupped in confirmation. "I want to go."

I looked at her, looked at the barman approaching, and looked at Alan and Archie, who were by then deep in conversation with Alan's father.

"I see Mr. Karslake is in for his nightcap," said the barman.

"What does he drink?" I asked.

"Same whisky as Mr. Blythe, sir."

"Then, I should like a whisky each for Mr. Blythe and Mr. Karslake, and another I.P.A. for his son."

"Very good, sir. Nothing for yourself and the lady?"

I shook my head.

"I'll just take these over, then I'll come back and walk you back to your accommodation."

Luciana nodded. "Don't get any ideas, though."

"I just want to make sure you get home safely. Scout's honour."

Luciana did not see fit to question whether I had ever been a scout or not. For the record, I had not.

If Miss Fortescue-Ripley-Jones, however, was not in a spot of bother while she was standing in the bar, she certainly was when she stepped out into the chilly, autumnal air. Luciana staggered in an impressive arc, periodically becoming a tri-ped to maintain a level of uprightness. My sobriety was also sorely challenged, but I managed to dash across and catch her, when a fall looked inevitable.

"My hero," she gasped, looking up into my eyes.

"Right place, right time." I hauled her up to her feet. "Let's get you back. Hold onto me."

Luciana retained balance and drew her coat around her. "I'm fine now."

We walked the first couple of hundred yards in silence. Every so often Luciana swayed outward, then steered herself back toward me.

"Careful; you'll trip."

If she heard me, she didn't acknowledge it, and swerved from the path onto the grass. It was then, accompanied by a strange cracking noise, that she collapsed in a heap on the turf. I ran over to help her up.

"Are you alright? Nothing broken?"

"Yes," she sobbed: "the heel of my favourite shoes!" She tore them off of her feet, in a fit of petulance, and hurled them into the darkness.

"Come on. Nice and easy, let's get you off of that grass. There's a bench there."

She pushed me away: "Leave me! I can do it!"

"I know you can, but—"

"But, nothing. I'll get up myself." She pushed herself toward the vertical, then tipped over, backward. "Well, don't just stand there looking useless; help me up!"

By now, Luciana was in streams of tears. I picked her up and we box-stepped over to a nearby bench.

"Look at the state of me! I've good mud all up my legs, goodness knows what on my backside, and my mascara must look like spiders have run down my face."

"You look fine."

Luciana glared at me. "Can't you just be honest with me, for once? I'm tired of your empty platitudes."

"But, Luciana—"

"Tell me! Tell me, Cornelius! Tell me that I look a mess! Tell me that I'm silly for drinking too much! Tell me that I'm blind and they're just giving me parts because they want to take of advantage of me!"

"Luciana, no one wants to—"

She swung around an arm, and slapped me across the chest. "So, I'm undesirable, am I? Then there's no hope."

"Luciana, you're being—"

"Don't you dare! Don't you dare say 'silly'! I will show you, Cornelius Thryke! I will show all of you!" I guess she meant mankind as a whole. She was such a strong woman.

"I never said that."

"You never say anything! Look at me. You were supposed to look after me tonight. What a mess."

"I'm sorry."

Luciana didn't reply. She began brushing herself down, as if preparing to move off again.

I began to feel sick. "I want to look after you," I blurted.

She stopped brushing and looked at me. A cloud rolled away from the moon, and we were both lit in the glow.

My voice trembled: "I want to always look after you."

Our faces were parallel. I tried to read her expression: did it look like anticipation? Puzzlement? Fear? I gulped and tried to look meaningfully into those soft, blue eyes.

"Marry me, Luciana. Marry me."

It was the first and, until now, only time that I had ever proposed to a woman. While the years have solidified my heart, that moment is still etched upon it.

"Oh, Cornelius," she said, softly, "why would you say that? You're such a wonderful man."

I sought to postpone the pain. "Look, don't answer right away; think about it. Take whatever time you need."

Luciana stood. Her body began to turn and she stepped away, barefoot and backward, as if from something terrifying. Her tear-written face stared back at me, now with a fresh saline coating, no doubt caused by me. "Why did you have to say that?"

Then, she began to walk, soundlessly, the shock of my foolishness having returned her to full sobriety.

I suppose I should have gone after her, grabbed her and kissed her passionately, beneath the light of a celebratory moon. But, those sorts of thing only happen in films or books. In real life, the protagonist just sits there for half an hour, before walking back to a snoring trailer.

I didn't sleep that night.

Come morning, I was sitting outside the trailer, boiling the kettle on the little stove. It was an activity I liked to do. I found it calming, watching the little, purple flame leap around the sides of the kettle, with a low, serpentine hiss. I had never encountered a snake, but we were warned about them in Tunisia: horned vipers and cobras. Snakes bearing apples.

Cyril was the first to emerge, hacking and coughing, striking a match over a miser's roll-up, to kick-start his lungs.

"Morning, Cyril. Tea will be up in a minute." I said this with a degree of solemnity.

Cyril hocked, spat and came to sit on the upturned crate: condensed milk, unsweetened; 48 x 16oz.

"That's just what the doctor ordered," he said. "Though, you look like you could do with something stronger."

I snorted: "There was enough of that last night. I don't mind telling you I spent a fortune. Did me no good, though."

"You didn't get a handful, then?"

The remark grated with me, but I swallowed back my ire. It was a comment that one might expect to receive in that company – no use pretending it wasn't. Or, that she was some sort of princess – even though, to me, she was.

"No, far worse than that." Maybe if I laughed it off, perhaps that would help.

"What could be worse than that? You didn't punch Alan Karslake, did you? Word around the place is that he could use a stiff dig."

Spout steam. Nearly there. "No. Though, I admit, there were times I wanted to."

"Well, what then? No feminine involvement? Okay, that's bad. No fisticuffs, especially with entitled shirkers? Okay, while I would have loved to have seen that, it didn't happen, and you're still in a job this morning, a few bob lighter, with a bit of a baggy head. You'll get over it."

"I asked her to marry me."

For a few seconds, all that could be heard was the hiss of the gas stove. The trailer door opened again and Bob slipped out, into the dewy dank of the morning.

"Are you alright, Cyril? You look like you've seen a ghost. Ah, morning, Corny. You've got a brew on, you hero."

"Tell Bob what you've just told me," said Cyril, in a slow, staccato monotone.

"What's going on, fellas?" Bob sat on the low stack of tyres: 550-16; fill to 22 psi. "Good evening, Corny?"

"You tell him, Cyril," I said.

Bob looked at his young confidante, as if sniffing the air for clues.

"He," started Cyril, "as in Cornelius…"

"Yes, yes, I know who he is!"

"He. Asked. Her. To. Marry. Him."

"Who asked who to do what, now?" Bob seemed confused.

Dodger now emerged from the trailer – stately, but far from plump. "Morning all," he said, amid a yawn.

"Don't interrupt, Dodger," snapped Bob. "Come and sit yourself down. Corny's got the tea on."

As bid, Dodger descended the makeshift steps and sat on the stuffed potato sack: Harvest Days – happy days.

I reached for the teapot, warmed it from the large kettle and swirled it to the ground. Steam rose in a satisfied *ssss*. One spoon. Two spoons. Three spoons.

"Go easy with that, Corny: it's got to last," stated Maintenance Bob. "Look, what has happened? Come on, Thryke; we're all friends here."

And, they were. Sometimes, even now, all these years later, I wonder what happened to Maintenance Bob, Cyril and the young Dodging Daniel. They were the salt of the earth: decent, honest chaps; nothing mendacious, nothing false.

"I asked her to marry me."

"Who," said Bob.

"Luciana!" cried Dodger, punching the air. "I'm going to a wedding!"

"Who's Luciana?" asked Bob, understandably.

Cyril, thankfully, took up the explanation: "Think back, Bob – a couple of days ago. That blonde we saw in the catering tent, with Blythe and Kerslake junior."

"Oh, rather! Ding dong!" Bob gazed off into the distance, then jolted back: "What of her?"

"Well," continued Cyril, "if you were listening, boss, you'd know that, last night, lover boy asked her to marry him."

I poured the angrily boiling water into the teapot, turned off the stove and left the pot on top to mash.

"He did what?" said Bob.

"Exactly," said Cyril.

"What did she say?" asked Dodger. It was the one question I didn't want but, admittedly, it was the only question that really mattered.

"Nothing," I said, glumly.

"Nothing?" echoed Cyril and Bob, in choral harmony.

"Nothing."

"Let me get this straight," said Bob: "you asked a fantastically beautiful and eligible woman to marry you, and she said nothing?"

"She didn't say 'nothing'," I protested, pointlessly; "she said *nothing*. She remained silent on the matter. But, I got her shoes." I indicated a pair of defective high heels, sitting on an oil drum.

"Oh, well that's alright then: he got her shoes," exclaimed Bob, "though, Heaven knows what he's planning to do with them."

Cyril laughed. Poor Dodger just looked confused.

"I'm just going to fix them, that's all," I retorted. "One of the heels snapped and had her over – nothing more than that."

"Forget the shoes!" screamed Cyril. "Let's not focus on the shoes – I hardly think that is the most important consideration here. What happens now?"

I remained hunched over, staring at the teapot. "I don't know. What would you chaps do? I've ruined everything."

Chins started to be scratched, as I began to ready the mugs for the brew. It was what we all needed, especially me. It wasn't far past six o'clock, after all.

"I'm just going to keep my head down for the time being," I reported. "She goes home for a week or so today, anyway, so there are just a few hours to get through. Then, I can be back working with you chaps, like normal."

Cyril and Dodger, still scratching their chins, nodded sagely.

Meanwhile, Bob shook his head: "I fear not, Master Thryke. Don't forget, you have to be over in wardrobe by eight."

And, he was right. In all of the excitement – if that was the right word – I had totally forgotten that I was due to appear in the film that very day.

As it was, I had my tea and was breakfasted, showered and shaved in plenty of time. The lads circled in around me and made sure I got there with time to spare.

EDITOR'S NARRATIVE
Quentin Prowler

The film that Cornelius was about to take part in was *For the Corps*, directed by Basil Karslake (released 1946, Echinus Studios). This is widely known as the picture which launched the career of Luciana Fortescue-Ripley-Jones. Attentive readers will know that Luciana was not credited under her full name for this or future movies; rather, the baronet's daughter used the abridged moniker of Lucy Ripley for all further showbusiness engagements, becoming something of the celebrated femme fatale.

Within the Thryke papers, we are lucky to have some documentation relating to the release of *For the Corps*. Again, this is the form of correspondence, this time between Cornelius and his mother, Vera. I am delighted to be able to recreate those letters here. Of particular note, and forming a touching piece of historical evidence, the enveloped letter from Vera contains a faded ticket stub – I believe that this is the very ticket she bought to attend a screening of *For the Corps* at the Belmont Picture House, in Apple Qualmsbury, a short bus ride from home.

Dear Cornelius,

On Wednesday last, your sister accompanied me to the Belmont Picture House in Apple Qualmsbury. You may not

know this, but I have seldom been to the picture house in my lifetime. Your father, may God rest his soul, did not approve of picture houses, believing them to be the work of the necromancer, so he never took me. I went once or twice, to see the newsreels during the war, but I was to gather most of my intelligence from the wireless. Due to the vagaries of the omnibus timetable, we decided to try for an afternoon performance. A few other ladies from the parish happened to be upon the same transport, including Mrs. Pomfrey and Mrs. Wild. I had only told a few select acquaintances of your success, but it appears that most of the village had made the journey across to The Belmont. The cinema thanks you, and the bus company thanks you, too.
But, I digress, dear son.

I felt giddy as they lowered the lights. I feared that I might nod off and miss your debut. It gave me such pride when you appeared on the screen. Your face must have been two yards high! You delivered your commands with such authority. Some said you were too fierce, but I say you were just right. Well done, my dear boy!

Martha and I stayed right to the very end. When your name came up on the screen, the projectionist stopped the film, so that we could pick it out, from amongst the others. A little cheer went up when people eventually found it. I was so very proud.

While your face may have aged, as we all have, when I saw you, there was sorrow in my heart. I fear I must address this by letter, or I never shall. Please find some forgiveness for a foolish woman. In my grief, I pushed you away. I know, in my heart of hearts, that you were not responsible for the death of Henry. He answered his country's call, as did you. You were both such brave boys.

While my heart still mourns him, and shall continue to do so every day, please, dear son, do not feel there is not a welcome for you here. I wish it, and Martha wishes it.

Please write soon, and maybe think of a date when you might be reunited with your loving mother? I cannot be sated by your face upon a screen alone, as much as it fills me with pride. For I am, and always have been, so very, very proud.

Your loving Mother.

*

My dear Mother,

Thank you so much for your letter.

It meant an enormous amount to read it. I have carried around the guilt of Henry's death for many years now, but to hear you say that you do not blame me has eased that burden a little. I still wish that I could have been there, if only to hold his hand as he passed, to see him through those last moments of fear.

Sometimes, I think that I should have been in France, and that the shrapnel of that blast should have pierced me and saved a worthier life. Or, perhaps, my whole unit might have been there, instead of slogging up through the boot of Italy. We were not so far away. Could our commanders not have sent us to the aid of Henry? Could we have found and made safe the awful weapon that took him from us?

It is evening now, as I sit by lamplight to write this. It has been another long day. Last week, we finished a film called A Vale of Villains. *Look out for it, because I have a small role in that; I portray one of the bank tellers, during the robbery scene. I also play one of the policemen, during the denouement, but you do not see my face, and I am not credited for that.*

I am still lending a hand with Maintenance Bob, Cyril and my young friend Dodging Daniel. They are happy to remain out of the limelight, but do not begrudge me my time in front of the camera. They are good chaps, really, and I have been lucky to find a situation with them. I still enjoy tinkering with the broken equipment, between scenes.

We are working on a picture called Little Tim at the moment, then almost immediately after that finishes we begin a sleuthing movie called A Lord is Murdered – I think you will definitely enjoy that one! Your favourite, Archibald Blythe, plays Cramshaw, the master detective. An up and coming actor, by the name of Dickie Loughborough, is coming in as Cramshaw's sidekick, Butters, and Lucy Ripley has her first starring role, as Lady Jennifer. It is another Karslake production for the studio, so we will all be in good hands. It's been exciting working with another director on this shoot, but Echinus has become synonymous with the Karslakes, don't you agree? It will be good to see all of the old gang once more, particularly Luciana. She stayed away from me during the filming of this picture, even if I had fixed her shoes! It's a long story, Mother, and one I will not bore you with here. Perhaps on my next trip home.

Please pass on my regards to Martha. I am guessing that she still resides with you. I have not been the most loving of brothers, where Martha is concerned. This situation is something for which I need to take some responsibility. Perhaps I shall write to her. Yes, I will sit down tomorrow and *pen something, yes. Do not read this bit of your letter to her; I should like it to be a surprise. And, I promise that I will not enclose frog spawn with her envelope!*

I will sign off now, Mother. You will never know what your letter has done for me. I promise I will write more frequently from now on, and I shall certainly come and visit at the earliest opportunity, given that it is convenient to you, of course.

Your loving son,
Cornelius.

In the same batch of papers was this letter, which was redirected through the studio. I include it here, because it will be of general interest to the reader.

Dear Corny,

As you may remember, I am not one for writing letters, but here goes!

I didn't half get a shock the other week, when I took Mavis to the pictures. I was sitting there, minding my own, if you know what I mean, when who should pop up on the screen but our very own Cornelius Thryke! I said to Mavis: "Here, Mavis, I know him. We trained together in the Army! His name's Cornelius Thryke. Well, look at him now!" She didn't say much, because she was eating a toffee, but I think she was impressed!

For the rest of the film, I was wondering if my eyes were deceiving me, like. But, how could they be? Your boat was six-foot square! I was sure it was you. Everyone was standing up when the names started rolling, so I couldn't be 100% sure, but I had to try and see. I have written you this letter, so do reply if I am right, and these words somehow find you. I don't want to have to go and see the film again, do I?

You're probably wondering who this is actually from, unless you've gone right to the end to see who signed it. Yes, you've probably done that, so I don't need to do this bit, but I'm caught up in the momentum now, see? It's me! It's Jack Bristow! We were at Brington and Crumpton together. Do you remember? Of course you do! How could you forget someone who you made crawl through pig shit? Cor, the pong! I went through the whole war and never did anything to match that.

Did you know I've got Mac working with me, too? I've started up a little building firm. Lord knows there is plenty of work, so we're pretty much flat out. I'd offer my old mate Corny a job too, but it looks like you've found a way to avoid real work! Typical Corny!

I heard that Jenkins never went to war, not after his knee injury. Last I heard, he was running a poulterers, somewhere in South Wales. That only leaves Ginger of the original gang; no one seems to know where he is. Some say he didn't make it; others say he went into the priesthood. I know which I would like to believe.

Well, if you get a chance, come across and say hello. You're only in Borehamwood (if my cinema eyes did not deceive me), and I'm just here in West Ham. It's not far. Come along.

With best wishes, your comrade in arms,
Jack.

Part Five:

Reflections

EDITOR'S NARRATIVE
Quentin Prowler

Vera Thryke, beloved mother of Henry, Cornelius and Martha, and wife of Bartholomew, died on 18th July 1965. She was only seventy-four years old.

Diary entries do exist, and Cornelius wrote extensively throughout the last few days of Vera's life. However, it is worth noting that, following the day of her passing, no further diaries exist until 1st January 1966. In his grief, he just stopped writing.

As ever, I shall leave it to Cornelius to take up the story...

THE MEMOIRS OF CORNELIUS THRYKE.

XII

Mother had been admitted to the General Hospital in Thelmesbury. It had a pulsing white interior, under bright, murmuring strip lamps. Around it scurried starched matrons, stiff cerulean nurses and Brylcreemed doctors, all carrying clipboards in a flurry of never arriving. Mother had been an outpatient there for some time, and I had taken her there, once or twice.

I had purchased a car in '64, a turquoise-green Ford Anglia with a white roof. I had passed my test in the Army but hadn't driven much since. It didn't take long to get used to things again, however, though the roads were no place for the faint-hearted. As time passed, I began to hear fewer horns. I was working all over the place, on film and stage mainly, plus the odd role on the newfangled television, so it had made sense to take a motor vehicle. It also meant that I could be at Little Sodbury, with a higher degree of flexibility. So, when I could, I ran Mother to the hospital. It was not a journey one would wish to make by bus and, besides, they either got you there five minutes late or three hours early. No, a car I had to have.

I received the message at my digs that Mother had been admitted by ambulance. It was a Friday, so I guess that made it 9th July 1965. I arrived in Thelmesbury in the early evening – about 7 p.m., I think.

A kindly woman directed me to Mother's ward, and I set about picking my way through the bleached, institutionalized corridors. I saw the sign for Bluebird Ward and pushed at the large, white double doors. I stepped through and leapt clear as they sprang back fiercely, oscillating into still silence.

"May I help you?" a nurse asked. Maybe in her thirties, dark of eye and hair, she was pencilling notes at her desk.

"My name is Cornelius Thryke. I am here to see Mrs. Vera Thryke; I'm her son."

"I see." She looked at me as if I were an inconvenience. "Visiting hours end at eight o'clock sharp. I shall take you to Mrs. Thryke, forthwith."

"Thank you, Nurse."

"Ward Sister: Ward Sister Evans. Now, follow me. Have you come far, Mr. Thryke?"

"From London, Sister."

"Ah, yes, you must be the actor; Mrs. Thryke mentioned you. Here we are." We stopped before a drawn curtain. This barrier was deemed offensive by Ward Sister Evans, and she flung it back with a ferocity which made the cloistered incumbents jump.

"Kindly leave these curtains open! They are to be touched by medical staff only. Are you medical staff?" The comment was directed at my sister, Martha, who looked at the ground.

"No, Ward Sister."

"No, Ward Sister," repeated Sister Evans, in a clipped tone. I liked her. I liked her very much. Anyone who would put Martha in her box was alright with me.

Mother, it appeared, was slightly dozing. This situation was also, apparently, seen as offensive.

"Mrs. Thryke," said the nurse, sharply, "your son has arrived. He has travelled quite a way to be here." She turned and walked past me. "Eight o'clock," she said, sternly. It was already half past seven. I really liked her.

"Cornelius, is that you? Is it really you?" said my mother, dramatically, as her eyes flicked open.

"Yes, Mother, it's me: your son, Cornelius."

"Oh, really!" exclaimed Martha. "This isn't a Victorian novel; stop talking like that! Yes, Mother, Cornelius is here. Finally."

"Oh, he's a good boy. Isn't he a good boy, Martha?"

Martha, who was by now in her fifties, fixed me with an icy stare. If she hadn't been wearing those awful winged spectacles, the effect might have been much worse.

"I rode in the ambulance, Cornelius," she said, very matter of fact. "But, even so, I still found time to pop out and buy Mum these grapes and other bits."

"You're a good girl, Martha. Isn't she a good girl, Cornelius?" said Mother, seemingly on a pre-set loop.

I smiled. "Yes. Yes, she is, Mother. Now, how are you feeling?"

"Not too chipper, I'm afraid."

"Has the doctor been?" I had recently finished playing a doctor in a London play. "Perhaps I could talk to him."

"He came past on rounds," said Martha, "which you missed. Perhaps you were queueing at the fruiterers around the corner?"

"What did he say?" I ignored Martha's barbs.

It was Mother who replied: "They're going to keep me under observation – isn't that what the doctor said, Martha? And, they're going to try and manage my pain. That's right, isn't it, Martha?"

"That's right, Mum." Martha tucked the blankets under Mother's chin and smoothed them down.

She then looked at me, and there was a softness in her eyes – something I had not seen in quite some time. "How are you, Cornelius?" she asked.

"Between jobs at the moment, but otherwise well. How are things with you? The bakery treating you okay?"

"Martha is courting," crowed Mother.

"Mother!" protested Martha.

"Tsk! I'm too old and tired to be keeping confidences. You deserve a bit of happiness."

And, bless her, the old dear was right. It was true, I'd served the country for five years, but we had all made our own sacrifices. "She's right."

"And, what would you know?" spat Martha. "You've been off playing soldier and standing in the background of films for twenty-five years, whilst I…"

Her voice trailed off. Sister Evans was glaring, from a few beds down.

"Will you take me home tonight, please?" I guess it was all she could think to say.

"Of course," I replied, piously.

It was a particular relief when eight o'clock came around. Nurses attacked from both sides, chivvying the lingering in the direction of Ward Sister Evans.

"Wait for me down in reception, Martha. I'll be right down."

As you know, there have been few moments in my life when I have played the lothario. But this, to my shame, was one.

"I say, Staff Nurse Evans?"

She glared and walked over. I felt rather bilious. "I just wanted to say thank you, to you and your team, for everything that you are doing for my mother."

"It is our job, and we do it with pleasure, Mr.... er..." She raised a clipboard that she was carrying and began to scan it. A lesser man would have bolted. But I knew a little about acting.

"Thryke," she concluded.

"Quite. Tell me, if visiting hours conclude at eight p.m., what time, if I may be so bold, do you finish?"

"I shall be here until six a.m., Mr. Thryke. Your mother will receive the best of care. Now, if there is nothing else?" She began to walk away.

"Well, there was, actually."

She huffed, stopped and turned. Was that the hint of a smile, lingering on her face? I hardened my resolve and, I'm afraid, I rather babbled: "I would like the opportunity to take you to dinner. By way of gratitude."

"Mr. Thryke, I hardly feel that would be appropriate."

"Do we always have to do what feels appropriate?" Oh, dear.

Ward Sister Evans looked me square in the eye, and I began to quake. She was more fearsome than any Panzer!

"I have duties to attend to."

I nodded and began my tactical withdrawal. She swept past me with elegant aggression. "Visiting hours recommence between two and four, and then again between six and eight," she added, as a parting shot.

"There you are. Where have you been?" sighed Martha, as she spotted me approaching, via sets of gabbling double doors.

"Sorry, I was just checking visiting times for tomorrow. You must be tired. Come on, let's get you home."

Back in the car, I pulled out the choke and turned the ignition. She juddered into life. Martha sat hunched, crow-like, with her handbag clutched upon her lap. I glanced at her and pulled away. Soon, we were traversing the dusk of the quiet roads, on our way back home. Her home.

"Will you stay?" she asked suddenly, breaking the silence.

"May I?"

"It will have to be the sofa, I'm afraid. It doesn't seem right to give you Mum's room."

"Don't worry. I've slept on worse."

"Yes, I imagine you have. Do you still think about it?"

"About?"

"The war. I didn't mean to belittle it back there. I know what you faced."

People always said that.

"It's alright," I said. "And, yes, not a day goes past when I don't remember. It's the faces, mainly; I remember the faces. It's my way of honouring them. I hope, in a strange way, that they never fade."

We reached a junction. I checked and made my turn.

"There's one face I do remember, though." I left my statement hanging, hoping to draw Martha out, just a little.

"Whose?"

I leant forward and quickly looked at her again.

"What are you doing, Cornelius? Keep your eyes on the road."

"Just checking. It's quite gone now."

"I fear the only thing that is quite gone is you, Corny!"

I laughed, heartily. Martha hesitated, then began to laugh too.

"The face I remember, always, was yours."

"Mine?"

"When we were children. I was never the best brother to you, Martha, and I'm sorry. Do you remember, when we went off trekking – you, Henry and I?"

"Dearest Henry."

For a few moments, we sat in silence, our thoughts bouncing to the dull rumble of the engine.

"Yes, dear Henry," I said. I flipped the indicator stalk and slowed the Anglia for another turn. A car whooshed by and I drove out behind it.

"There was that one trek: we ended up at that beautiful pool. And I, to my shame…"

"Split my head open with a rock."

"I thought it was just a clump of mud."

"Well, that's alright, then: Cornelius thought it was only a clump of mud."

"But the scar has quite gone."

"Yes, that one. But, how many more do I have? Do we both have? Dear Henry." Martha still had a remarkable gift for evoking the maudlin.

A distant doe, its eyes flashing, crashed back into the trees.

"Did you see her?" I asked.

"At least she knows where she's going."

"What does that mean?"

"Well, you got us lost, didn't you? You told Henry that you knew the way back, but you didn't, did you? You had us wandering half the night. And me, with my pinafore dress caked with dried blood – blood that wafted under the noses of hungry woodland predators." Martha's talent for the maudlin was only surpassed by her unmatched, world-beating magnificence in exaggeration. She really, really was… well, you get the idea.

"Hungry woodland predators?"

"Yes! What if I had been carried off by a pack of ravenous foxes?"

We both laughed again.

I reflected. I was not sure if I had ever spent time alone with my sister.

"Then, they would probably have made you their queen."

We drove on, for perhaps a mile. The outliers of the village were approaching: painted farmhouses and outbuildings; all rendered grey.

"He beat me, you know," I said, suddenly.

"Who did?"

"Father. On that day I got us lost. Mother whisked you indoors, and Father took a switch to me."

"I know."

She reached over and placed a hand on my arm. Shortly after, we pulled up outside the cottage.

I woke in the morning, knowing that I was getting too old for sleeping on sofas, but also cognizant of the glorious aroma which was gyrating around the room. I could hear the fizz of the fry, and suddenly I felt famished. I quickly pulled on my shirt and trousers, and padded, in stockinged feet, to the kitchen.

"Oh, you're awake. I'm doing us a breakfast," said Martha. "There may not be time for a proper lunch, as you're taking us to the hospital."

Clearly, I would need to be assertive and set out some ground rules.

"Okay," I said. There would be time aplenty for upsetting her later – after I had eaten. And, perhaps today I could do as she wished – just to show willing.

"Have they caught that train robber yet?"

"Sorry?" Martha was beginning to tong the bacon onto the plates.

"He escaped from prison on Thursday. Went over the wall at Wandsworth, with a couple of others."

"I've been too busy to listen to the wireless."

Mother and Martha, while they had been ensconced in the cottage, had staunchly maintained the same lifestyle they had since Father passed, in 1932; there was no television and no telephone. Not that I craved these things, but the winter nights had to be terribly long.

"Now, sit at the table and have your breakfast."

Mother slept through most of the Saturday afternoon visit. I wandered into one of the men's lounges, to hear that Edrich was doing frightfully well at Headingley. I think he made an unbeaten triple-hundred, while I'd sat at the side of that iron-framed bed, listening to the clack of Martha's needles.

Four o'clock finally came, and we walked out in silence. It had not been a joyous visit, yet I knew Martha would wish to return for the evening.

"Look, Martha, there's scarcely going to be time to drive home and come back. Why don't we see if we can find somewhere to get a bite to eat?"

"We are coming back at six?"

"Yes, we'll get you back for then."

In the end, there was nowhere that was serving food, unless we wanted to sit down in a restaurant, and Martha wasn't keen on that. We just ended up wandering around.

"How about a drink?" I asked hopefully, looking at my wristwatch. "It's nearly five-thirty."

"No."

"Look, Martha, I know you're anxious about Mother, but we haven't eaten since breakfast. More importantly, we've not had much in the way of liquid refreshment."

"We'll have a cup of tea when we get home."

"Martha, I'm not sure how long I can keep coming up and back twice a day. Perhaps if we came for the evening, at least we could have lunch. You might even be able to do some hours at the bakery, and I have work to be—"

"Mother is dying in there!" Her eyes were like daggers. "That might not mean much to you, but it means something to me, despite the mistakes she made."

I looked at my sister. I wasn't shocked at her vitriol against me – that had always been there – but... was there? Was there some of that same judgement directed at our mother? How had she erred in the eyes of my sister, the moral judge and jury of the Thrykes? I decided not to press it further.

"We're none of us perfect."

"We must be getting back, Cornelius. We have a duty."

It was the following evening – the Sunday – and we were travelling back. We both knew by now that Mother would not be coming home – all we could hope for was that her passing was peaceful.

"I want to go earlier tomorrow: first thing," said Martha, perched in the passenger seat, her sharp nails worrying the surface of her bag.

"Eh?"

"I'm going to find bed and breakfast lodgings, near to the hospital. That way, I am close, and you can come and go as you wish."

"Now, look here!" I barked. "Don't think that you have a monopoly on grief! How dare you push me away, your very own brother, after all I've done!"

I glanced at her, as I negotiated the swerving lanes. My remark had struck. Remorse washed over me.

"I'm sorry: I shouldn't have shouted. We're both under strain. Maybe I could take a room, too."

"As you wish. Though, God sees that disgusting display you are making around the ward sister. It reveals the fibre of your character."

Martha was a true champion at inducing righteous shame. Sometimes, I wished to find that she was a little more human – that she were a secret drinker; that she kept multiple men in the wardrobe; even that she cheated to win third in the village jam-making contest would be enough! Lord, make her fallible so that, in her weakness, I might dally with Ward Sister Evans.

"She almost smiled at me today."

"Ward Sister Evans has better things to do than smile at you!"

"Yes, she is doing a wonderful job, making Mother comfortable. They all are."

Martha didn't reply, and we drove the remainder of the journey in a stuttering silence. Mouths opened, mouths closed, but the air remained free from words.

Martha and I both found rooms at The Halcyon Bed and Breakfast, on that Monday morning.

"I often have people staying for the hospital," said the landlady, Mrs. Beaufort, in the hushed, reverential tones of an undertaker. "I can offer an evening meal, for a small, additional charge – all home-cooked. I serve it at four-forty-five sharp, so that it is between the visiting hours."

"That sounds delightful, Mrs. Beaufort. Martha?"

She waved a hand in my direction, as if shooing me away. It appeared that she was scanning the expansive and comfortable lounge for dust and graven images.

"We would be delighted to take you up on the tariff for dinner, bed and breakfast, Mrs. Beaufort. I must say this really is a charming place that you have here."

"Thank you, Mr. Thryke. I do my best. A home from home, that's what I like to provide. You will find everything to be in order here, in your hour of need."

The landlady gazed over to the mantle. I snuck a peek in the direction of her misty eyes. There was a photograph of a man in a frame; he wore an Army uniform.

"And, our rooms?" I asked, interrupting her heart-strung reverie.

"I'll prepare them presently," said Mrs. Beaufort, with a small jolt. "In the meantime, please feel free to relax in the lounge, or come and go as you wish."

"Martha?"

"We shall go for a walk."

"We shall go for a walk, Mrs. Beaufort. Thank you so much for your understanding and hospitality thus far."

"Very good, Mr. Thryke; Miss Thryke." And, with that, she scurried out of the room.

"Seems like a nice lady," I said.

"She keeps a reasonable house," replied Martha, sniffily.

"Yes, and look," I swept my arm back, with the gusto of a stage magician: "a television set – a nice one, too. And a phone in the hall. I really should get the number; we can give it to the hospital. Plus, I really must ring Marjory."

For those who do not know, Marjory had been my agent since the late 'forties – one could say that we were growing old together. In our prime, work had found us both, in a torrent. But, now I was older (I had turned fifty in 1965), the roles were becoming lesser; I could no longer portray the dashing leading man. Marjory had sent me for new headshots, back in the winter, and described my face as "interesting". The film industry was still booming, and I still spent a good deal of time at the studios, but now my costumes were that of the butcher, baker and candlestick-maker; they were hardly commensurate with my standing.

"I want some leading roles, Marjory. Can't you get me up for anything bigger?"

"I shall try, dearie, but the priority is to keep you working; keep your face up there. It's easier to find the roles if people sort of know who you are, than if they don't at all."

"I understand that, Marjory, but I am an experienced actor. I should be turning offers down, not scrabbling around to find them."

"What about more theatre? You like theatre."

"Well, yes I do – helping to bring the young ones through. But, I'm a film actor; that's what I'm primarily famous for."

"I'll try and get you some more theatre, then."

Sometimes I felt that Marjory didn't listen to me. It has been a constant source of friction and, dare I say it, a missed opportunity. She is not a great agent, but she is my agent. Our conversations and meetings always went this way.

"What about television, dearie?" she would suggest. "There are some quite big opportunities in television."

"Marjory," I would say, with a mix of exasperation and resignation, "just see what you can get."

So, on that Monday, in July of 1965, I attended afternoon visiting hours with Martha. Mother was drifting in and out of sleep, and was rambling with increasingly rare moments of clarity. After a while, I had wandered off again, into the television lounge.

"Ah, here you are, Mr. Thryke. You realize this facility is meant to be for patients?"

I turned around. Ward Sister Evans was looking at me. Only, it wasn't Ward Sister Evans; this one was smiling. "How are you faring?" she asked.

"Slightly better than the Kiwis," I said, pointing to the screen: "they're taking a frightful pasting. The commentators are so convinced of the outcome that they have resorted to extolling the virtues of chocolate cake."

"I don't really follow cricket. And, I seldom watch television – excepting last night: the Sunday film."

"Oh, really? What old thing did they drag out last night?"

"It was called *The Butterfly Gang*."

I turned away from the television and smiled – gently and handsomely, I hoped. "Well that's not all that old, and it is a great film."

"Well, you would say that: you were in it! I knew I had seen you somewhere before. I thought you were one of those people who just have a strangely familiar face; I didn't realize that you had been in films."

"Well, I could tell you all about it, but I guess you're busy now." *Try again, Thryke!* "But, how about over dinner? What time do you finish this week?"

Sister Evans was still smiling. Could it be?

"I am finishing at six o'clock this week." I could see the wheels were still turning; there was pondering taking place. If my devilish charm and fame were not doing it, perhaps convenience would.

"Well, how about tomorrow, maybe at eight? It would be my way of thanking you for your hard work, plus it would mean you wouldn't have to worry about finding yourself something to eat; you could just relax and unwind. Do you know anywhere nearby that is good?"

"Mr. Thryke, were you not an actor, I would imagine you would have made a fine travelling salesman."

She was yet to turn me down flat. I reached into my pocket and withdrew a small card.

"Oh, I meant to give you this: it's the number of the establishment where we have taken temporary lodgings. Leave a message when you decide where we're going."

And, I strolled out, back to the ward, with a bounce in my step.

"Where have you been," demanded Martha, "looking like the cat that got the cream? Don't you realize that your mother has been asking for you?"

I curled my fingers around the frame at the foot of the iron bed. The clipboard rocked forward, and I immediately felt like the worst man in the world.

When I told Martha that I would not be accompanying her to the hospital, on Tuesday evening, I felt even worse and, to be fair, I deserved every twist, squeeze and stab of that feeling.

"I don't think I'm going to come tonight," I said, exhaling laboriously. I dropped my spoon into the empty pudding basin and patted my stomach, contentedly.

"Why not?" asked Martha, a look of anguish crossing her face.

"I'm feeling rather tired, I'm afraid."

Martha tutted. "I'm not surprised: you've just polished off a double helping of toad-in-the-hole and treacle pudding and custard."

Martha was right. Mrs. Beaufort did have a proclivity for ensuring that none of her guests went hungry; breakfast alone had forced me to consume more sausages than we used to get in a week. I have always had a weakness for a good, home-cooked meal – I imagine it is because I have had so few in my life. But, no cooking ever matched that of your... mother.

"I would hate to appear rude; Mrs. Beaufort has toiled away at this for hours."

"Stop being silly, Cornelius. Go and have a wash, and I will meet you down here, as usual. The walk to the hospital will do you good: help you work off some of that gluttony."

Martha was right, particularly as I had cornered myself into the need to eat again, that night. I was heading for trouble on all fronts. Perhaps I should let down Nurse Evans; leave her standing? Pretend that there was a medical emergency? No, wait – that wouldn't work.

I could always tell Martha the truth: *Martha, I am taking Ward Sister Evans out for dinner.*

"Martha," I started. She glared at me. "I just can't tonight. I'm finding the whole thing so terribly distressing; it's bringing on one of my heads."

I didn't know what "one of my heads" was, but it sounded like the kind of thing that Martha would understand.

"One of your heads?"

"Please, Martha, just let me have this evening to myself. I promise I shall come twice tomorrow."

So, now I was bargaining? But, there was no bargain to be had – just living with my own conscience and the eternal judgment of a disgruntled sibling.

"I doubt there are many visits left, Cornelius, yet you would throw one away, because you feel bilious from over-consumption! You are and have always been a deeply selfish man, Cornelius Thryke. But, as you wish."

She threw her napkin down onto the tablecloth – rage encapsulated in the never-sound – stood and began to walk out of the dining room.

"I just hope you can live with yourself. I shall say no more." The door closed behind her.

I sat and reflected; I saw Mother in her hospital bed. Martha was right: I was selfish. I was, unquestionably now, the worst man in the world.

The door opened again.

"Martha, I—"

"It's only me, dear: Mrs. Beaufort. Did you enjoy your meal?"

"Oh, it was quite wonderful, Mrs. Beaufort – quite, quite wonderful. My compliments to the chef."

"Thank you, Mr. Thryke. Oh, and I do so like to see clean plates."

It was multiple clean plates, in my case.

"The proof of the pudding, and all that."

I really shouldn't have said "pudding": I blew out. I noticed that I was beginning to break out in a light sweat: the brain had obviously released the memo that the stomach was expected to eat again.

"Has your sister gone already?"

"Yes, gone to freshen up before her hospital visit."

Mrs. Beaufort, with an eye for detail, compounded my sense of grief. "Are you not going this evening, Mr. Thryke?"

I smiled and beckoned her in, conspiratorially. "I'm afraid I have other pressing business to attend to this evening. But, where Miss Thryke is concerned, I am sure I can count on your discretion?"

Twenty-five years in the acting business had taught me that doctors, priests and landladies were all bound by the seal of the confessional. But, if a look of disgust can be fleeting, I think that Mrs. Beaufort had perfected it.

"I'm sure I don't know what you mean, Mr. Thryke," she snapped. "Now, I must see to this dirty crockery."

She couldn't have known but, in my turmoil, I felt that there was an unnecessary emphasis on the word "dirty". Perhaps, if I was the cad that everyone assumed I was, I had better go out and prove it!

Martha left at 1745 hours precisely. From behind my third-floor net, I watched her stride away, indignation in every step.

I crossed to the sink and looked at myself in the mirror. My face had become looser, of late, my cheeks were like wattles and my ears were fair hairier than they had ever been. I began to fear that Ward Sister Evans was more interested in dynamic Cornelius Thryke (1948), rather than this, the comfortable Thryke of 1965. I pulled in my stomach and smoothed my hands across my hair.

"You'll have to make it up to her. You'll have to make it up to them both."

Mirror-Thryke gazed back, knowing I was right, but still living under the delusion that this nurse might actually be attracted to him.

"Luciana!"

As I dressed, I figured I could see Luciana Fortescue-Ripley-Jones, lounging on the candlewick. I was shocked into silence. I had no idea from where that notion had sprung.

"You don't think she likes you, do you?" she said, with a derisive snort.

I didn't dignify the apparition with a response.

"I mean, she's an attractive woman, and you've hardly got a glittering track record there, have you?"

I applied the polish to my shoe. I still carried out this procedure with the precision that my first corporal had shown me.

"He has a track record in sin!" – Father, now sitting beside her.

"Now, this doesn't work," I protested: "it's not like both of you are even dead. One or the other – that I can understand – but not both!"

Luciana placed a hand on Father's knee. "Never underestimate the power of a guilty conscience. Eh, Reverend Thryke?"

"The power of the devil is within him!"

"No, it is the scent of a woman, and that is far, far worse."

I arrived outside the hospital at 1945. I had taken a somewhat circumventive route.

Martha had indeed been proven correct: a pleasant walk was all I needed to shift some of the delightful stodge that I had onboarded earlier. At least, that is what I hoped.

But now, there was another problem – I kicked myself that I had not foreseen it. I had arranged to meet Ward Sister Evans at eight o'clock.

Visiting finished at eight o'clock.

Yes, you have seen it. There was potentially a window of disaster.

If Sister Evans was a little late, as women could often be, there was the danger that Martha would leave and see me waiting or, even worse, see me greeting Sister Evans, and whisking her off for dinner. On top of this came the crashing realization that it had all been so avoidable. I could simply have come on the visit with Martha and made sure I left just before eight; I could have been honest about the whole thing.

I slunk back into some bushes, near to the hospital entrance. At least camouflage would offer me some sense of protection and wellbeing.

"What are you doing in there?"

I sprang back to the present. Some highly-trained individual had skilfully seen through my disguise.

"Ward Sister Evans, how delightful to see you. I swear, I wasn't hiding."

She laughed. I must have looked ridiculous. "Well, come on out. And, you can't keep calling me Ward Sister Evans all evening, can you?"

I stepped out of the shrubbery and brushed myself down. "I don't know; it rather suits you."

"Well, it's my work name. You wouldn't want me to call you by whatever character you are playing now?"

Currently, that would be nobody. "I guess not." I gallantly offered her my hand: "Good evening. I am Cornelius."

"Beverley," she shook my hand, demurely. There was none of the well-meaning aggression with which she delivered her duties. And, her hands were remarkably smooth.

"Cornelius? Cornelius?"

"I'm sorry, Beverley, I'm afraid I drifted off for a moment there. How may I be of service?"

She squinted at me, in the slowly fading light.

"I know you had your heart set on going for dinner, but would you mind if we just went for a drink, instead? I'm not feeling terribly hungry."

My heart went into raptures of celebration. My brain, however...

"Oh, I had been looking forward to some dinner. But, if you don't want to eat, that's fine by me; it will just be nice to spend some time with Beverley."

"Oh, I feel rotten now."

"Don't, please, it's fine. This is my way of saying thank you to you, so it should be via with what you feel most comfortable. A drink it is. Perhaps you could lead the way?"

Beverley began to drift slowly from the hospital entrance. I glanced at my watch, placing a hand lightly on her back, to guide her along, but it was too late: in a gaggle of the righteous, Martha was just exiting the hospital doors.

"Isn't that your sister?" asked Beverley.

"Yes."

"Why is she glaring like that? She doesn't look happy."

"Oh, she must be thinking about something. That's the look she gets when she is lost in thought."

"Really? I'd hate to see her when she was really upset, then."

To me, Martha seemed to slightly hover and glide across the ground, spitting fire like some hybrid of a corvus chimera, adept at knitting and crafts. Martha floated alongside us, and I prepared for the flaming broadside.

"Ward Sister Evans," said Martha, tersely, with a nod. "Quite recovered I see, Cornelius."

I smiled, weakly. "We're just going for a quick drink, as a way of thanking Beverley," I said. "Perhaps you would like to come with us?"

It was not a proud moment, but it was all I could think of. Judging from her eyes, if Martha could have incinerated me on the spot, I believe that she certainly would have.

"Disgusting," she spat. "You are a beastly man."

She then turned to Nurse Evans and said, politely: "Shall we be seeing you on the ward tomorrow afternoon? I imagine you will have to be up early for your shift?"

Beverley just smiled and gave an almost imperceptible nod. Then, with a flap of her wings, Martha disappeared into the night.

"Would you care to explain?" said Beverley, turning to me.

"Not without a drink."

We found a table in a quiet public house, and when I returned with the drinks, Beverley was still looking quizzical.

"So, what was eating your sister?"

"We just have a different view on life. She is very devout and has a definite picture of things; I go more with the rhythm of life. It annoys her."

"And, what specifically annoyed her today?"

I exhaled, heavily. It was time, at last, to be honest.

"I didn't go to visiting this evening. I made some excuse, so that I could come out with you. Does that make me a terrible person?"

She sipped her port and lemon, and weighed up the situation. "You went this afternoon?"

"Well, yes."

"Then, relax; you're doing your bit. You'd be surprised how many poor souls lie there for weeks, without a single visitor. In the end, they just give up."

I thought of Mother, now lying alone.

"Though, I imagine your sister is more upset that you felt the need to lie to her. All so that you could meet me." Beverley picked up her glass to hide her mouth, but I could see that her eyes were smiling. "Don't you get on?" she asked.

"I try," I answered, "but not as much as we might. Our father didn't like us, and Martha felt that she should take his place." I puzzled for a moment. Why was I telling a complete stranger all of this?

Beverley lit up a cigarette. "Sounds a bit like my family." Seeing what must have been my look of mild surprise, she held up the smouldering item: "Oh, this? I only smoke occasionally, when I have a drink. Do you mind?"

"Not at all."

"So, I guess you're going to be getting it in the neck tomorrow, then?"

We chinked glasses, and I nodded at the inevitability of it all.

"You said 'us', back then?"

"Sorry?"

"'Us'," replied Beverley; "you said your father didn't like *us*."

"Ah, yes: Henry."

"Henry?"

Beverley was a good bit younger than me, and a great deal more attractive; if our evening were to be likened to a sporting event, onlookers would consider that I was playing considerably out of my league. Would it be wrong to stack the deck with a little sympathy? Was this who I was?

"He was our older brother. He was killed during the war."

"Oh, I'm sorry."

"No, no, it's okay: you weren't to know." *A little more?* "I... I... No, it's silly."

She reached across and placed her hand on mine. "No, go on, really."

"Well, I always thought they blamed me – Mother and Martha. You see, Henry was in a reserved occupation, but a sense of duty made him follow me into the Army; he wanted to do his bit." *And, bring it back around to me.* "We both did."

"Yes," she smiled, "I imagine you looked rather dashing in your uniform."

"Could we talk about something else? You don't want to go over all of my woes. Tell me, how long have you been in nursing?"

"The best part of twenty years. It's all I've ever done."

"Twenty years? You must have started when you were ten!"

She looked at me, as she scrunched up her nose.

"Don't with the mindless flattery; you don't seem the type. I'm always hearing it," she said, gently, with genuine fatigue in her voice. "That's the only reason why I agreed to come out with you tonight: you seem a bit different."

"Do you get a lot of male attention?"

"Well, either they're *eurgh*, or they stare from miles away, and dash off whenever the frightening ward sister comes near. Then, along comes a film actor. Not one whose name I could remember, but one whose face I knew that I knew, you know?"

"Ah, so it was *The Butterfly Gang* that did it! I always have fond memories of that film. I could always play off the swarthy villain, but I much preferred to be the suave, cool officer."

Beverley was now leaning in, her chin resting in her palms, elbows on the table, the light catching her captivating citrine eyes. "I bet you have got some stories," she said.

"Oh, I don't know."

"Go on, tell me one. I shall be the soul of discretion."

I pondered for a while. I was hardly the raconteur, with heaps of exciting tales and titbits. There were some actors that I knew, who were always in the right place to deliver a cutting epigram or *bon mot*. Not me; I was usually queuing for tea.

"Well, there may be one, but you absolutely cannot share it."

Bringing Beverley into a confidence was another caddish action, I am afraid. On that particular evening, my intentions were entirely dishonourable.

"Oh, I shan't! Brownie's honour!"

"Were you even a brownie?"

"Of course! Guide's honour!"

I let out a low hum of doubt and considered my next steps.

"Please," she said. "You can trust me! Share whatever juicy morsel you have hidden, you dark horse."

I drummed the table dramatically, with the fingers on my right hand, while my left slowly raised the glass to my lips.

"It's probably not even that interesting; only to me does it have any pep."

"Try me."

"Well, I suppose it does involve a tremendously famous movie star." I was in danger of over-egging the pudding; Beverley might slip the hook at any time. "I..." I began, grandly, "once asked Lucy Ripley to marry me."

I felt awful as soon as I had said it, as if it were a great betrayal.

"Lucy Ripley? No way!"

"A world-renowned actress – yes. A great beauty – yes," I continued. "I swear, it's true. It was just after the war; we were both just starting out."

"Well, what did she say? How did it happen?"

I gazed at Beverley, from beneath arched eyebrows. "She didn't say anything; she just walked off. There had been a lot of alcohol consumed, I am afraid. But, I shall never forget that night... how she looked, under the glow of the midnight moon."

"Sounds like you still care."

"Of course! I care about everyone. Not too dissimilar to you. Would you like another?"

"Are you trying to get me drunk?" asked Beverley.

"Do I need to?"

"Yes. I'll take another."

I got back to the bed-and-breakfast just before six the following morning. I clearly remember looking at the door, wondering how I was going to affect entry, when it opened. Mrs. Beaufort was standing there, in a checked pinny.

"Good morning, Mrs. Beaufort. A lovely morning."

"Looks set fair for sunshine, Mr. Thryke."

"I... I like to get out early sometimes – have a brisk walk, you know."

"Of course, Mr. Thryke."

"I'll just..." I shimmied past, avoiding the swirling gulf of my rapidly diminishing standing, "...a bracing wash before breakfast, I think."

When I eventually entered the dining room, a few of the other guests were already there, which was a blessing, as they could shield me from another of their number: Martha. I decided that bright and breezy was the order of the day.

"Morning, everyone."

A stationary salesman (who was not) and a couple down from Huddersfield both nodded. I joined Martha at the small table, where she was sitting.

"Good morning, Sister. Did you sleep well?"

"I did not. Could you?"

"I had a satisfactory night. May I?"

I took a piece of toast from the rack and began to spread it with butter. "Shall I pour the tea?"

"As you wish."

It was going to be a long day – though, the highlight would

undoubtedly be going to the hospital that afternoon: Beverley would be there.

"Yes, a nice cup of tea – that's what is called for."

After breakfast, I went for a walk. The birds seemed to be singing a little bit louder that morning. I sought out a florist. But, how many bunches? One, two or three?

In the end, the cost settled the issue and I purchase two bunches. Do not ask me what they were – flowers are flowers to me – but they had a pleasant aroma and made my nose tickle.

"Here," I said to Martha, as we were walking to the hospital. "Could you take these? They're for Mother."

Martha accepted the flowers, smelt them and seemed to unwind a shade.

"And, who are those for?" she asked.

"Sister Evans."

Martha considered for a moment. "You like her, don't you?" Her words softened her further.

"Yes." We walked a few steps farther. "I didn't mean for it to happen, you know. Look at me; it's so silly at our age."

"I don't think so."

Then, I remembered: Martha was human, too. "Do you miss your chap?" I asked.

"Barry? Sometimes. It's more for companionship, really. Though, I've spent more and more time looking after Mum, recently."

"Well, perhaps you'll be able…" I stopped. "I'm so sorry."

"There's no need to apologize, Cornelius; we both know how this ends. I'm just glad you'll be here."

Martha took my hand and squeezed it. We carried on, perhaps for another fifty yards, before the embarrassment of closeness got too much.

"Unless I'm out with another fancy woman," I added.

"Cornelius Thryke, I doubt there is a town in this whole realm which has two women who would go out with you."

The walk from reception to the ward was a long one, which went past various departments and their maelstrom of staff. Porters pushed, cleaners cleaned, nurses nursed and doctors docked; the pace was swift, but not frenetic. I had played a few doctors over the years; I had the gravitas of a senior consultant by then. I observed them as they went by, coated in surety and white. It was with the quiet confidence of a doctor that I would present the flowers to Ward Sister Evans.

Martha and I exchanged a glance as we approached the stiff double doors of Bluebird Ward. I had that feeling, rising from the pit of my stomach to the back of my throat, toppling, turning and twisting. I injected a little hop into my last few steps and pushed back a door for my sister. She smiled and passed by, and I followed, my heart palpitating and leaping. I approached the desk.

But, something was wrong. That was not Beverley. Not unless her hair had become three shades lighter since yesterday.

I cleared my throat, and the nurse looked up. Martha came and stood at my side.

"I was looking for Ward Sister Evans."

"I am Ward Sister Moltenbough. Can I help you?"

"No, Ward-Sister…?"

"Moltenbough."

"Yes, quite. I was specifically looking for Ward Sister Evans. I wanted her to have these." I presented the flowers and placed a hand on Martha's shoulder-blade. "As a thank you, you see – for looking after our mother, Mrs. Thryke."

"Mrs. Thryke?"

"Yes, I am Cornelius; this is Martha. Mrs. Vera Thryke is our mother."

The new ward sister stood up and walked around the desk.

"If you go and wait with your mother, I shall ask Doctor to see you presently. I shall take those, Mr. Thryke. Unfortunately, the staff here should not accept gifts of this nature. If it is alright with you, I shall give these to a patient who has not been fortunate enough to receive any flowers."

"And, Ward Sister Evans?"

"Moved to another ward. I am sorry, I must be getting on. Now, if you would attend Mrs. Thryke, I shall ensure Doctor comes by as soon as he can."

She swept past, leaving Martha and I standing in a state of confusion.

"A doctor, Cornelius?"

"Quite."

When we got to the bed, a grey Mother was not moving. Her

lidded eyes had sunk back into wide sockets, which were encircled with black. Her breathing was laboured; each lungful was fought for, gasped in and expelled with a whistling sigh. Her arms lay on top of her bedclothes, ram-rod straight, but fragile, like twigs. She was the perforated skeleton of a bird. Martha and I approached, one on each side. We both took a hand and a seat, and waited.

I don't know how long we both sat, our heads bowed in silent contemplation, but it was too long. Was the end approaching? Was she in any pain? Had Beverley moved ward deliberately? Did she ever really like me? Did I want to go back to work?

"Mr. and Mrs. Thryke?"

Martha jolted and I stood up.

"I am Cornelius Thryke. This is my sister, Martha."

"Ah, very good. I am Doctor Rajiv Chatterjee. I am the consultant looking after your mother's case."

"And how is she, Doctor?"

"Well, as you can see, she is currently heavily sedated. She was very restless this morning and finding it difficult to settle."

"But, how is she?" I asked again.

"Mr. Thryke; Mrs....?"

"Thryke," replied Martha; "I am Miss Martha Thryke."

"And, Henry? She was calling for him, this morning."

"Henry is our older brother," said Martha. "But, unfortunately he was killed, during the war."

"I see. And, Bartie? She seemed most agitated when she mentioned that name."

Martha turned to me. "It's Father!" she said. "She can see them. Father and Henry are close; they are waiting for her."

"Doctor…?" I asked.

"Such episodes are common, considering the drugs that we are administering to your mother. But, I must advise, your mother is gravely ill now. I am afraid to say that your mother's organs are beginning to close down; she is preparing for the end."

Martha threw her head forward and began to wail over the bed.

"How long, Doctor?"

He shook his head, sadly; "That, I cannot foretell. It could be hours or it could be days. Your mother, as you know, is a very strong woman, Mr. Thryke."

"But, she isn't suffering?"

"We are making her as comfortable as we can."

"Thank you, Doctor."

"Speaking of which, I have taken the liberty of making a few enquiries. This hospital is lucky enough to have some private rooms – one is to become available tomorrow. I have arranged for your mother to move there, if that is agreeable to you?"

I shook him warmly by the hand. I had only spent a few minutes in the presence of this gentle doctor, but I knew I would always remember him. "Thank you, Doctor. Thank you for everything."

On Friday morning, I awoke in the comfy chair which had been thoughtfully placed in Mum's room. My whole body ached and I felt like I had not slept for a week. I looked over to Martha. She had her hands clasped, as if in prayer, her head bowed over the shape in the bed.

"Any change?"

"Her breathing is becoming shallower. The nurse gave her something an hour or so ago. You were asleep."

"I'm sorry. I dropped off."

"You must have been tired."

"Why don't you try and have a little nap? I promise, I'll wake you if anything happens."

"I couldn't."

"You must, Martha. Please, come and sit here."

We swapped seats. My sister had aged terribly in that week. She shuffled over and we hugged at the midpoint – it was a moment I often think of.

If Martha slept at all, it was not for long. About an hour later, the hospital chaplain came by, to offer us comfort. My sister, sensing a spiritual presence, leapt to her feet – curiously, it was only afterward that she opened her eyes.

"She is getting ready," he said, quietly.

We all stood at the foot of the bed. A serenity had fallen over our mother. Martha reached for my hand and we beheld her, as children once more.

The unmistakable rattle of release came at just after ten a.m.

It might only be an embellishment of memory, but rays of sunshine beamed in and illuminated her as she went. If Father died in the darkness, Mother passed in the light. And, she went as she had lived: a woman of virtue and without sin. It was a beautiful passing. I hope that I am to be granted similar peace.

EDITOR'S NARRATIVE
Quentin Prowler

The death of Cornelius Arthur Thryke, back in 1977, came as a shock to many. It is covered in some detail in the book *Gone to the Dogs*, which was compiled from a series of interviews carried out by the late Eric Whisky and his nephew, Gavin. It is described in heart-breaking detail by Kenneth Burlington, a fellow actor in the much-loved sit-com. I will not cover the circumstances of his passing here, needless to say. Cornelius was only sixty-two years old.

Martha Thryke lived on to the ripe old age of one-hundred and one. She died in a nursing home, in Wimborne Minster, in 2015.

But, we have one more twist in our tale.

In the August of 2018, I received the following letter. I shall present it here, in full, very much as I received it:

Dear Mr. Prowler,

I was only a little girl – perhaps eight or nine – when I first became aware of the actor, Cornelius Thryke. Mother and I would sit on the sofa and watch Gone to the Dogs *every week – it was my favourite show. If you do not remember it, it was set in a greyhound stadium and, each week, the staff would get up to a new set of hilarious shenanigans. Cornelius was my favourite actor. He played the stadium manager, Arthur*

Chataway. He used to come across as pompous and bad-tempered, but I thought there must be a seam of warmth in there somewhere. The other girls in my class would mock me: they were all in love with Kenneth Burlington – at least, until the morning break the following day, then it was back to dreaming about Les McKeown and the Bay City Rollers. Don't get me wrong, I loved the B.C.R.s, but I was more into Eric Faulkner. I just wanted people to know that Arthur Chataway could be nice. At least, that was my theory.

When Cornelius Thryke died, in 1977, I remember seeing it on the news and feeling quite sad for a while. I remember Mum looking at me strangely, as if she didn't understand what was going on. I had always been searching for the paternal influence of a man in my life. I had never known my father, you see. Mum was still very coy about him and, while the gaps between me asking her grew longer, he was always there, at the back of my mind. I guess that is why I was drawn to the strong character portrayed by Cornelius Thryke in Gone to the Dogs.

My mother died in 2010. In her final weeks, she finally told me the information that I had desired for all those years. Her name was Beverley Evans. Mr. Prowler, I must ask, do you have any inkling of who she was? Have you come across her name in your papers? You see, as I am sure you have guessed by now, my birth name was Wendy Evans. I am Cornelius Thryke's daughter.

While, sub-consciously, I suspected that my father had died (my mother was eighty-three, and would only say that he was a deal older), when Mum told me who he was, I grieved all over again. It was worse knowing that I had seen him – had watched him through the screen – and been naturally drawn to him. Mum's reaction to the whole affair made a lot more sense then.

Did I, deep down, really know? If I had walked past him in the street, would I have stopped and felt his presence? I thought about it so much, I really did. I can only conclude that it was something from my mother that transferred to me: when she watched Gone to the Dogs, *maybe her heart reached out to someone that I hope she once loved – if only for a little while. Father was just a face on a screen, and one who faded after his death. I bought all the videos and watched them until the tape grew snowy and thin. Then, I replaced them with D.V.D.s. – my husband, Trevor, bought them for my birthday, and I wept as I unwrapped them.*

It was then that we started the detective work. We bought a membership to one of those genealogy sites. It felt strange digging into the past of this family but, as my husband pointed out, it was my family. We started with Dad, then worked back to Bartie Thryke and Vera Summers. It was surreal, but there I was, looking at the names of my grandparents. From there, it was easy to find Martha and Henry, my aunt and uncle. I also found out that I had lost my uncle during the war. It wasn't hard to determine that Cornelius – Dad – had a sister, Martha.

For a long time, Martha intrigued Trevor and I. We struggled to find any marriage records, or any record of her death. I was hoping that she may have had children, and that there were some cousins somewhere, but the trail went cold. We thought that we had found some extended family in Wiltshire, and we swapped emails for a time, but they turned out not to be related. Bless them, though: they still send me a Christmas card.

Then, one evening, it was weird. Trevor and I were sitting at the computer, shooting zombies, when an idea occurred to us both, almost simultaneously. What is the most obvious reason that we could not find marriage records for Martha? Yes, because she never wed. And, why could we not find any death certificate? Because she was still alive! It went through me like a bolt of lightning. Everything started to come together, then unravelling again from there.

We tracked Martha down to a nursing home, near Bournemouth. We spent a few months getting the necessary permissions and arranging a trip to go and see her – I am ashamed to say that I was like a cat on a hot tin roof during this time; Martha was approaching her one-hundredth birthday and, having only just discovered her, I did not want to lose my paternal aunt to the inevitable progression of time. As it was, Trevor and I ended up driving down on Saturday 26th October 2013, two days before Martha Thryke's centenary. The nursing home welcomed us with open arms, as they were afraid that there would be no family present to celebrate such a milestone. So, despite the fact that we were two days early, the home put on a little party, in honour of their oldest guest.

We found Martha to be fully in command of her faculties, and most indignant about the whole thing.

"It is not my birthday until Monday! Why am I having a cake now? Do you see a telegram up on the shelf, you foolish girl? Take that cake away! And, who are these people? Why is she smiling at me?"

"This is Wendy, the lady we told you about. She believes that she is your niece?"

"Niece?" Martha shot her eyes over to me and looked me up and down. "You say that you are Cornelius's daughter?"

"Yes, Miss Thryke."

"Hmm, I see no resemblance. He had no money, you know."

Yes, I found her rude and unnecessarily cruel, and I had no idea why she would be. But, I had to know. I had to go further.

"I am not interested in money, Miss Thryke," I pleaded.

Her eyes scratched over me again.

"Evidently, my dear. Svetlana! Svetlana! Take me back to my room please."

A nurse began to wheel Miss Thryke away. I looked over at the matron, who shrugged as if to say we'd tried, at least. As Martha's chair reached the doorway, she raised a hand to halt.

"You, niece, you stand there just as your father would have done: useless! I suggest that if you want to know a little more, then you had better accompany me to my room. Your husband can wait here and amuse himself with my premature cake."

I looked at Trevor and he looked at me. He was boiling with rage. He had never heard me spoken to in such a surly manner, but we both knew what I had to do.

"Go," he said.

We arrived at Martha's room. It was immaculate.

"Sit there, child." She indicated a small, winged chair, its extremities draped with antimacassars. I sat.

"So, you claim to be the daughter of Cornelius. But then,

who would claim to be that who was not?" she cackled to herself.

She was only a little old lady, but I was terrified. Who knew what demons she could summon up, with but a click of her gnarled fingers?

"My mother was Beverley Evans, Miss Thryke. Perhaps you know her?"

"I do not." The response snapped out and was unreflective.

"She was a nurse. She would have been working at Thelmesbury General Hospital, around the time that she met my... your brother."

Something in my statement wounded her. The malevolence dropped away from her voice.

"Thelmesbury?"

"Yes."

"Our beloved mother died in Thelmesbury, in July of 1965."

"I was born in April of 1966." I began to count the months on my fingers. Could it be? But, Miss Thryke did not hear my reply.

"There was a nurse – I remember. Cornelius took her out. But, she disappeared. Cornelius was crushed – I liked that."

"Ward Sister Beverley Evans?"

Martha looked at me again.

"Come closer, child. Closer."

A cold hand clamped around my chin.

"Yes... yes, maybe," she said. "But, what use?" She pushed me away, scratching my cheek. "All the faces have faded now; they are all but formless spirits."

A shiver went up my spine.

"Then, your brother is my father. You are my aunt."

Martha let out a burst of vile, witch-like laughter, which chilled me to the bone – as if she saw one last chance to snare me.

"Cornelius may well be your father, but I shall never call you niece!"

"I don't understand."

"A bastard daughter of a bastard son!"

"Now, just you wait!"

"No!" There was a finality in her tone which stopped me in my tracks. "You just wait!" She turned her back to me and made good to deliver the blow.

"Cornelius Thryke was not my brother – not full, anyway. Nor was that illiterate, Henry. They were the sinful offspring of Biggleswade Smart, the wandering priest with the wandering eye. They were not pure Thryke – not like I. They were bastards, and so are you!"

I felt violence rise within me, whoever that "me" even was. My fists clenched. I swear I would have launched myself upon her, had the door not opened.

"Is everything alright in here?" It was Svetlana. "I heard voices raised."

"All is well," said Martha, dismissively. "Whoever this is was just leaving."

I got up. My whole body was shaking. Martha turned back to watch me go, never taking her eyes from mine, as if weighing me up, like some terrible Egyptian God.

"One last thing."

I stopped. Tears were streaming down my face, I was so enraged.

"What?"

"His papers and all of his effects are held at the Little Sodbury Museum. They were keen that I went and got them for many years. But, they are your problem now. Good day."

The door closed behind me. I never went back.

So, now you know the reason for my letter: I am the daughter of Cornelius Arthur Thryke, film and television star. I would be so grateful if you would permit me to spend some time in your archives, so that I might get to know my father a little better, and perhaps to see if there is anything of my mother there.

It has taken me a long time to write this letter, but I am ready to take up the journey once more.

Yours most sincerely,

Wendy Francis (Mrs.)

When I read this letter, I sat in the archive and I wept.

AFTERWORD
Quentin Prowler

When I began to travel in the shadow of Cornelius Thryke, I started as the arbitrary keeper of a collection of boxes. Little did I know that I would follow him through school, into the Army, into film, television and out the other side. The vaguely-recalled face from *Gone to the Dogs* became a man. What is more, he became a man that I respected and liked.

It is that fondness and respect which shattered me, when I read Wendy's letter. For now, I saw Thryke's life for what it was: an odyssey of tragedy.

He never understood why Bartholomew Thryke mistreated him so. I now understand why. He was a boy searching, like Telemachus, for the love of an absent father. Fate cast this burden upon him; he did not ask for it.

Yet, as we read the pages, certainly of his boyhood diaries, his father, Biggleswade Smart, appears larger than life. A willow wielding hero, strong and tall; a true man of the country. The eternal wanderings of Biggleswade Smart now have a much, much more tragic intent.

I urge you, please, go back and re-read the passage about the fishing trip, once more. It is all there, so poorly hidden in plain sight, that it is a wonder Cornelius and Henry did not trip over it and fall headlong into the river.

Perhaps we must even re-appraise the Reverend Bartholomew Augustus Thryke. Is he a hero, or a villain? He kept his sons with disdain, but keep them he did. In the 1910s, such a scandal would have been immensely destructive. Reverend Thryke kept Vera and her two boys from the jaws of such shame, in exchange for the profoundly symbiotic relationship with Martha. How long Martha knew, we can only speculate. Perhaps she always did.

The tragedy of not knowing his father was doubly compounded by Cornelius not knowing that he had a wonderful daughter.

Wendy and Trevor have been my guests at the Little Sodbury archives on many occasions since, and our afternoons together always end in the same way: with floods of tears. Wendy has got to know the father that she never met – perhaps to love him a little, too. I have had the privilege to watch that relationship grow. I think he would have been an extraordinary father, had he the chance, like he was a special soldier, actor and, to me, a friend.

I am happy to share that both Wendy and Trevor have had the chance to read these pages and to recommend small changes, here and there. In a sense, this book is my reply to the beautiful and deeply emotional letter that Wendy wrote, back in the late-summer of 2018. I never met the father but, through his daughter, I feel closer to the man.

It is perhaps not the book that I originally envisaged, but then Cornelius Arthur Thryke was not the man that I initially imagined.

He grew out of his own story, in his own words. It was a tale that was funny, exhilarating and sometimes moving. But, hey, that's life, is it not?

I shall leave you with a quotation from the gentleman himself. It is taken from the last known interview given by Cornelius Thryke, "The Man that Nobody Knew":

"Life has this property – and, it happens so rarely – when it offers you the opportunity to move along a path. In my extended years, I have learnt that it often takes tremendous courage to grasp these chances. So often, in this course of my life, I have recognized these moments only after it was too late, and have wallowed in the indignity of regret – just for a while, you understand."

Cornelius Thryke,
p.388; *Gone to the Dogs: The Story of Britain's 14th Most Successful Sit-Com.* Simon Gary, 2019.

I am still available to curate this story on television.

Quentin Prowler, 2020.

FILMOGRAPHY OF CORNELIUS THRYKE

A Vale of Villains (1946) – *uncredited*

Little Tim (1946) – *uncredited*

A Lord is Murdered (1946) – *uncredited*

The Butterfly Gang (1948)

Major Orpington Goes to Court-Martial (1949)

Farewell to Thrasher (1949)

The Gentleman Burglars (1950)

Operation Sea Dog (1951)

The Gentleman Burglars Strike Again (1952)

Six Feet Under (1954)

Gone Thrice Before Sunset (1957)

M is for Microfilm (1960)

Television:

Gone to the Dogs: Series 1-5 & Christmas Specials (1973–1977)

ALSO BY SIMON GARY:

If you have enjoyed this book, then reunite with Cornelius Thryke as he plays Arthur Chataway, in the hilarious fictional 1970s sit-com *Gone to the Dogs*.

Gone to the Dogs: The Story of Britain's 14th Most Successful Sit-Com will draw you into the lives of the cast and writers of this wildly funny and bawdy television programme. Cornelius is joined by such acting luminaries as the "cheeky chappy" himself, Kenneth Burlington; Hollywood-bound Kathy Fields, future M.P. Leighton Hughes; and, the ever-popular celebrity chef and agony aunt Valentina Thorpeworth. The cast are brought together under the fatherly eyes of writers Ray Spatchcock and Harry Munroe. The collective lives of the group intertwine, then tragically unravel, as this tremendous comedic bastion waxes and wanes.

A book you simply must read.

"The dialogue is wonderful and charming, and Gone to the Dogs *is a funny, dramatic and ultimately very moving book; I enjoyed it very much, and it has drawn my attention to a very satisfying author."*

Matt McAvoy